'Joe Lansdale's zany and irresistible new novel brings back the madcap Hap Collins and his partner in crime, Leonard Pine . . . Fast paced and extremely funny, *Captains Outrageous* sees Joe Lansdale writing at his very best' Vic Buckner, *Crime Time*

'Colourful, profane and with an injection of black humour that borders on bad taste, this is another high-octane race through the Texas badlands, with a rising body count and thrills galore. A rewarding romp' Maxim Jakubowski, *Guardian*

'This is his 23rd novel . . . What is even more remarkable about the Texan is that the quantity doesn't affect the quality of his work, which remains remarkably high . . . Regular readers, like myself, will not be disappointed . . . a finely developed sense of the ludicrous . . . the humour usually adds to, rather then detracts from, the suspense. He can switch from belly laughs to stomach-churning violence on the same page but the reader rarely needs to suspend his or her disbelief'
Ewing Grahame, *Glasgow Herald*

'It's vintage stuff, a heady mix of brawling, smut and general waywardness from a consistently entertaining writer' *Uncut*

'This is the sixth outing for Hap and Leonard and it is as humorous and exciting as the others in the series . . . This is a standout thriller that shows Joe Lansdale at the top of his game . . . *Captains Outrageous* is amazingly well written and entertaining. I look forward to the next Hap and Leonard novel' Jude Davies, *Waterstones Enigma*

'This is real in-your-face stuff and not for those of a sensitive disposition. But it does give rise to many a belly laugh'
Michael Painter, *Irish Times*

By Joe R. Lansdale:

The Hap Collins and Leonard Pine novels
SAVAGE SEASON
MUCHO MOJO
THE TWO-BEAR MAMBO
BAD CHILI
RUMBLE TUMBLE
CAPTAINS OUTRAGEOUS

Novels
ACT OF LOVE
THE MAGIC WAGON
DEAD IN THE WEST
THE NIGHTRUNNERS
THE DRIVE-IN: A B-Movie with Blood and Popcorn, Made in Texas
THE DRIVE-IN II: Not Just One of Them Sequels
COLD IN JULY
CAPTURED BY THE ENGINES
TARZAN'S LOST ADVENTURE (with Edgar Rice Burroughs)
FREEZER BURN
THE BOAR
WALTZ OF SHADOWS
BLOOD DANCE
THE BOTTOMS
THE BIG BLOW

Juvenile
TERROR ON THE HIGH SKIES

Short-story collections
BY BIZARRE HANDS
STORIES BY MAMA
LANSDALE'S YOUNGEST BOY
BESTSELLERS GUARANTEED
WRITER OF THE PURPLE RAGE
ELECTRIC GUMBO
A FISTFUL OF STORIES
ATOMIC CHILI: The Illustrated Joe R. Lansdale
THE GOOD, THE BAD, AND THE INDIFFERENT
VEIL'S VISIT (with Andrew Vachss)
PRIVATE EYE ACTION, AS YOU LIKE IT (with Lewis Shiner)
THE LONG ONES
HIGH COTTON

Anthologies (as Editor)
BEST OF THE WEST
NEW FRONTIER
RAZORED SADDLES (with Pat LoBrutto)
DARK AT HEART (with Karen Lansdale)
WEIRD BUSINESS (with Rick Klaw)

Non-fiction
THE WEST THAT WAS (with Thomas W. Knowles)
THE WILD WEST SHOW (with Thomas W. Knowles)

Joe R. Lansdale is the author of over two hundred short stories and twenty-three novels in the suspense, horror and Western genres. He has edited several anthologies of dark suspense and Western fiction. He has received the Edgar Allan Poe Award, the British Fantasy Award, the American Mystery Award and six Bram Stoker Awards from the Horror Writers of America. His novel *The Bottoms*, which is also available from Orion, won the Edgar Award for Best Mystery Novel (2001). *The Bottoms* and *Mucho Mojo* are *New York Times* Notable Books. He lives in East Texas with his wife, son and daughter. Visit THE ORBIT, the official drive-in theatre of champion MOJO STORYTELLER Joe R. Lansdale, located on the web at www.joerlansdale.com. Free stories changed weekly, plus Hap and Leonard links.

Captains
Outrageous

JOE R. LANSDALE

PHOENIX

A PHOENIX PAPERBACK

First published in Great Britain in 2002
by Weidenfeld & Nicolson
This paperback edition published in 2003
by Phoenix,
an imprint of Orion Books Ltd,
Orion House, 5 Upper St Martin's Lane,
London WC2H 9EA

First published in the USA in 2001
by Warner Books, Inc.

A CIP catalogue record for this book
is available from the British Library.

ISBN 0 75381 674 1

Printed and bound in Great Britain by
Clays Ltd, St Ives plc

Author's Acknowledgments

The second chapter of this novel is loosely based on a true incident involving my friend and martial arts student Paul Britt. Hap's fictional adventure is just that, a fictional adventure. Paul Britt—policeman, martial artist, master instructor of Shen Chuan—is a real hero, responsible for saving a young woman's life.

I have tremendous respect for those who are true exponents of law and order. My best thoughts and wishes go to you, Paul, and to the young woman whose life you saved. May your magnificent breed multiply and may the likes of the savage you fought diminish and in short time vanish from the face of the earth.

Also, acknowledgments to Betty Ann Taylor and the fearless crew from the Nacogdoches Humane Society who decided a cruise would be nice. It wasn't.

A small part of this novel is loosely based on my short story "Master of Misery."

CAPTAINS
OUTRAGEOUS

This is the worst trip, I ever been on.
"Sloop John B,"
New England Maritime Song

1

I MADE A LAST ROUND and met Leonard in the break room. He had his security guard cap cocked at a jaunty angle and was standing in front of the soda machine, counting out change.

When I came in he said, without looking up, "You got a quarter?"

I gave him a quarter.

"Any chickens try to break out?" I asked.

"Nope. None tried to break in either. How about on your side? Any trouble?" Leonard pushed the button on the soda machine and a Dr. Pepper dropped out.

"No chicken problems. I saw a suspicious wood rat out by the trees, but he didn't want any part of me."

"Well, I can see that."

I went over and made myself a cup of free decaf because I'd just given Leonard my last quarter. I put lots of free creamer in it. The coffee at the chicken plant needs lots of creamer so it doesn't taste like something dead.

I stirred the coffee in the Styrofoam cup with a plastic swizzle stick and sipped it. It still tasted like some-

thing dead, only with creamer in it. I dropped the full
cup in the trash and we went out to Leonard's pickup.

We had been working at Deerstone's Chicken Processing for about six months, and it wasn't so bad. We
had the three-in-the-afternoon-to-midnight shift. Mostly
you just walked around and made sure there weren't any
holes in the fence and nothing was out of place and you
didn't see workers packing their car trunks with frozen
chickens.

It beat one chicken plant I tried to get on at. They
didn't want me as a security guard, but thought I'd be
great out at their farm, masturbating roosters for sperm to
impregnate hens. No joke. They really did that, or so they
said. I tried to imagine if they had you do it with tweez-
ers and gloves, or if you had to do it with a naked thumb
and forefinger. Perhaps it was better for the chickens that
way.

When you spent a lot of time walking around outside
a dark building and inside where chicken slaughter was
going on, you thought about all kinds of possibilities. And
in the middle of the night, edging on toward the big
twelve, a lot of dumb ideas seemed reasonable.

The guard job had come through an acquaintance who
was quitting and said they needed two. I had to get gun-
certified, way it's offered in Texas, and Leonard, who already had the certification, got the job with me. We were
the last hard bastion between the chickens inside the processing plant (most of them already dead, headless, de-
feathered, and on hooks) and the outside world who
wanted them.

Let me tell you, these chicken people aren't messing
around. They're serious about their fowls. They got all
kinds of processing methods they hold dear and don't
want stolen.

Processing plant across town, the one wanted me to

jack off chickens, lived in mortal fear of spies from Deer-stone's. So fearful, in fact, Leonard and I liked to imagine they would send their own chickens over for secrets. You know, dressed in black ninja outfits, going over the fence and the wall, with metal cleats on wings and feet, climbing through ventilation shafts, ready to pluck out secret information after formidable nunchaku battles in elevators and dark places with Deerstone's own chickens.

Yes sir, sort of made you feel proud when you went home at night, put your dark green guard suit, hat, and holstered handgun on a chair, lay down in bed, smelling of chicken, knowing you kept the world safe from meat processing thieves. That and the fact you got a decent check every two weeks and a sexy uniform to dazzle the female population.

Well, decent money depends on what you've been doing before. Bouncing sometimes paid better, but you had to hang out with a bunch of drunks in a smoky joint full of naked women, and after a while the naked women were just bothersome. You wanted them to put clothes on. I can't explain it. It's just one of those strange things in life. You start to think you wouldn't have to bounce in the first place, throw drunks in the parking lot, if they didn't serve alcohol in there and have naked women running around shaking their tits and sticking their bush in everyone's face.

Then you realize if the place wasn't like that, you wouldn't have a job. It's a bit like being a preacher. If there wasn't any sin you'd be hosing down oil at a filling station. Which, come to think of it, in either case, bouncer or preacher, was sure to be a more honorable profession.

Way I felt lately, naked women were one of life's miseries. I hadn't seen my woman, Brett, naked in some time. Fact was, I wasn't sure she was my woman anymore. And what I had done for her had changed my life, made me blue and sorry and sad about the needs of the flesh. It was my feelings for her, both emotional and physical, that had got me in some business that had resulted in deaths. I dreamed about those people at night. They came to me in bursts of gunfire, powder smoke, and screams. Their faces were huge and they howled at me with mouths open so wide I could see fillings in their teeth, and beyond that, the abyss into which we all go.

What I had done had a certain justification, but certain justification and justification aren't the same thing. I had been on the edge of violence before, and had acted in self-defense before, but in this case I had gone in with the full understanding and the design that I might have to take human lives, and had. I had left there wounded with blood on my shoes.

Since Leonard had been with me on this horrid escapade, I asked Leonard if he had the same problems, the same dreams. His answer was simple. The dead people were assholes.

As for dreams? No.

After it was over, me and Brett kept in touch, made love a few times, had dinner together, went to movies. But there was something missing. Like a hamburger without the fixings. Part of it was the fact she was trying to bring her daughter, Tillie, back to normalcy.

Problem was, Tillie liked being a whore, just not a whore against her will. I guess it beat wanting to grow up and work as a politician.

Truth of the matter was, Tillie was one hell of a good whore. She was pulling down big change over in Tyler, where the Baptists liked sex good as anybody.

I liked sex too, but Brett wasn't for it anymore. Not really. Last few times I had felt as if I were having a kind of desperate aerobic workout. You do it 'cause you think you're supposed to and it's good for you, but you don't like it, and you end up sweaty for little to nothing.

I felt as if Brett ought to have a light on, be reading a magazine, have a pair of scissors at hand so she could clip coupons. Making love to her was kind of like I was trying to beat something to death with my pelvis that was already dead.

Frankly, it wasn't the kind of loving made a man feel hard as steel, or even firm as Greek Age bronze.

Unspoken, we bled sex out of our relationship, and pretty soon we bled the relationship out of it. I had talked to her by phone a few times. She dropped by the plant at dinner break with Kentucky Fried Chicken once, but it was all pretty uninspiring. If I remember correctly, we talked about KFC's biscuits most of the time. They're good biscuits, by the way, but they can't beat Popeye's, and neither's biscuits quite match up to a loving relationship.

After that, I saw her once more. Then all went quiet on that front, and I had pretty much decided from here on out it was the bachelor life for me.

Sex and chicken processing. Two of life's great mysteries.

Leonard drove me around the big chicken plant lot to my car. We did this every night. I parked on one side, he on the other. If we went out the front door, he gave me a ride to my car. We went out the back, I gave him a ride to his. We could have parked side by side, of course, but we liked to add a little adventure to our lives. And it gave us a few minutes to talk about whatever we felt like talking about. Most of it just stupid stuff about the chicken plant, a quick survey of our present lives.

Since I had moved out of his place, we only saw each other at the job site these days. Weekends I enjoyed punching the heavy bag, skipping rope, and feeling sorry for myself. It had one side benefit. I had lost weight. I hadn't been so trim since I had a stomach virus and a full week of vomiting and diarrhea. Only now I felt better and wasn't gaining it back and I could live life without having to always be near a commode.

Leonard had a boyfriend he was seeing, and that kept him busy. I had met the guy and he seemed all right. He was a lead man at the aluminum chair factory. He wasn't quite as macho as Leonard, but he wasn't a skipper, as Leonard called the more effeminate gays. He was black as tar, flat-nosed and thick-lipped, balding, solid built and a little younger than Leonard. Or as Leonard liked to joke, he's big and way black, likes slow walks in the park, and he's got a eight-inch dick.

Leonard, as always, liked to cut to the chase.

This guy, John, he liked to just hang out mostly, and that's what Leonard liked. That and the sex. They went down to the gym, lifted weights three times a week, went to movies and read books in bed. Probably talked about chickens and aluminum lawn furniture now and then. When it came to John, Leonard was pretty free with his vanilla cookies. I guess being a best friend and damn near brother you don't get vanilla cookies so easy. With Leonard, you got to be like a date or something, a lead man at the aluminum chair factory, eight inches of dick and a willing disposition.

John was probably the best thing that had happened to brother Leonard, but it sure put a cramp in my life. No woman. No friend. Just a heavy bag to punch and lots of cheap food eaten with spoons out of cans.

I didn't have a TV either and I had read all my books and didn't have money for more. I was putting what money I had into paying for my new domicile and keeping up my half-ass pickup. I had traded in a banged-up Chevy Nova with hardened gum stuck beneath the dashboard and a rotting pack of rubbers in the glove box for it. Those rubbers and the gum had come with the car, and I had been more than glad to pass them on. The pickup was only better than the Nova in the pollution department. The Chevy Nova had damn near been a mosquito fogger.

All I had of my old life was an ancient stereo and a few playable records I'd rescued from the mess of my home after a tornado. I had one CD that had been given to me, but no CD player.

As Leonard drove me around to my car, we were heavy into a philosophical conversation. He was telling me about his love life. I said, "You like John 'cause he's got eight inches?"

"Yeah."

"That's kind of shallow, ain't it?"

"Yeah."

"You're jerkin' me again, aren't you?"

"I'm tellin' you it's the same as when you buy a burrito. Big is better than small."

"Size doesn't mean a thing."

"You say. What would you know? You ain't a dick man."

"No, but women say it doesn't matter."

"Women are liars. Hey, you like titties?"

"What?"

"Titties?"

"Yeah. And I see where this is going. I like any size tittie. Long as it's a friendly tittie."

"But you like big titties?"

"Yeah, but you're not roping me into some bullshit here. I don't think a woman's got to have big hooters to be worth something."

"Yeah, but if she's worth something and has big hooters, you like that, don't you?"

"Well, yeah, but that doesn't prove anything."

"It proves you like big titties."

"It doesn't prove that big titties are important."

"I say this. I say you could maybe, at least for thirty minutes, like a woman you didn't really like long as she had big titties and was willin' to shuck drawers. Am I right?"

"Leonard . . ."

"Am I right?"

"I don't think I'm that shallow."

"Let's say you're in the mood, and she's in the mood, and she hasn't got visible scars or oozing sores, and she looks pretty good and she's got them big titties. We're not talkin' marriage here, or takin' advantage. We're talkin' she's willin' and she's not too damn smart—"

"Whoa!"

"Just listen. Say, she's got like an IQ of, oh, I don't know. We won't put her in like some kind of home for folks can't figure left from right, but let's say we're talkin' someone's not gonna challenge Einstein in the smart department."

"That's most of us."

"All right. You get that one. Say, she's not any smarter than, say, a postal worker. You know, ones at the counter with their mouth open, always put up a sign says NEXT WINDOW when you walk up to their slot."

"I can see that."

"Say, she's, you know, that kind of dumb. And she's willin'. Let's even say she ain't the best-lookin' thing. I don't mean she's got her nose on the back of her head. She doesn't scare people. But she's got this shape, and them big ol' titties. She wants you to throw her the sausage. Now, you're tellin' me, even if she ain't so pretty, and not so smart, she wanted you, you wouldn't fuck her?"

"All right, I might."

"Might, hell. You'd be on that stuff like a duck on a June bug."

"But I might do it if she didn't have big breasts. I mean, she's pleasant-looking enough."

"Then you're sayin' you'd bang anything?"

"I'm not sayin' that."

"All right, you're not sayin' that, then you're sayin' you like big titties."

"I think this conversation is rigged."

Leonard pulled up next to my car.

"Well," he continued, "I like a big dick. Think about it. A big tit really doesn't do you any good. You get to suck on it, or whatever you heteros do. Roll it around in your palms or rub your head with it. Whatever. Frankly, the thought of it kind of disgusts me. You're not accomplishing anything there. Just buy a beach ball."

"It's not like that, Leonard."

"Now, a dick, there's somethin's got a purpose."

"I'll be going now, Leonard."

I opened the door, got out of the pickup. Leonard punched in his Johnny Cash cassette, waved at me, and drove off to the sounds of "Delia."

Just as I unlocked my car door, tossed my cap on the seat, and was about to climb inside, I heard a weak voice in the nearby patch of woods beyond the fence.

"Help me."

2

THE VOICE HAD COME from the trees beyond the great chain
link fence that surrounded the parking lot. Nothing else
was said, but I could hear a whimper, as if a puppy were
dying under an automobile tire.

There wasn't much of a moon, but besides the whimper I could hear and see movement in the trees. I just
couldn't make out exactly what it was. I opened my truck
door and jerked on the headlights, and what I saw horrified me.

Between two trees a young man was looking at me,
startled, like a deer caught in headlights. His hair was
mussed and full of pine straw and leaves, his face was
smeared with something. He had hold of a woman's wrist.
She was on the ground, nude, her head turned slightly
toward me, her dark hair spread out like a stain on the
leaf mold. After a moment of glaring at me, the guy turned
his attention to her and began stomping her, like he was
trying to smash an insect. It was a horrible sound, way
his booted foot came down on her soft face.

There wasn't any way to get through the fence, and
it was too far to go around. I thought about pulling my

gun, but I'd done the gun thing already and was wearing scars from that, filling my head nightly with dark bad
dreams. I was determined not to do it again. I leaped at
the fence, climbed over, dropped to the other side.

No sooner had I landed than he came for me. He was
hot to trot, and in my headlights he looked like a bad
dream. What I had seen on his face was blood and dirt,
and I figured the blood wasn't from him. I caught a glimpse
of the woman—a girl, really. One of her hands quivered
like an animal in a trap.

He charged me and I sidestepped, slapped at the back
of his head with both hands. He went past fast, slammed
into the fence, turned, came at me again. I side-kicked
him and knocked him back, but he didn't go down. He
leaped at me and I brought an elbow up and under his
chin, but all that did was make him fall back a pace.

He jumped on me like a spider. I spun around, bent
forward, and he flipped over my shoulder. He hit the
ground, came up as if he had bounced off a trampoline.
I hit him repeatedly, but he kept coming. The only thing
I had fought before with this much tenacity and ability to
absorb damage was a rabid squirrel, but the squirrel had
been much smaller and Leonard had been there to help
kill it.

I got him by the back of the head with one hand, the
chin with the other, stuck my index finger in the soft spot
on the side of his neck. He went around and down, but
pounced up. We hammered at each other and I caught a
good one over the eye. He came in for a tackle, and I
hooked my arm under his neck and let his momentum
carry me back. I stuck a foot in his balls as we went. He
went up high and came down hard on his back. I rolled
him over on his stomach, still holding on to his neck, trying to choke him out.

Out of the corner of my eye I saw the girl, lying there

in the pool of yellow from the headlights. She was covered in blood, and one eye was nothing but a dark wet hole. Her head had literally been driven into the ground.

I kept choking him, but it didn't seem to be bothering the bastard. I didn't get it. This guy was half my size, not overly strong-looking, and I knew what the hell I was doing.

Up he came, and out of the choke, and wheeled on me. I started kicking his shins and inside his thighs and his groin, but he kept struggling.

I kicked him one last time and decided I liked the gun after all. If just to discourage him. I pulled it, an automatic. It didn't slow him down. He charged and I jammed it forward into his face, hitting him with the barrel. I struck him with such force the barrel slide was knocked back and it ejected a shell, but still he came, trying to get the gun. I should have shot him, but didn't. I avoided him and tossed the gun over the fence.

He bellowed like something out of hell, came on hard again, and I wished now I hadn't been so ethical. In that moment, had I had the gun, I would have emptied it into him. I was so frightened I thought of trying to break away and climb the fence for the automatic. But there wasn't time for that now.

I hit him with a slipping elbow to the side of the face, dropped my arm and hit him with a hammer fist in the balls, went for a hammerlock, but that was like trying to put a lock on a rubber hose. I couldn't hold him. I jabbed a finger into one of his eyes, and for the first time I got the right response. He went back, holding his face. In an act of desperation I leaped up sideways with both feet and hit him in the chest with the force of my entire body.

I at least succeeded in knocking him down. I got up, scared. In this rare moment of breathing room, I considered again going for the fence and the gun, but he went for it instead, leaped, grabbed the links, began to climb over.

I grabbed the fence, started scuttling too. He beat me over by a second or so. I threw myself over the top and landed in front of my pickup. The automatic had fallen on the far side of the truck, and he was going for it. I put a foot on the bumper of the pickup, sprang onto the hood, pushed off with my foot and rolled over the roof, hit in the bed on my feet, leaped from the truck onto him, hit him hard in the back just as he was reaching for the gun. He missed his grab, went forward, getting a parking lot full of asphalt across his face and chest. He got up with me on his back, my arm around his neck. He whipped me off of him like a dog shaking off water.

He turned, and since we were away from the head-lights, and there was only a little light from the parking lot, I couldn't see his face well, but there was asphalt hanging from his raw cheeks and his lips looked to be nearly scraped off. He began to beat his chest like Tarzan and yell. He turned, put both hands on the tailgate of my truck, and sprang into the bed, made the roof of the truck, yelled, "I'm a swinging dick," and did a back flip onto the parking lot, hit hard. He hopped up from that and ran between me and the truck. I picked up the automatic, jumped into the truck. I was hoping the lights hadn't run down the battery. It cranked. I backed out and went after him.

He was bearing down on Ella May. Ella May was a heavy black woman who worked in the department where the chickens were run through a neck slicer. On her shift she wore a hooded yellow slicker and high black boots, sat on a throne surrounded by a lake of blood, and it was her job to slit the throats of the survivors with a lit-tle hooked knife. She didn't have her yellow slicker and boots on now, but that knife was her own.

As he charged her, she jumped back slightly and the knife came out and she cut him, deep. I could see blood fly up between him and her in my headlights. He ran right over her and kept running. He could have rushed around the building and out the open front gate where the shift was changing, but he charged the fence, ready to climb over. I put the pedal to the metal and bore down on him. He was already near the top. I hit the fence hard enough to knock him loose. He fell backward, smashing my windshield. I jerked open the door, leaped out, grabbed him off the hood, slammed him against the side of the truck, and kneed him in the balls two or three times.

He still succeeded in hitting me in the face. I wavered consciousness but didn't go down. Ella May had come up on the other side of the truck and she was scrambling across the hood. She got him around the neck and stuck that curved knife in his cheek and pulled for all she was worth, splashing blood and exposing his teeth.

The guy reached up, grabbed the blade and tore the knife away from her. I got on that knife quick, latched a figure-four on his arm, swung him around and down, and butted his nose with my forehead.

"I teach you to jump on me, motherfucker," Ella May said. She came off the hood and landed on his legs, then came around and started kicking him in the head.

I was beginning to swoon. Black spots swirled in my vision like gnats in the river bottoms. The two security guards who were my and Leonard's replacements showed up and everyone dog-piled the bastard. We got him rolled over and handcuffed. One of the guards, a black guy I didn't know, said, "You all right?"

"There's a girl," I said. "He was attacking a girl. Other side of the fence there," and I pointed.

"I'll call some law," the black guy said.

I leaned against the truck. Ella May was kicking the

guy still. He lay on the ground and took the shots without so much as a grunt. "Motherfucker, run over my ass. I'll teach your cock not to stand up."

One of the guards got hold of her and pulled her back, but she kept fighting. He finally pushed her up against the fence and held her arms behind her back and used his handcuffs on her. All the while, she was screaming.

"Handcuffs! Handcuffs! I'll kick your dick over the fence, cocksucker."

"Calm down, Ella May," he said.

"Calm down, my ass. Motherfucker run over me . . . You're hurtin' my arm, goddamn it. I'll remember your ugly face."

The headlights from my truck, the lights in the lot, the darkness between and around them swirled together and I remembered feeling hot, trying to bend over to breathe better, trying not to faint, but when I bent forward I just kept going.

3

Ouch," I SAID. "Take it easy."

Leonard was poking at the deep cut over my eye with the tip of his finger, examining the stitches.

"One of 'em looks to be sewed too loose," he said.

"It'll do," I said.

I was sitting on a gurney in a little room just off of the emergency room hall. An intern had just sewn me up and left. Now there was just me, Leonard, and John.

A cop, a friend of mine, Charlie Blank, had been in earlier to take my side of the story. He left shortly after Leonard's and John's arrival.

The young woman who had been beaten was in intensive care, and word was she wasn't doing too well. One thing was certain, she had lost some teeth and an eye.

"Well," Leonard said, "you did say you saw a wood rat out by the trees."

"I just didn't know he was so mean."

"Yeah, he wasn't as afraid of you as you thought."

"I don't think this sonofabitch was afraid of anything. I tell you, Leonard, he was the toughest dude I've ever fought. I'd rather fight three guys than fight him again, and me with a pipe wrench. I think Ella May wants a piece of him, though."

"Ella May," John said, "hasn't got the sense of two nickels rubbed together. I've known her all my life. Before she was cutting chicken throats, she worked at the aluminum chair plant with me. She put the damn riveter through her fingers two or three times. I'm surprised she hasn't cut her own throat at the chicken plant."

"I'm not accusing her of intelligence," I said, "just her willingness to fight. Come to think of it, her and this guy, they'd make a great tag team they wanted to get together. They'd be unbeatable."

"Good thing she wasn't on his side tonight," John said.

"She hadn't been there," I said, "that sonofabitch would have gotten away. I wonder how bad messed up he is. I'd feel better he looked worse than me."

"Well," Leonard said, "it ain't like you got to worry about your native good looks."

"What I'd like to know," John said, "is what's this guy's story?"

"Whatever it is," I said, "it isn't a fairy tale. More like a horror story, I figure."

"Speakin' of horror stories," Leonard said, "that shirt Charlie had on, where in hell did he find that? It looked like it had been used to wipe up paint."

"It's colorful," I said.

"Colorful is a nice word," John said.

In that moment I realized since Leonard had been seeing John he dressed nicer himself. Nothing fancy, but a little slicker. John always dressed that way, like he was going to a casual prayer meeting.

"Charlie just looked like hell in general," Leonard said.

"He's divorced and not happy about it. He gave up cigarettes because his wife wouldn't give him any unless he did. Turned out she was seeing a guy on the side who smoked. It really got his goat. Worse yet, now he finds he can quit smoking. Thing bothers him most, besides the wife gone, is he's gotten hooked on this shitty *Kung Fu* television series. He said when he got to taping it while he was at work, looking forward to it at nights, he knew he had crossed the line into dark depression."

"I don't know," John said. "Nothing to do, it's not so bad."

Leonard and I looked at him.

"I mean, I watch it sometimes," he said. "I got nothing else on tape, you know. Now and then."

We kept looking at him.

"Jeez, guys. I'll quit. Promise. Really."

I took a couple days off from work, enjoyed being a hero for about fifteen minutes. Me and Ella May. I wondered how she was doing. Probably still cussing and wanting to fight.

Night it happened I was so wired I didn't sleep, and the next day I was still wired, and the next night too. I was not only wired, I hurt too. I felt as if I had been wrapped in duct tape and rolled down a rocky mountainside into a brick wall with my nuts in my teeth.

Friday some of it passed and I got a good night's sleep, slept in late without the bad dreams, and was a lot less sore. Saturday morning, near eleven, I was up in my sweat pants, T-shirt, and bare feet, making coffee.

My new place was in town, a duplex. It was upstairs with a connecting kitchen/living room, a small bedroom, and a bathroom with a toilet that sagged into the floor when you sat on it. I figured some morning I'd be in there taking my morning constitutional and find myself flying through space, down to the bottom floor, having firemen dig my corpse out from under busted ceramic and a pile of shit.

There was some good news. The duplex was cheap. Mostly because the bottom floor was burned out. Before I moved in, according to the landlord, some drunk had left a frying pan on the stove and it and the grease and the chicken leg floating in it caught on fire and the blaze spread through the kitchen/living room like a yeast infection. The drunk had been sleeping on the couch at the time. He was in some kind of burn center, probably wishing he'd just opened a box of crackers and pulled the tab on a can of beanie weenies.

The place wasn't going to be rented for a while, not until the landlord fixed it up, so he let me store some stuff down there in the only rooms that weren't burned, the bedroom and the bathroom. Long as there wasn't someone under me, the duplex wasn't so bad, though now and then the burn smell would come up through the floor and stink the place up, make my eyes water, wake me in the middle of the night, and I'd get up to make sure I hadn't left something on the stove myself.

All in all, it was all right, though living in town wasn't my preference.

Anyway, I was making coffee and thinking about toast with jelly for breakfast, when I heard a car drive up. I went to the kitchen window over the sink, looked out. It was Charlie Blank. He was getting out from behind the wheel of a clean white Ford. A middle-aged, gray-haired guy in a brown suit got out on the passenger's side. He looked up at the duplex as if he were observing some prehistoric hovel. Of interest, but surprised people once lived there, even more surprised to think someone might be squatting there now, perhaps supping on mastodon marrow.

Charlie, as usual, was wearing a colorful Hawaiian shirt,

slacks, tennis shoes, and a sports coat the color of mustard, or if you really want to get technical, baby shit. A straw boater had replaced his felt porkpie. The new hat, I presumed, was part of his spring ensemble. The shoes he had on were the kind you might dress a juvenile Frankenstein monster in, black, thick-soled, and solid enough to drive a nail. He had a greasy brown bag in one hand.

I listened to them clunk up the stairs and opened the door before they could knock.

"My man," Charlie said.

"How are you, Charlie?"

"All right. I got someone needs to see you. Can we come in?"

"What's the password?"

"I'm throwing out your old parking tickets."

"I don't have any."

"Well, if you had some."

"Come on in. Sorry about the place, maid's day off."

The guy in the suit hadn't cracked a smile, not even a sly grin. I couldn't tell if he was humorless or if Charlie and I were just boring. Probably the latter.

I motioned them to the couch. It had come with the place. It had one spot that nearly sagged to the floor. I had slipped a piece of plywood under the cushions there, and though it no longer sank, it was seriously hard on the ass.

"Coffee?" I asked.

"I could use some," Charlie said, then to the man in the suit. "You?"

The man shook his head.

Charlie gave me the bag. I put it on the table and opened it. Doughnuts.

"The stitches come out soon?" Charlie asked.

"Pretty soon."

I pulled down nonmatching cups, poured coffee. Charlie sat on the couch and drank his, I leaned against the sink. The man sat by Charlie with his hands in his lap, looking around. It was as if he was avoiding placing his arms or hands on the sofa for fear of contamination, or a possible attack from a rat hidden in the cotton.

"I'm just living here till they get my condo built," I said.

He turned toward me. This time he did smile. Nothing to get excited about, but teeth were involved.

"This is Elmer Bond, Hap," Charlie said.

The name hit me. That had been the girl's name, the one that had been stomped by the maniac. Bond. Sarah Bond.

I switched my cup to my left hand, stepped over and shook his hand. "I presume you're kin to Sarah Bond."

"Father," he said.

"I'm sorry about what happened. How is she?"

"Not good. But better. She'll live. She lost an eye. There'll be extensive plastic surgery. But, thanks to you, she'll live, and the bastard who did this to her is in custody. I hope he decides to hang himself, but if he doesn't, I hope they give him the needle. I'm not very sympathetic to him."

"I wouldn't expect you to be," I said.

"Mr. Collins," he said. "I—"

"Hap. My dad was Mr. Collins, and he didn't like being called that either."

"Hap. I came here to thank you personally for saving my daughter's life."

"You're welcome."

"I want to show my appreciation by giving you a check for a hundred thousand dollars."

"Do what?"

"A check, for a hundred thousand dollars. I'll write it out now."

"Hey, you don't owe me anything for that."

"I'd like to give it to you anyway."

"That's a lot of money."

"Not to me. It's a drop in the bucket. I'm wealthy, Hap. Money is not a problem. A hundred thousand is not a problem. I'm not paying you for doing what you thought you should do, I'm showing my appreciation. Thanks and a handshake is very nice, but a hundred thousand dollars is better. I did the same for Miss Drew."

"Drew?"

"Ella May," Charlie said.

"I don't want to be paid, Mr. Bond."

"Elmer. If you're Hap, I'm Elmer."

"I don't want to be paid, Elmer."

"Certainly, I can't wrestle you to the floor and make you take it and spend it on yourself, but hear me out. My daughter is sixteen years old, Hap. Sixteen. A baby. She was attending a church function. Just got her driver's license. Has hardly been driving at all. This . . . human . . . No . . . this animal, this thing. A man named Bill Merchant, he knew my daughter. They went to school together, though he dropped out his junior year. He's a few years older. Did you know that he's only eighteen?"

"I knew he was young. One of the reasons I was amazed at the way he fought."

"Drugs," Charlie said. "Pills. Alcohol. Ritalin. Lots of Ritalin."

"I thought that was a medicine for hyperactivity," I said. "Attention deficit."

"It is," Charlie said. "If you have those problems. But if you don't, it works like speed. Bruce Lee couldn't have beat that guy that night, Hap. He was on that and everything else."

"I want to finish," Elmer said.

"Sorry," Charlie said. "Please."

"He had just been released from a juvenile facility. He was there for rape. This happened shortly after he dropped out of LaBorde High School. He's been a problem kid all his life. When I say just released, I mean the day before. For whatever reason, he parked his mother's car outside the church and began to drink and take pills, or whatever it was he took. When Sarah came out, he spotted her, and perhaps because he knew her, or because she's pretty—or was pretty—he went over to speak to her, pulled her in the car in front of half a dozen witnesses. He drove her to a little stretch of woods on the edge of town, pulled her out of the car, into the woods, and raped her. She escaped. He chased her. The woods came out against the chicken plant fence. He caught her there. He raped her again. He bit . . . Do you hear me, Hap? He *bit*, one of her nipples off, then he began to beat her and stomp her. He stomped her face in, Hap. In! Just like it was made of cardboard. Crushed her jaw, her cheeks. Knocked out teeth, and he stomped out her eye. Stomped it out. She's going to have to have a glass eye. A fucking glass eye."

"Easy," Charlie said.

Elmer had started to tremble. Tears were running down his cheeks, and I was just about to cry myself.

"My daughter was beautiful, Hap. She wanted to be a model. They'll fix her some. Her face will probably be all right, for the most part. She'll have a glass eye, a false jaw and teeth. That's just one bad side. Worse, she'll have this asshole who did this to her inside her head the rest of her life. But you know what?"

"What?" I said.

"She'll remember you too. You'll be there too. When she gets well she'll want to see you. She said you're her knight in shining armor. You came over that fence when she had given up all hope. She knew her life was gone, and you saved her, Hap. You fought the dragon, and you defeated him."

"With help," I said.

"You laid him low. I only regret you didn't kill him."

"It crossed my mind," I said. "I had it to do over, I don't know what I'd do."

"But you saved my baby, Hap. I want you to take the money. God, may I use your bathroom to wash my face."

"Sure." I pointed it out to him.

When the water was running in the bathroom, Charlie said, "Take the money, Hap. It would make him feel better. And it'll make you feel better. You could use it. This is a break you deserve. For Christ sake, take it. And hand me one of those doughnuts."

A moment later Elmer came out of the bathroom. He reached in his pocket and took out a small photograph of a beautiful young woman. "That's Sarah," he said. "Before the beating. Look at her. She was beautiful. And inside, she's even more beautiful. More than her face, he stomped on her spirit."

"I can't find the right words," I said. "All I've got is I'm sorry. And I'm glad I was there. I only wish I had been there earlier."

"And I have to wish you had killed the sonofabitch, but what you did stopped him from killing her. That's the important part, Hap. You saved her life."

Elmer looked at the photo once more, put it back in his pocket. He looked teary again. He said, "I'll take that cup of coffee now."

I got down a cup and poured him some. When I gave it to him, he said, "I want you to take the money. I want you to go on vacation, or buy something for yourself, take a month off from the chicken plant. Take that buddy of yours"—he turned his head to Charlie—"what's the name?"

"Leonard," Charlie said. "Leonard Pine."

"Charlie told me all about you, Hap. About you and Leonard. I want you to take the money. Please take the money."

"I'll take the money, Elmer. But as for the vacation and the month off, I don't think so. The chicken plant frowns on that sort of thing."

Charlie grinned.

Elmer said, "No it doesn't. Not in this case. I own the plant."

4

LEONARD AND I were shooting pool with John at the LaBorde Rec Center, which in spite of its name is not for kiddies. It was a place where you could buy a beer, shoot some pool, see football games and boxing matches on a huge television, and watch guys scratch their nuts and try and pick up women. And from time to time guys try to pick up guys and women pick up women.

The bartender, Marlie, was a bull dyke with a flattop and a body the size and shape of a small sumo wrestler, or if you prefer, a three-hundred-pound potato. Fortunately, she didn't dress like a sumo wrestler or a potato. She always wore gray coveralls with the sleeves cut out, so you could see her big biceps and tattoos, like: MOTHER NEVER LOVED ME, AND SO WHAT?

Marlie owned and ran the place. She was noted for her uneven temperament. I had seen her use a taped axe handle to subdue rowdy customers, and she had a mean left hook and she didn't mind kneeing a man in the balls either. Saturday nights, the Rec Center could get pretty rowdy, and so could Marlie.

Marlie always looked as if she were about to break

out into a string of obscenities. Which, of course, she often did. Stuff like: "Quit fuckin' up that pool cue, you limp-dicked cocksucker," and "Do that again, motherfucker, gonna wake up peein' through a tube."

She had a girlfriend who looked like a *Vogue* model.

Leonard and I were the lousiest pool players ever produced. We were playing colored and stripes. I was stripes, Leonard was colored. He thought that was funny.

I took a shot and knocked my last striped ball in the hole, eased around to shoot in the black one. Leonard had two colored balls left, red and green, and neither in a good position. I grinned at Leonard as I lined up the shot, an easy one.

I boosted the ball with the stick. It went in the hole. I said, "That's another ten cents you owe me."

"Damn," Leonard said. "What is that now, forty cents?"

"Fifty."

"You're not countin' the first game, are you?"

"Why not?"

"That was a warm-up game."

"You didn't say anything about a warm-up game. Did he say anything about a warm-up game, John?"

John shook his head, said, "And you owe me all the games I beat you, Leonard. Don't try and weasel."

"I'm not weaslin'."

"I call it weaslin'. Hap?"

"Weaslin'."

"I just think you ought to have least one warm-up game," Leonard said.

"John, we do that, does that mean I don't owe you first time you beat me?" I said. "Could that be a warm-up game? You want to do that, I'll go with Leonard."

"Everybody owes," John said.

"Yeah, you say that," Leonard said, "'cause you're the only one hasn't lost a game."

John said, "My turn. It's you and me, Hap. Loser racks."

Leonard fed some quarters into the slot on the side of the table and the balls were released. Leonard gathered the balls, racked them.

It was my break, but I let John go first. He burst, and I never so much as picked up my stick after that. He ran the table. When he was finished twenty minutes later, he said, "Ten more cents."

I looked at Leonard. "Give him a dime out of the money you owe me."

John held out his hand and Leonard gave him the ten cents.

"That's a beginning," John said.

Leonard bought beers for himself and John, got me a Sharps. We sat at a table and watched some women shoot pool. One of the women, a blonde with black roots, had a large but well-formed butt, like the kind R. Crumb draws. The other one was tall and thin with brown hair and big doe eyes. They were in their thirties, attractive. They were interested in two guys at the bar, however, and they were playing pool with them in mind, moving their butts so that those two got a good view.

I kept an eye on them, just in case I might pick up a few pool-shooting tips.

Leonard said, "It's so interesting to watch a straight guy work. The way you casually observe those women, check the men out over at the bar, know they are the object of those two gals' attention. Then I get to see you feel sorry for yourself because the women don't know you're alive. It's all so . . . curious. And pathetic."

"Yeah," John said to Leonard, "like you haven't been checking those guys out over there."

"I suppose," Leonard said, "I did turn an eye in their direction."

"I think it was both eyes," John said. "Don't turn it there too often, okay?"

"Okay," Leonard said. "Besides, those guys are straight."

"Well, don't overdo the looking anyway," John said.

Leonard reached out and gave John's hand a pat, then turned his attention to me. "So he offered you one hundred thousand dollars and a month off from the plant? And a month for me?"

"Yep."

"He didn't happen to offer me a month off from the aluminum chair factory, did he?" John said.

"Sorry, John," I said. "He doesn't own the aluminum chair factory."

"Maybe he'll buy it," John said.

"It could happen," I said.

"I'm guessing since the owner's name isn't Deerstone, then there isn't a Deerstone," John said.

"There was. He sold out to Bond nearly twenty years ago," I said. "But they kept the name because it had commercial value."

"We get our jobs back when the month's up, I reckon," Leonard said.

"Of course," I said. "Frankly, I feel funny taking his money. You know, I didn't intend to, and I tell myself I did it for the guy and because Charlie convinced me, but I know deep down, hell, not that deep, that I did it because I wanted the money."

"Hap, you're about the least money-oriented sonofabitch I know," Leonard said.

"That's because winning all your dimes, I don't have to worry about money."

"You don't worry about money," Leonard said, "because you're goodhearted and haven't got enough brains to worry about it. Hell, you didn't do what you did for money. That was just an unexpected end result. You don't need to feel guilty because you took it. You'd have done it had you known the girl was a pauper and that motherfucker was not only going to fight you like a tiger, but was going to win. You'd have gone on ahead anyway."

"I'll take all that as a compliment. Except the lack of brains part."

The blonde with the black roots and the big firm butt was on our side now, the rear of her white shorts pointed in my direction. They were not only short shorts, but they flared dangerously and I could see some of the soft meat up there and a hint of pubic hair. I shifted subtly in my chair for a better look.

"Your turn to buy," Leonard said to me.

I took a last look at the shorts and what was in them and went over to the bar. Marlie came up, "What'll it be?"

I sat on the bar stool, said, "Two Miller Drafts, a Sharps."

"You drink the Sharps, don't you?"

"Yes."

"What for?"

"I like it."

"It ain't a diet thing?"

"I like it."

"It ain't a diet thing and you drink it?"

"I like it."

"Why?"

"There's no alcohol in it."

"Hell, I thought that was why you drank beer, 'cause there's alcohol in it."

"Sharps isn't beer. Not really."

"You're tellin' me."

"Can I just have the Sharps?"

Marlie finally got the beers and the Sharps. She said, "Those two gals, the one with the big ass, she's making my clit hard."

"Oh," I said.

"Them's the facts," Marlie said. "Problem is, the blonde, the one with the dirt in her part—"

"Dirt?"

"The black roots."

"Oh."

"She's interested in the guy at the bar there, one turned toward her, smiling. She's interested in his tuber, which, from the looks of those pants, is about the size of a banana."

"I didn't think that sort of thing interested you."

"It don't, but I check out the competition."

"Well, no offense, but you can't compete with that if that's what she wants. I mean, you know—"

"Hap, you can't compete with that either."

"How would you know?"

"Like I said, I check out the competition. I first saw you, I just passed my eye over you. You don't worry me none."

"Oh, thanks, beat up on the heterosexual. Besides, aren't you with Miss *Vogue*?"

"Hey, what can I say. I got a rovin' eye. I get older, I'm startin' to realize I like my women a little trashy. I don't even mind they smell a little."

"On that note . . ."

I carried the drinks back to the table.

"I'm glad you took the money," Leonard said, "because now I get to go on vacation, and I say we go on a real one."

"What about me?" John asked.

"See you when I get back," Leonard said, smiling, patting John's hand again.

5

I ACTUALLY WENT BACK to work at the chicken plant for a couple weeks, made arrangements for time off. I felt guilty about the whole thing, taking off a month with a hundred thousand dollars because I had saved someone's life. I felt more mercenary than heroic. Leonard, who had done nothing, felt great. He wanted a vacation.

A week into my two-week notice of vacation, me, Leonard, and John made plans at my duplex while I cooked, and slightly burned, a pizza.

John's suggestion: a cruise.

"A cruise?" Leonard said. "You mean, hang out with a bunch of rich old people who want to look at countries from a boat so they don't have to deal with other cultures? Man, you know I saw somewhere one of those cruise lines is making their own island. You know, like *Fantasy Island* meets *Love Boat*. This way you don't have to deal with those pesky locals. Don't have to have a nigger rub up against you."

"They're not all like that," John said. "Most of them stop in different countries for a day or two. Thing is, it would be relaxing. And you could actually go some places you might not go, might not could afford to go to. These cruise lines, you can pay a thousand apiece, plus some expenses, and you get all your food and lodging provided. It comes out about like a good hotel with room service."

"Maybe just a month off around here is good enough," I said. "It'll save me money."

"Yeah," Leonard said, "this place is swinging. Besides, I've spent enough money on you, now it's time you spent some on me."

"Oh, that's nice. That's very friendly."

"It's true."

"Didn't I just give you a quarter for a soda the other night?"

"Yeah, and I'm forever grateful."

"Look, I got some stuff here." John, who was dressed in a sports coat, as usual, took a folder out of his inside pocket. "This isn't one of the big cruise lines. In fact, the boat is an old Argentine Navy boat that's been revamped for cruises. It's not real expensive."

"Man, you been thinking about this cruise stuff yourself," Leonard said.

"For years, to be honest."

"Go with us," I said.

"Hey, I'm not fishing," John said. "I couldn't go if I wanted. No one's giving me time off where I am. I spent that time already. I got to be around. But you could maybe go on the cruise and tell me about it. Turns out all right for you two, I might could take one. Me and Leonard might could take one. Something romantic."

"Leonard's about as romantic as a hand job," I said.

"I'll ignore that," Leonard said. "So, John, we're the cruise guinea pigs."

"Kinda," John said.

I eyeballed the brochure. I had never really considered, or even thought about a cruise, but now the idea was starting to appeal. "Maybe it's too late to get on this one, it leaves, what? Two weeks?"

"You could call them," John said. "Their number is on the brochure."

I'm not exactly sure why I was convinced to do the cruise, maybe because it was so alien to me. The closest my family had ever come to a cruise was a rowboat down the Sabine River with fishing poles.

At first I thought spending a few thousand dollars for such was foolish. That was a good chunk out of the hundred-thousand-dollar check, but the more I thought about it, the more I wanted it. I wanted to step outside my life and enter into another. I wanted to leave chickens and disappointment behind. It wasn't like I was leaving anything of importance, even Brett was out of the picture. It might be nice to masturbate in an exotic location for a change.

Growing up, my parents had continually put aside things like trips, vacations; only rarely went to movies and ate out at Dairy Queens to save money. Maybe they had to. But they had never had a hundred thousand dollars in their hand at one time. What would they have done?

I knew what they would have done. They'd have thought first of me, second about survival, and last about a vacation. They'd have banked the money, kept working, and maybe driven over to Tyler to visit relatives. My dad might have gone fishing.

I wanted to do different. I wanted a radical change.

But I hesitated, and I knew why. Brett.

Last week of work before my vacation started, on a blue Monday, early morning when I should have been sleeping off the night shift, I called Brett. If nothing had changed in her schedule, she'd be home from the night shift at the hospital.

She answered the phone.

"It's been a while," she said.

"Yeah. I don't know exactly what to say, but I miss you."

"I miss you too, Hap. It's just . . . Well, I don't know. My head's all confused. It's not like I'm seeing anyone else. It's not like I really want to see anyone else. Life is just a mess."

"Yeah."

"I feel guilty too."

"How?"

"After what you did for me. I thought things would be great, back to normal. They aren't."

"Yeah."

"It's not you. I promise. I still feel for you, it's just that what I feel is so buried in shit. So buried in all manner of stuff. Can you understand that?"

"I think so. We did discuss those Kentucky Fried Chicken biscuits pretty good. I thought we had a moment there."

She laughed. "Oh, Hap. That's what I miss most about you."

"My humor?"

"The stupid shit you come up with."

"Oh, thanks."

A beat.

"Don't forget me," she said.

"I won't."

"Let's don't say it's over."

"Sure."

"Bye, Hap."

"Bye, Brett."

A couple minutes later, I called the cruise line. They

had space. Me and Leonard would soon be on our way to Mexico, Jamaica, and the Caymans.

Yeehah.

Brett. Brett. Brett.

6

IT WAS A PRETTY INTERESTING WEEK. I paid off the little bit I owed on my worthless truck, had my stitches taken out, went by the hospital late morning to see if I could look in on Sarah Bond, and they let me. She had just been out of intensive care a couple of days, still in serious condition, able to see visitors, but not long.

I slid in there and saw her sleeping. Her head was swollen, her face was dark blue, and her lips were puffed and cut and there were stitches all over and wire contraptions and tubes and such. Her hair was oily and pulled up and clipped. A portion had been shaved and in that spot was a red swelling in the shape of a boot heel. Her eye was patched over with a large gauze pad.

It hurt me to see her.

"Thanks for coming by."

I turned. It was Elmer Bond. He was entering the room, had a Styrofoam cup of coffee in his hand. He was wearing a charcoal gray suit this day, a colorful tie, a kind of off-color white shirt. He looked like what he was worth. Several million bucks.

"Elmer," I said. We shook hands.

"She's actually much better. They keep her pretty doped. The pain. Then she's got to deal with the recovery, therapy, you name it. It could go on for a damn long time. Bless her heart. Her mother can't even look at her. She goes into hysterics."

"I just wanted to drop by and see her, you know."

"Yeah."

"I'll be checking from time to time."

"I kind of wish she was awake," Elmer said. "I think she'd like to see you. I'll tell her you came by."

"Sure. Like I said, I'll check back. Maybe when she's out of the hospital. Now that I think about it, it's best she doesn't see me, anything to remind her of the other night might not be so good."

"She'd want to see you."

"Give her my best, will you?"

"Sure. You enjoying your time off?"

"Just starting. I'm going to pay off some bills and go on a cruise."

"Something you've always wanted to do?"

"No, not really, but I got talked into it by a friend of a friend. I'm going to take Leonard with me."

"Have the best time possible. And Hap . . ."

"Yeah."

"You ever need anything. Anything. Come to me. I'll do the best I can."

"Thanks."

"Enjoy every penny."

"Sure."

I took a last look at Sarah and went out of there, on down the elevator, out to my car, her shattered image in my head, tears in my eyes. In that moment I wished I had just gone on and shot and killed the cocksucker.

*   *   *

I drove over to Charlie Blank's place. He was off that day and had invited me to lunch. Marvin Hanson was going to be there. Former lieutenant on the LaBorde police force. He had been in a terrible car accident, then a coma, and had finally come out of it. After months of rehabilitation, he was much better, but in a wheelchair. The only time I'd seen him since the accident was at his house, and he was comatose then. I regularly asked about him, kept up with him through his best friend, Charlie.

After their separation, Charlie had let his wife have the house. He was living in a trailer on a couple of acres he was buying. It was a pretty nice area, actually. Out by the lake with some trees. When I drove over there it was a warm day and Charlie was sitting in a lawn chair by an outdoor grill and a picnic table. Hanson, looking very thin and pale for a black man, was sitting in the wheelchair. He was wearing a baseball cap that said ASTROS on it. When he saw me, he gave me a kind of sly grin.

"You and Leonard burned anything down lately?"

His voice was a little weak, and he talked out of the side of his mouth, as if his face and lips were too tired or lacked the muscles to form words.

"No, haven't had any matches," I said, shaking his hand, which was surprisingly strong. "How're you feeling?"

"Like I drove my car into a goddamned tree, that's how."

I sat down in a spare lawn chair. I could smell meat cooking on the grill.

"What are we having?" I asked.

"Steaks," Charlie said.

"Man, that's uptown."

"Not where I bought this meat. I said we were having steaks, I didn't say they were any good. I got a feel-

ing this meat might have come off horses found dead at
the pony rides."

"You're looking pretty good," I said to Hanson.

"Liar," Hanson said. "But had you seen me before,
you'd know I really am."

"I did see you before, but you were, to put it politely,
sleeping."

Hanson nodded. "It's been hell. Good thing about it,
me and my wife have reconciled and the feeling's come
back in my dick lately."

"Then your worries are over," I said.

"Not quite. I want to have sex, it's an ordeal to get
situated, and though I got the feeling back and the ol'
weenie has got some steel in it, I haven't got any thrust-
ing power. By the time me and Rachel get set, I'm worn
out."

"He's getting some tingling in his legs," Charlie said,
getting up to fork and turn the steaks. "That's a good
sign."

"That's great," I said.

"I'm working with a physical therapist, and I'm study-
ing martial arts. Shen Chuan and Combat Hapkido. There's
a guy here teaches both systems to the disabled. I'm a
little too weak right now to learn much, but it's helping
me out. It's building strength in my wrist and arms. My
physical therapist recommended it."

"That's good," I said.

"I won't be going back to work at the cop shop,
though."

"I'm sorry."

"I'm not. Not the least little bit. I wasn't all that loved
anyway."

"I hear that."

"And, Hap, I suggest you watch the kind of trouble
you get in from now on," Charlie said, " 'cause I'm quit-

ting myself. Turned in my notice. A month from now, I'm on my own."

"No shit?"

"No shit."

"Me and Charlie are forming a business," Hanson said. "Private Investigations. Charlie's the legs, I'm the brains."

"Ho ho," Charlie said.

"Damn," I said. "Real private eyes. Charlie, does this mean you're gonna get sapped a lot and fall into dark tunnels and get laid all the time by strange blondes with long sleek gams?"

"I can do without the sap part," Charlie said, "but the rest of it sounds all right."

"You guys are serious?" I said.

"Hanson and Blank, Private Investigations," Hanson said. "Has a nice ring to it, don't you think?"

"Blank and Hanson, Private Investigations," Charlie said, "has a nicer ring to it. Don't you think, Hap?"

"You're not getting me in on this."

"We'll flip for the name," Hanson said.

"Not if you're flipping the quarter," Charlie said.

"I think that's great, guys. Really."

We ate the steaks, a salad, and some bread Charlie had warmed in the trailer oven. They drank beer and I drank ice tea.

Charlie had been joking. It was good meat and well prepared, medium rare with a touch of salt and pepper. We ate, talked, and laughed a lot. When the meal was over Charlie went inside the trailer and made some coffee. Me and Hanson bullshitted a little. Charlie made a couple of trips out. First he brought coffee for Hanson and me. Then coffee for himself and a Tupperware container filled with Hostess Twinkies and cupcakes. "I damn near pulled my thumb out of joint trying to open this damn Tupperware lid."

"Childproof," Hanson said.

"Probably," Charlie said. "You know, I shouldn't eat this shit, but I got like a serious problem about it. I like it."

We ate Twinkies and cupcakes and even though Charlie had told Hanson about my adventure at the chicken plant, I told it again, then I told them about the cruise.

Charlie said, "Well, finally, you and Leonard are off to do something where the worst trouble you can get into is cutting a fart in the dining room."

"Yeah," I said. "Ain't it grand?"

7

JOHN HAD TO DRIVE us over to New Orleans to catch the ship. We got there a day early and took a hotel near Bourbon Street and walked along and watched people wander about. I had once been there during Mardi Gras, and the place was nuts. People everywhere, women exposing their breasts, yelling, floats, the whole nine yards. But this night was not a total waste. We did get to see some guys wearing makeup, hear some great jazz music over at Preservation Hall, and we ate some good crawfish at a place called Mike Anderson's Seafood.

On the way back to the hotel a drunk naked man took a leak against a wall and staggered into a bar and didn't come out.

"Do you think he just went in and ordered a drink?" Leonard asked.

"I wouldn't doubt it," I said, "and I wouldn't doubt they gave it to him. He's probably in there sitting at a table sipping whiskey with one hand and playing with his ding-dong with the other."

"For an old Baptist boy," John said, "this is just a little too close to Sodom and Gomorrah for me."

"Yeah, Hap," Leonard said, "we better get John back to the hotel before he wakes up naked in an alley with a black leather whip handle up his ass."

We went to the hotel and took our rooms. Me in mine, John and Leonard together. Where we were staying was in the French Quarter, and because of that, we were paying more for location than convenience. The joint was clean and not nearly as primitive as my place, but then again, I was paying one third of my monthly rent for one night in this cracker box and down below I could hear drunks who seemed more than happy to collect like crows and sing show tunes beneath my window.

I even went to the trouble to open my window and yell at them once. One of the drunks, wearing a gold lamé shirt and pants so tight his dick looked like a cucumber in Saran Wrap, looked up at me and said, "Oh, honey, lighten up."

He was right. I was tense. I also hated hearing those morons sing under my window. He and his crowd moved on, and across the street I saw a tired black prostitute trudging along in a red dress that started just below her navel. Her wig was slightly askew and her shoes looked designed to hurt her. She walked in a manner that didn't invite business, but appeared more an invitation to a fistfight. She clicked on down the street and out of sight.

I watched TV for a while and thought about Brett. The last thing I remember was seeing the first fifteen minutes of the remake of *Cat People* and wishing it was the original, and then it was morning.

We met in the lobby, went over and had bignets and coffee at the Café du Monde, and took a short cruise on a riverboat that took us past the place where the tour guide told us *Hard Times* with Charles Bronson had been filmed.

We arrived back at the dock early afternoon, had lunch

at a hamburger joint, went back to the hotel, got our luggage and John drove us to the dock. When we saw our ship, the *Sea Pleasure*, sitting in the water against the dock, it was a little disappointing.

"I was expecting something bigger," Leonard said.

"It's big enough," John said.

"Well, it isn't like on TV," I said. "You know, like those commercials where everyone is dancing on board and fish are jumping and there's a rainbow and stuff."

"It's a smaller cruise line," John said.

"You mean cheaper," Leonard said.

"Does that mean we don't get the dancing fish and the rainbow?" I asked.

"We get a fish floating belly-up under a rain cloud is my guess," Leonard said.

"You guys are always such pessimists," John said.

"That's because pessimistic things happen to us," I said.

"Yeah," Leonard said. "Like our cruise boat is smaller than everyone else's."

We were standing outside John's car with the trunk open. A couple of guys in white steward suits and hats had come over to take our bags. Leonard and I didn't want them to. Considering we only had one apiece, we figured we could handle it. They stomped off without our bags or the tips we might have given them.

"They look disgruntled," I said.

"Long as they keep it to themselves," Leonard said.

Leonard reminded John how to care for his pet armadillo, Bob. Bob had been with Leonard for a year now, and the damn thing was like a dog. It stayed in the house during the day, holed up under the bed or on the tiles in the bathroom right by the toilet. By night Bob roamed the woods and rooted holes in Leonard's yard. It came when Leonard called and would curl up in his lap. I always liked to remind Leonard armadillos were the only animal that could carry leprosy, other than man, but this had no impact on him. Leonard liked that big armored rat.

"Well," John said, "have a good time."

Leonard and John kissed. I felt a little uncomfortable. Two men kissing still sort of jacks me around, especially with me standing next to them. Too much East Texas Baptist background, I guess.

Leonard, knowing this, said, "John, give Hap a little peck on the cheek."

"No," I said, holding up a hand. "I wouldn't want to steal any of your sweetness away from Leonard."

Leonard cackled and John smiled. Leonard said, "At least we didn't give each other blow jobs in the lot here. Isn't that what everyone expects of queers? Blatant sexuality in public places?"

"That, smooth dancing, and interior decorating abilities," John said.

Leonard and John hugged and kissed again. John got in his car and drove away and Leonard and I hauled our bags into the terminal. We stood in a long line there, showed our passports and papers, got our room key, eventually boarded the ship.

Our room wasn't quite as small as a Lilliputian clothes closet. There were two very narrow beds and a wound-colored curtain that opened on a solid wall. Since we were in the middle of the ship, I should have expected that, but somehow I had hoped for a porthole and a sea view.

Then again, since I didn't really like water that much, especially the ocean, I decided I was better off without the porthole. Then I started to wonder what in hell I was doing on a ship. Just reading *A Night to Remember*, I had gotten seasick.

How had I talked myself into this? I had done some

dumb things, but outside of agreeing to rescue a whore and kill people in the process, this was the dumbest thing I had ever done.

Well, there was the time I talked Leonard into going to Groveton during a flood to deal with the Ku Klux Klan. And there was the time we tried to get a stolen treasure out of the Sabine River bottoms. My idea again.

Come to think of it, my life had sort of been a series of dumb ideas. Some of them mine, a few Leonard's. Hell, I had even voted Republican once in a Texas governor's election.

We put our suitcases on the bed and took out our clothes and hung them in the closet, which was a gap in the wall with a metal bar for a clothes rack.

We put our suitcases in there too. It was a tight fit. We put our shaving kits in the bathroom. I took time to brush my teeth and put the book I was reading, along with my reading glasses, on the nightstand, which was bolted to the wall.

We sat on our beds across from one another. I looked over the itinerary they had given us as we entered the ship.

"Well, here we are," Leonard said.

"Yep," I said.

"We haven't left dock yet, have we?"

"Nope."

"Are you bored as I am?"

"Reckon so."

"They have movies on this ship?"

"I read how they did when I got the original stuff from the cruise line, but this itinerary they gave us, I was just glancing through it. Looks like we don't have movies. Wait a minute. Here's a few, but you watch them on the TV."

"TV?"

"I don't believe I stuttered."

"I heard they had theaters, regular movies, you know."

"John tell you that?"

"He did."

"Did he say they had them on this ship?"

"He don't know from this ship."

"There you are. We got the tub of cruise lines. Our luck is still in, Leonard. Only it's bad luck."

"Oh well. What are the movies?"

"*The Postman.*"

"Oh Jesus."

"*Harley Davidson & The Marlboro Man.*"

"I seen all this shit and didn't like it on the big screen. I could get my money back on that *Postman,* I would. Least the other one had some good fistfights. Or was it gunfights? It kind of runs together. But that *Postman,* I thought maybe I was in some kind of purgatory with popcorn. Someone had locked the door there would have been suicides. What else is there?"

I read off the two remaining movies.

Leonard said, "That last one sounds promising."

"It says it has subtitles."

"God. Next to sitting next to someone wants to talk about crystals and astrological signs and the nature of their diseases, I like subtitles better. But just."

"French subtitles."

"Guess that beats subtitles in Ebonics."

"Hey, we didn't go on a cruise to watch television or movies, did we?"

"I did."

"That's not the proper spirit."

"What kind of spirit is proper? I thought I'd just hang out, read, and watch movies."

"You can. On TV."

"Yeah, maybe one movie out of four."

"You git what you git."

"I wanted a big screen, Hap."

"People in hell want ice water."

"How long before dinner?"

I glanced at the clock on the nightstand, then the itinerary. "Two hours. You hungry?"

"No. Not really. Anything else going on?"

"Shuffleboard will start shaking in about half an hour."

"Want to go up on deck?"

"Sure, maybe we can swim back to land before we actually disembark."

"There's a thought."

We locked our cabin, went up a flight of stairs, then another, and finally onto the deck. It was a pretty afternoon out, starting to gray some, but there was still plenty of light. Our ship had started to sail.

We leaned against the railing and watched the New Orleans dock retreat.

"Didn't a ship run right into this dock once?" Leonard said.

"Yep," I said. "Couldn't stop."

"In a hurry to get back to land, I figure."

"Think it's too late to swim for shore?"

" 'Fraid so."

We stood on the deck until the dock and New Orleans were out of sight and the brown water turned blue. Then there was no more dock or New Orleans visible, just the water and our ship pushing into the Gulf and the night coming down soft and the Gulf air sweet with the occasional bite of dead fish, and there was the Gulf itself, washing hard against the ship, washing us steadily with the assistance of a great engine, on out to the deeps.

8

We stood out there by the rail and talked and watched the night fall on the blue water, first making it purple, then black. The wash of it against the side of the ship was hypnotic, and once we got past our initial sensation of feeling like mice trapped in a tin can, we began to relax.

We finally went back to our room to wash up and brush our teeth and shave. It was just something to do. We were finishing up this when there was a singsong whistle on our cabin's intercom. It was followed by a voice telling us all to meet on the deck to find out which was our lifeboat and to learn what to do in case the ship sank, other than drown.

We went out on the deck for our words of wisdom. Essentially, the wisdom was, the big boat started sinking, in an orderly fashion, you got in a smaller boat that was supposed to be lowered over the side of the larger sinking boat. That was about it.

A little later, back in our room, the whistle sounded again, this time with an invitation to all passengers to have dinner, and it ended with the words: "Bon appétit."

We wandered outside and saw the cattle call moving in the direction of the dining room. According to our information, there were two dining rooms. One that served more formally, and presumably better food, and another that was a kind of buffet.

The menu that came with our cabin information said the meal in the main dining room was lobster this night, and we both wanted that.

When we got to the dining room, a fellow in a white coat, white pants, white shirt, and a black bow tie was kind enough to tell us we couldn't come in without coats.

"Why not?" Leonard said.

The door usher, or whatever his title was, was a tall man with dark skin and dark hair with a bald spot at the crown. He looked about thirty and wore his uniform with all the grace of James Bond in a tux. He said, "It's required."

"What's it required for?" Leonard said. "Are we gonna spread it on the ground and eat off of it?"

"Leonard," I said, "let's just go back to the room and get coats. It's easy to solve."

"You'll need a tie as well," said Mr. White Coat. Then, after a moment's reflection: "There's no use coming back without a tie."

"What if I borrow yours?" Leonard said.

"We have security on board," said the man, finally showing a bit of nervousness.

"It's all right," I said. "We'll put on a coat and tie."

I took Leonard by the elbow and turned him around. We started down the corridor, back to the cabin.

"Let's eat in the buffet area," I said. "They don't require anything but that you don't go naked."

"You sayin' we're not good enough to eat in there?"

"No. They're saying that. Leonard, everything is not

personal. Them's the rules. You're one goes on about rules all the time, and those are the rules."

"Yeah, but those are stupid rules. And since when am I one for the rules?"

"All that Republican shit," I said.

"I just don't think I ought to be made to wear a coat for a meal I paid for."

"I paid for it."

"Whatever. But it's paid for. It didn't say anything about a coat and tie in the brochure."

"It said evening wear is suggested."

"Ah ha! Suggested."

We were back at the cabin. I unlocked the door and we went inside and sat on our beds across from one another.

"I'm hungry," I said. "I want to eat. Where are we going to eat?"

"I want my lobster."

"Then let's put on coats and ties."

"I didn't bring a tie."

"Now that you mention it, neither did I."

We put on sports coats and went back. Leonard had the brochure with him. White Coat stopped us at the door. "I see you have coats, but you still need ties."

"No, we don't need them," Leonard said.

White Coat said, "Those are the rules, sir. I did not make them up."

Leonard showed him the brochure. A line was forming behind us. The man looked at the brochure. He said, "Yes."

"It says coats and ties are suggested," Leonard said. "You can suggest it, I can choose not to do it."

"And you can choose to go to the buffet."

"I paid—he paid—for us to go on this cruise. Let us in."

A Filipino fellow in white shirt, black pants, and black bow tie came over. He asked what the problem was. White Coat told him.

"It's suggested, Phileep, not required."

White Coat grew red-faced.

"Thanks," Leonard said, walked past White Coat and I followed. Leonard said to White Coat, "Dick cheese."

I told the Filipino who was showing us to our table, "We're not trying to be a pain—"

"No problem," he cut in, leaning close to me. "He's an officious little fuck. All the staff wishes he'd fall off the boat and get eaten by sharks."

We wound our way between tables of mostly elderly people and were placed at a table with four other diners. Wine was served and menus were brought.

The Filipino was headwaiter on the cruise. His name was Ernesto. He was a short solid-looking guy with black hair well combed except for a sprig that was determined to hang down on his forehead.

Ernesto stood at the table and smiled and talked to us all about what specials were being offered. It was kind of cool really. They didn't do that at Burger King. He leaned down and spoke to Leonard and Leonard, smiling big, talked back to him in a whisper. I caught the words "Thank you" in there somewhere.

Ernesto went away and our actual waiter came and took our choices and left. Ernesto showed up again three or four times. Talked to us all, talked to Leonard a little more. Just chitchat stuff. I finally got a line on it. He was gay and somehow knew Leonard was. What was it? A secret handshake? A mark in the middle of the forehead only gays could see?

When Ernesto finally went away and the food came, I leaned over to Leonard, said, "What would John think?"

"We're just talking. He's friendly."

"Is he gay?"

"I think so."

"You look pretty happy."

"We queers just love to make contact. We have secret messages about the nature of the universe that we only pass along to one another. Sorry, Hap."

We ate. The food was not as good as I had hoped, and the lobster was downright awful. I thought it might be a big boiled cockroach.

We chatted with our table partners. One of the men was wearing neither coat nor proper tie. He was a big white-haired Texas guy with a Western shirt and bolo tie. Fit the stereotype. So did his wife, who was about fifty, maybe ten or fifteen years younger than he was. She wore a kind of Western-cut dress, which didn't look bad on her. She was attractive in a plastic surgery kind of way. Her hair looked like a beehive wrapped in a bleached blond sweater. They looked rich. Their names were Bill— he went by Big Bill—and Wilamena. Right out of Central Casting, both of them. I liked them immediately, even if he was a little loud. I asked him how he had gotten past the coat-and-tie Nazi.

"I gave him five dollars. I figured it wasn't worth five dollars to walk back to the room."

"They haven't got the right to keep you out anyway," Leonard said.

"Yeah, but five dollars keeps him happy, me happy, and no animosity."

"This here is our twenty-fifth wedding anniversary," Wilamena said, "and we ain't gonna let no suit-and-tie monkey throw it, ain't that right, Big Bill?"

"That's right, honey."

A plump matronly looking lady with glasses said, "The ship has Argentine papers, so they're allowed to sail in

Cuban waters. We're going to go right by Cuba. Won't that be interesting?"

We agreed it would. Bill said, "We can buy Cuban cigars too, in Mexico and Jamaica, but we got to smoke 'em on board."

"Frankly," Leonard said, "I ain't buyin' nothing from them commies."

Things went quiet for a moment, then Big Bill, who obviously wanted to defend Cuban cigars but didn't want to be thought a commie or mess up a wedding anniversary, said to me: "Pass that wine bottle, will you, son?"

After dinner, on the way out the door, Leonard leaned over to White Coat, said, "You work cheap. Five dollars is no kind of money. I think you ought to go up to six-fifty, and give a blow job with it."

White Coat did not respond. He just looked as if he had eaten a persimmon and it was caught tight in his bowels.

Down the hall on the way to our room, I said, "Commies?"

"Did I sound like Joe McCarthy?"

"A little."

"Well, you know what, Cuba is a communist country. They haven't ever given us anything but the back of their hand. Fuck them and their goddamn cigars."

We went back to the room. It had been made up in that short time. The TV was on the floor.

"Why's that?" Leonard said.

"Guess he dusted and forgot to put it back."

I put it back and we watched *The Postman* for a while. It put Leonard to sleep. I got up and took off his shoes and covered him, turned off that Flying Dutchman of a movie, undressed, and went to bed.

I lay there for a while and looked at the ceiling and

thought about Brett. I thought about other women in my past, two of them dead. I certainly had the touch.

About midnight the ship began to pitch and I realized why the TV had been placed on the floor.

9

LEONARD AND I were up at the same time. I flicked on the light.

Leonard said, "Oh God," and dashed for the toilet. I heard him in there upchucking, which prompted me to do the same. I let fly into a trash can all my bad lobster, wine, and culinary accouterments. It wasn't all that good going in, but it certainly had smelled better than it did now, and it had looked better too.

The ship leaned way port and I felt as if it would never right itself. I let out with an involuntary cry. I heard Leonard yell in the bathroom, then I heard him upchucking again.

The ship came up high and went starboard and it was all I could do to hold the trash can so the contents didn't slop out.

A little later the commode flushed and Leonard came out and lay on his bed and moaned.

He said, "Oh, God, kill me. Kill me now."

"Fuck the seasickness," I said. "I'm scared to death."

I managed to set the TV on the floor, and by bouncing off the wall, I made it to the bathroom where I poured the glorious contents of the trash can into the commode and flushed it. I sat the trash can in the little shower stall, but it rolled out and I hit the wall and banged the back of my knee against the commode.

I lodged the trash can between the wall and the commode and tried to make it back to my bed. I understood what was meant by sea legs now. I didn't have some. In fact, I'd have given anything for us to have run up on a spit of land, a reef, any damn thing solid.

I just knew we were going to flop so far to one side we'd never right ourselves. I kept thinking about that movie *The Poseidon Adventure,* where the ship turned over and trapped people underwater.

I swear, at times it felt as if that damn ship were actually lying completely on its side, then it would fling itself upright and go the other way. You could hear the ocean banging on the sides of the ship. It made you realize how fragile, what a paper cup the thing was, and it made you realize even more how fragile you were as a collection of blood and bone. All I could think about, after that realization, was just how dark and deep the goddamn ocean was.

I managed to wobble, fall, and crawl over to the closet, reach in a side pocket of my suitcase, and pull out Dramamine tablets. I punched a couple out of the aluminum side and gave Leonard one. I took the other. No less than two minutes later Leonard said, "Hell, give me another one of them sonsabitches."

I did. I took another. It wasn't easy swallowing them dry, but now that I had found my bed again, and was clinging to it like a raft, I couldn't bring myself to let go and make for the bathroom.

Frank truth of it was, I was scared blind, shitless, and paralyzed. No argument. When it comes to the baddest sonofabitch on the block, nature wins hands down every time. Well, nature and that eighteen-year-old guy I had fought.

It wasn't until early morning that the ship ceased to pitch. I had felt horrible all night, slept fitfully, even whimpered a bit. Leonard had whimpered too, so I felt better about it. My manhood was still intact, because he wouldn't tell if I didn't.

Leonard slept while I washed up, brushed my teeth, and started for the deck. On the way up, I discovered a middle-aged woman and two children sleeping on the landing near the hatch door that led outside. The woman sat up from the pallet she had made and looked at me as I reached the door.

"We nearly sank last night," she said. "I thought it would be better if we were close to the lifeboats."

"It was scary," I said, "but not that bad." I was braver, now that it was all over.

"Oh, yes it was," she said.

One of the children, a little girl, lifted up on an elbow. A teddy bear tumbled out of her covers. She looked about nine. She said, "Mama said *fuck*."

"Dear," the woman said. "Ssshhhhh."

"I said it several times last night myself," I said. "Some other things too."

The woman gave me a nervous grin. The little girl smiled. The other kid, girl or boy, I couldn't tell way the kid was wrapped up in the covers, didn't wake up. I went out on deck.

It was clear now. The water was bright blue and so was the sky and the sun was a great fat wafer of burning gold. The shadow of the ship lay on the clear water like an organized coat of oil. It fled with us as we pushed onward, probably running about twenty-two knots.

There were others on the deck, leaning against the rail

like me, and there were some in lawn chairs against the wall of the deck, and there was a young couple with chairs close together, kissing, looking as if at any moment they might strip and go for broke. No one looked as if anything had been out of the ordinary last night. And truthfully, it probably had not. For a landlubber like me, a big wave seen at a distance is frightening enough, let alone knocking and swinging about a ship I'm in. For all I knew, the crew might well have found it relaxing, like a rocking chair.

While I was standing there, looking out at the water, Big Bill came up and lit a cigar. "That was some night," he said.

I turned and smiled at him. He was dressed in blue jeans, a cowboy shirt with the sleeves rolled, and house shoes. His gray hair coiled and rumpled in the wind like some invisible hand wadding up stringy cotton.

"I'll say it was some night. I lost my lobster."

"Not much of a loss. Sort of ruined the honeymoon atmosphere in our cabin, that's what I'm trying to tell you. We were just down to business when all that started. Pretty soon were just two naked bodies rolling around on the floor clutching at each other saying *shit*."

"Worse ways to go," I said.

"I suppose that's true. I got upset, got dressed, came out for a look, like it would do me good to know. Waves were washing all along the deck here. Scary. I went back in and up front and outside. Waves were jumping over the deck, way up there. It was one spooky experience, I guarantee. Cigar?"

"No thanks."

Leonard came on deck then. He greeted Bill, who offered him a cigar.

"Is it Cuban?" Leonard asked.

"Nope. Not this one."

Leonard took it and lit it. He said, "You know there's a woman behind the door there, on the stair landing with two kids?"

"Saw her when I came out," I said.

"Me too," said Bill. "She was there last night when I came out for a look. I was surprised they hadn't locked the doors. Safety seems a little scant to me."

"Her little girl informed me Mama had said *fuck*," I said.

"Yeah," Leonard said, "she told me the same thing."

"Me too," Big Bill said. "You know, this cruise stuff sucks. I'm excited for when we get to Mexico and dock. I want to get some land under my feet and an enchilada in my mouth, wash it down with some tequila. Me and Mama might like to dance too. You know, I was out here early to smoke, and they were pushing a covered body along the deck in a wheelchair, took it through that door over there."

"No shit?" Leonard asked.

"No shit. I asked one of the crew what happened. He said an old guy died last night. Apparently the old fella had taken this cruise several times, thought he'd like to do it one last time, and last time it was."

"I can't believe anybody does this on purpose twice," Leonard said.

"He croaked in all that high seas business," Bill said. "My guess is it scared him to death. They got him in a meat locker or something down below."

"I can see it now," Leonard said. "A sheet-covered corpse in a wheelchair in the food freezer with our dinner lobster and a bag of green peas in his lap."

"Maybe it wasn't the rough seas killed him," I said. "Maybe it was the food."

On that note, we went to eat breakfast in the buffet dining area.

*   *   *

Later in the day we shot skeet off the back of the ship. If there's one thing I can do it's hit a target with almost any kind of long gun. Leonard did fair, but I was really on, and me and Leonard got to betting with Big Bill and this other guy, a Yankee named Dave who looked to be about sixty and turned out to be my and Leonard's age, late forties.

I made about ten dollars off the deal, and Leonard made five. We used our gains to buy drinks for all of us in the bar. I was the only one not drinking liquor. We sat and drank and talked for a while. It wasn't anything special, just talk. Bill and the Yankee were all right if you didn't have to see them on a daily basis. Then again, there's days I feel that way about all Yankees, but I promise I'm trying to get over it.

Later in the day Leonard and I walked around the ship, bored to death. Finally we holed up in our cabin and read. I read from a good Larry McMurtry book about the size of a cement block. Leonard read from *The Adventures of Huckleberry Finn* and laughed out loud a lot.

We had dinner in the buffet room that night. Leonard had made his point and didn't care if he pissed the doorman off again or not.

The food wasn't any worse or any better than where we had eaten the night before, just more casual. I couldn't help but think about that dead guy, maybe in the food locker. Did they have a morgue on board? Maybe. Surely people died on these things now and then. Perhaps more than now and then.

We went to a bad floor show later. I had seen better high school productions. It was a tribute to rock and roll with a Filipino rock and roll band that had probably learned its material that afternoon. Little Richard would have had a heart attack, and I bet Buddy Holly was rolling over in his grave.

The singers were so awful they hurt my feelings and their dancing was a bit more like contained stumbling to music. I noticed however that I kept my eye on one of the female dancers who wore only feathers and had big tits, and I got to thinking about what Leonard had told me, and I had to sit there and do some deep soul searching. I kept my eyes on the tits just the same. I can get over bad dancing.

That night the sea was rough again, but not as rough as the night before. I went up once to check the night seas, and on the landing was the lady and her kids and the teddy bear. The kids seemed to think this was all great fun, but the mother had her back against the wall and she had carried a trash can out with her and she had that in her lap, puking. The teddy bear was hanging tough.

I opened the door, but when a mist of sea washed into my face, I closed it. Wasn't anything I wanted to see out there. I had taken to carrying a packet of Dramamine in my pocket, and I gave it to the lady and her kids.

"It takes time to work," I said, "but it does work. It won't do anything for being scared, however. You know, you'd really be more comfortable in your cabin."

"No," she said.

"Yes, ma'am. You're the boss."

I went downstairs and to bed. About midnight I began to think the woman had the right idea. Perhaps I should get our trash can and go up and join her to be close to the lifeboats. The sea really began to pitch us.

When morning crept up the sea still tossed but the day was bright and things seemed less frightening. About midday we came to the coast of Mexico. It was a thin strip of brown in the distance.

The sea was bad and the ship could not go into shore,

as there was no proper place for it to dock. The ship anchored and they sent out from shore what they called a tender—a small boat to haul us tourists in.

While we were waiting on the tender, we saw the snotty doorman from the dining area. He looked at us, then stuck his hand out to Leonard.

"I'm sorry about the other night."

Leonard nodded, stuck out his hand to accept the apology.

They shook. No one offered to shake my hand. I felt kind of left out.

The guy said, "Going ashore, huh?"

"Oh yeah," Leonard said. "What time do we need to come back?"

The man paused as if remembering.

"Four-thirty."

"Okay. Good."

"Yeah. Well. Have a good time."

"Sure."

The guy went down the corridor.

I said, "He's all right, I guess."

"No, he's still an asshole."

I had been to Mexico many times, but never this spot, so I was reasonably interested in going ashore. Besides, I was ready to do anything to get off the ship, and I thought maybe Leonard and I might get a good meal in a restaurant or café. We went to the purser's desk, signed up for a tour to some Mayan ruins called Tulum, then got in the departure line.

The tender tossed up alongside the ship and we had to walk out to the side of it on a rickety collapsible dock and try to jump on board when it wasn't leaping too high or too low on the waves. A woman nearly caught her leg between the boat and the ship but pulled it back just in time to the delighted screams and yells of those on our little platform and those who had already boarded the tender.

More screams and sighs came when a kid, eight or nine, tore lose from his parents and leaped when the tender went down and landed on deck with a thud and got up laughing. When his mom and dad got on board the tender they promptly whipped his ass to the delight of us all.

An elderly man vomited over the side and a young woman I had my eye on lost her straw hat to the wind. It hit the ocean, the waves leaped on it, and it was gone. I could have jumped in the water to save it so I could be her knight in shining armor and maybe get laid.

I balanced the idea.

Big waves.

Pussy.

Big waves.

Pussy.

Naw. Waves too big. Pussy uncertain. She might just thank me. And the idea of drowning with a woman's straw hat in my hand didn't appeal to me.

One thing, though, she didn't have big tits. I'd have to tell Leonard that later as an example of my maturity. I wouldn't mention the dancer from last night and what I had thought about her.

On board, Leonard and I seated ourselves next to Big Bill and his wife. We were then borne by a chugging motor and churning waves toward shore, tailed by black diesel smoke.

There were lots of folks throwing up over the side and one idiot thought a log floating in the water was a whale and started screaming about it. When the log bumped against the boat he shut up and looked straight ahead like maybe he had spotted an important smoke signal in the distance that only he could translate.

Our tender pilot seemed oblivious to it all. Logs. Whales. He didn't give a shit. He was probably more concerned about capsizing. Two guys with blankets and trinkets wandered about trying to sell them to us. No bites from anyone, but that didn't stop them from making the rounds several times, the prices dropping dramatically with each tour.

I looked back at our ship. A real cruise ship was anchored not far from it. It looked twice as big as the *Titanic*. Our ship looked like some kind of fishing lure next to it.

I wondered if that poor woman and her children on the landing were coming ashore with their trash can on the next tender. I wondered why I had ever thought this would be fun.

I wondered what Brett was doing right now. I wondered if she wondered what I was doing. I wondered if Tillie was making big bucks pulling the train in Tyler. I wondered about that poor girl in the hospital with her face stomped in.

Hell, I didn't have it so bad.

10

It was a short rough trip in high seas but we finally edged alongside the dock and got off to the sound of one woman praying.

The two guys with the blankets got off too and walked alongside us. They hadn't even noticed the pitch of the sea. You would have thought they had been on a rocking horse. The price for their goods, which was in American dollars, continued to drop dramatically as we walked.

Still, no bites from us or anybody. Their wares were damn near free by the time we stepped off the dock onto land. They went away with their stuff, dissolved into the crowd as if they had never been.

Tough way to make a buck.

It felt funny standing on solid land after being at sea for a couple of days. Funny, but good.

Leonard and I walked along looking at people and sights like the tourists we were. We stopped in a cantina and had some food. When we got up to leave, I saw the woman from the boat who had lost her hat. She had her dark hair tied back and was tall and quite lovely in white shorts and a blue halter top, had one of those Audrey Hepburn necks.

On the way out I put on my best smile as we walked by her table, said, "I saw what happened to your hat."

A string of hair had fallen out of her 'do and across her forehead. She looked up at me with dark sensitive eyes, said in a voice that even in Brooklyn would make you wince, "No shit. Who didn't?"

Guess she wasn't looking for love.

We went out and along the boardwalk by the sea. I had sort of hoped, foolishly, of course, that Leonard would let it slide.

"Well sir," he said, "it's good to see you haven't lost your touch with women."

Playa del Carmen is a fishing village on its way to becoming a resort spot, a kind of Mayan Riviera, but not quite. Underneath it all, behind and betwixt the new hotels, is still the small Mexican fishing village that it has always been.

We did the Tulum tour. Went out there by bus. It was about an hour from Playa del Carmen. There was lots of scrubby land and little shacks with tin roofs along the way. All I could think was there wasn't enough shade. It wasn't like where I came from, East Texas, wooded and wet. It was like South or West Texas. Bleak. Why had this land become populated? Had someone actually thought: Hell, ain't this great. Let's just stop here. To me, it looked like the spot where the devil went to shit.

Far as I'm concerned, any place you can see unobstructed by trees farther than you can throw a rock makes me nervous.

Maybe that was it. It *had had* trees, then some industrious types had come along, cut down the trees, killed the wildlife, fucked what they couldn't kill, and stayed because they were too tired to do anything else. Or a wheel came off a cart or something.

We stopped at a couple of places where you could

buy straw sombreros and the rare artwork of the area: little carved trinkets that said MEXICO on them. They were turned out in droves for all of Mexico and shipped across country by truck, but when you talked to anyone there, they were, to hear them tell it, the only ones who had these little items and they had of course all been made by hand, their very own hands. Since two or three feet away was another vendor with the same stuff, you had to wonder if they actually thought anyone really believed this.

They had some pretty neat chess sets carved out of obsidian, and I looked at those but didn't buy. I didn't need it and didn't want to carry it. Leonard bought a sombrero. It had a big wide band that read: MEXICO. He insisted on wearing it, even on the bus. He looked like an idiot.

Tulum was neat. It was built by the Mayans on a cliff overlooking the Caribbean. It was a fortress city, and you could certainly see how it served its purpose. A mountain goat would have needed grappling equipment just to start up the side of the cliff next to the sea. Before time took its toll, the city must have been quite snug with this barrier at its back and the great buildings of solid stones all around to protect it.

There was a temple called El Castillo that had two columns depicting serpents, and a real serpent, a large lizard that looked as if he might do close-ups for dinosaur movies, was crouched on the stone floor next to one of the columns. He looked at us in that slow lizard way, seemed to say, Hey Mack, you're invading my home.

Or maybe, like us, he was just a tourist and thought we were one of the sights.

We spent a couple hours there looking at the ruins, thinking about how the people there must have lived, then we took the bus back.

We still had a couple hours till four-thirty, so we went walking, looking at the sights, such as they were. Leonard

needed to go to the local post office to buy a card and
stamp so he could mail a little note to John. It was a real
chore just getting one of the two workers there, a man
and a woman, to come to the desk. They had a private
conversation going and appeared in no hurry to stop it.
They turned and looked at us like we were intruding, and
went on with their conversation.

"How do you say, Hey dickhead, in Spanish?" Leonard
asked me.

Finally the guy came over. Leonard made a few ges-
tures, indicating what he wanted. The worker spoke to
him in English, grinning as he did it. He then explained
how to say dickhead in Spanish.

Leonard paid him, got pesos in change.

The guy said, "Someone give you the hat?"

"Bought it."

"With your own money, señor?"

Leonard didn't respond to that. He went over and wrote
a short note to John using a windowsill as a desk. He gave
it to the guy behind the desk and the guy dropped it in
an out box and smiled at Leonard's hat some more. We left.

"It's a good hat," Leonard said.

"For what?"

"Keeping the sun off."

"It's more like an eclipse, Leonard. It looks like something goes on a stick over a table by poolside."

"You wanted one."

"Did not."

"Did too."

"I wouldn't be caught dead in something like that."

"It's just that I've got the balls to do what I want and
you don't, that's what's got you irritated."

"I'm not irritated."

"Are."

"Are not."

It was just one of our usual goofed-up days. We might as well have been home in the States. We were unpopular and pissed off wherever we went.

About four we went down to the dock to catch the tender back to the ship. The tender was there with our original pilot standing on the deck, helping people on board, but out in the bay, no ship. Least not our ship.

We talked to the pilot. Our Spanish sucked. His English was good. He told us the *Sea Pleasure* had left at three-thirty. For a moment I thought we hadn't changed our watches, crossed a zone or something, had lost an hour. But we had the right time.

Leonard said to the pilot, "You're sure?"

The guy, who was short and gold-toothed, said, "You see the ship you want, señor?"

Leonard took a theatrical look out at the water.

"Nope."

The pilot shrugged.

"Could it have sunk?" Leonard asked.

"Funny, you are, señor. I got to take people out to the real cruise ship now. And whatever you pay for that hat, it is too much."

We walked back up the dock, stunned.

"That lying little ferret," Leonard said. "I gave him an opening and he took it and told me the wrong time. I see him again, I'm gonna beat him until he has flashbacks."

"Of what?"

"Me beatin' him."

"Can I hit him a couple of times?"

"If there's anything left, of course. You are my best friend."

11

WE DECIDED we might as well plan on being in Playa del Carmen for a day or two, so we ended up at a little pink stucco hotel where we rented a double. The room smelled of damp carpet and the bathroom smelled of urine beneath the warped linoleum.

Upstairs we sat on one of the beds and sorted our money. Most of what I had gotten for my heroic deed was back home in the bank, but I had more in traveler's checks in my luggage on the ship, right next to my clean underwear and socks. I had some bucks in my wallet, two hundred dollars in traveler's checks, and a charge card with a low limit on it. Leonard had a hundred dollars in assorted bills and a very ugly hat.

"Okay, we got enough for a couple nights, maybe three we need to spend them," I said. "That also includes food, phone calls we need to make, and maybe some clean underwear."

"I didn't know you changed yours," Leonard said.

I ignored that, said, "Okay, so what's first?"

"I vote on the underwear for you, but I suppose the thing to do is call John, get him to arrange some plane flights, nearest airport and all that, then we find a way to get to the airport, fly to New Orleans, get a cab to where the ship will dock, get our luggage, cripple the asshole who lied to us about the departure time, break his dick in three spots, cover his balls in peanut butter, pack his asshole with a pound of pure cane sugar, and hold him down in an ant bed."

"Might I point out this is all your fault."

"That so?"

"If you hadn't fucked with him in the first place this wouldn't have happened. All you had to do was put on a jacket or go to the buffet."

"I didn't want the buffet, and I didn't want to wear a jacket."

"And you see the results."

"That pompous motherfucker just thinks he got off scot-free with me. Besides, you said you wanted to hit him some."

"I want to hit you some too. But we'll make a phone call instead."

We looked around the room. No phone. Downstairs they wouldn't let us use the one in the office and there wasn't a pay phone. Suddenly there was a language barrier. The desk clerk indicated he had no idea where we might find a phone.

I asked him if there was a Holiday Inn anywhere near. He just grinned at me. Now I was the Ugly American.

We went outside and around the corner and started walking in the direction of the post office. Had we seen a pay phone in the post office? We were uncertain. As we walked, Leonard's hat provided me with a lot of shade. Which I needed. I was pretty warm. Not as humid as East Texas, but still warm, and by this time it was late afternoon.

The post office was closed.

"What the hell?" I said.

"They keep their own hours," Leonard said.

We walked along the littered beach a ways and actually found an old-fashioned phone booth. But the phone was missing. Someone had torn it out. Some of the phonebook was there, though, just in case it was needed.

"Maybe we could just put a message in a bottle," I said. "Toss it in the ocean."

"I'm game," Leonard said.

The beach was nice, and we decided for no good reason at all to just keep walking along it. I think, subconsciously, we were trying to get away from town, as if that would take us away from our miseries. There was a long wooden dock, and we walked on the sand next to that and watched the boats, some with sails, some without, bobbing in the slate-colored water like tops. Above us seabirds soared, made noises like insane laughter.

As we walked, no phone booth materialized but we saw three men coming toward us. They were stocky guys. One of them wore a coat, which seemed odd for the weather. We veered left around them and they turned and spread out and said something in Spanish.

One of them, a guy with a thick mustache, showed us a knife and a big grin. He said something in Spanish we didn't understand, but the big knife was speaking loud and clear and needed no translation.

It was at that moment that I remembered some of the literature I had read on the boat: Don't wander off from the main areas. Play del Carmen is a beautiful, quaint little town with the amazing ruins of Tulum nearby. But off the beaten path, thieves often rob tourists at knifepoint on the outskirts.

"Bad day for this," Leonard said to the trio, but they just smiled at us. I watched carefully. The other two didn't pull knives, but one of them did pull a machete from under his coat. I had sort of thought that coat was suspicious.

I didn't feel up to fighting a machete, but I didn't feel all that inclined to give them my money.

"Dinero," one of them said.

"We've already eaten," Leonard said.

"He means money," I said. "Not dinner. Dinero."

"I know that."

"I think we should give it to them."

They were circling us, waiting on us to make some kind of decision.

"What if we give it to them and they cut us anyway?" Leonard said.

"It's still going to work out the same, they're going to end up with the money. We give them the loot, we got a chance."

"That what you want to do?"

I watched the guy with the machete ease around in front of me. Leonard and I had now ended up back to back, sort of rotating with the guys as they went around us.

All three were speaking Spanish, and shaking their hands at us like we should fill them.

"What I want," I said, "is to stick that machete up his ass, crank it around like I'm trying to start a prop plane."

"Stop moving, and let them make their move," Leonard said.

"It's the machete worries me," I said.

"What, the knife don't bother you?"

The guy with the machete grunted and his arm went up, brandishing the weapon. I went to him, got under his arm before it dropped, got a hand on his elbow, one on his wrist. I had tried to move to his outside, but couldn't, so I was inside. I held the wrist with one hand and shot my elbow into his face, flicked his wrist, and the machete went away and we went down, him on top. He tried to choke me, but I rolled out from under him and pushed him aside. He came up and had both hands on my shoulders. I kicked at his balls, but he moved his leg in the way, so I kicked to the inside of his legs a couple of times, real quick, and the second shot made him go down. I kneed at his face, but he grabbed my leg and we were rolling on the ground again. I flipped him over, landed on top, bit a chunk out of his ear and pounded him a couple times and got up.

I caught a glimpse of Leonard out of the corner of my eye. He had lost his hat and the mugger with the knife was standing in the middle of it. Leonard knocked the guy with the knife down, but the man still had the knife. The other guy grabbed Leonard's arms from behind, and Leonard stomped his feet and shins, and the guy was letting go as the man with the knife leaped forward and the blade went into Leonard's stomach. I let out a scream, then the guy I had been fighting was on me again.

I flicked my fingers against his eyes and he groaned and got out of my way.

Leonard was down and the guy with the knife was stabbing him again. I got there just in time to slide behind the guy, reach around, and rake both hands across his face, gouging one eye deeply.

The guy shrieked like a rat with a boot heel on its back. He turned, lunged. I went sideways and he went past. I hit him with everything I had, right behind the head with a hammer fist. He went down and didn't move. The guy who had been holding Leonard had him down now and was punching. Leonard brought a leg up and over the guy's head, swept him off, got up holding his stomach. He said, "Watch out!"

When I turned, the machete man had recovered his weapon. He was coming toward me. The other guy came at Leonard. Leonard scooped sand, threw it in his eyes, sidestepped, and shot out a sideways kick that took the guy's knee out. It cracked as loud as a bullwhip. He yelled even louder as he went down.

The machete man charged me.

He was so wild, all I had to do was move and he went stumbling past me. When I turned, Leonard had gone down from his wounds, was lying in the sand, bleeding, unconscious. Maybe worse.

I had done all right the first couple of times, but a machete is a machete, and all it took was for him to make one correct move and for me to make one mistake.

Somehow I was aware of the sun turning red, dying somewhere behind the city. A gull shrieked loudly overhead, cheering us on. Then the guy with the machete began to stalk me, slow and steady, the machete cocked at his side.

I glimpsed something in my peripheral vision. Another man. He wore a blue baseball cap and also carried a machete.

I was about to reach for my wallet, throw it to the guy, hope for the best, when the second machete bearer ran past me. I ducked, but he didn't swing. He just kept going, right to the other man with the machete.

Machetes clanged together. The man who had joined the fray on our side was good. He was not swinging wildly like the other guy. He was warding off the man's strikes with the flat of the blade, using his free hand to slap and grab. Pretty soon he had the other man by the arm and was pulling him down. Using the flat of the blade, he knocked our attacker unconscious.

Our rescuer promptly marched over to the two downed men. One of them was out, the other was clasping his knee with one hand, holding the other hand up as if to push our savior away.

Our fella said something in Spanish and the man on the ground began to crawl away, leaving his unconscious buddies.

The man turned toward me, the machete held by his side. I wondered if I were his next victim. He might have merely been eliminating competition. I eyed the machete lying on the ground, judged if I could reach it quickly.

Nope. Too far away.

The man grinned at me. He had a gold tooth and the sun caught the tooth and made it sparkle. He had on a thick white cotton shirt and pants, and sandals. Although he had moved well and looked younger while in motion, I could see now that he was seventy if he was a day. The hair under his baseball cap was gray, nearly white, and he had gray stubble on his face.

He turned to Leonard, knelt beside him.

I rushed over. Leonard was bleeding. He opened his eyes.

"Have they gone home?" he asked.

"In a manner of speaking," I said.

The man said something in Spanish, and neither Leonard nor I responded. He came back in English.

"Policía. Not good."

"They're police?" I said.

He nodded. "Off duty."

"Oh," I said. "That's good, Leonard. They're off duty."

"Oh good," Leonard said. "You know, this hurts. Bad."

"They are corrupt," said the man.

"No shit," Leonard said.

"They are from Cozumel. They come here to make extra money."

"Nice," Leonard said. "A part-time job . . . Look, I'm gettin' kind of queasy here."

"Come," the man said. "We must go. My boat."

We got on either side of Leonard, helped him up, carried him toward a fishing boat tied at the dock.

"What about my hat?" Leonard asked.

"Well," I said, "if you want it with a hole in the crown. One of those fuckers' feet went through it. If you had ears like a mule, you might want it."

"Typical," Leonard said.

We climbed on board the boat with some difficulty, stretched Leonard out on the deck and opened his shirt.

"Not so bad," the man said. "Had worse."

"Yeah, but it's me that's got this one," Leonard said.

"I will fix it. Beatrice!"

A very attractive, slightly heavy, thirtyish woman with shoulder-length hair dark as a miner's dream came onto the deck. She looked miffed. She wore a black short-sleeve sweatshirt, earrings with silver dangles, blue jeans, and black canvas shoes. She smelled like fresh soap and had a look on her face made me think she could have beaten puppies to death and enjoyed it. I noticed that the tip of her right pinkie was missing and the skin was puckered there and visible was the faint shine of yellow bone.

The man said something in Spanish. The woman looked at us, sighed, went back inside the cabin, reappeared with first-aid gear in a plastic box. She squatted beside Leonard, opened the kit.

The man took out some alcohol, some other disinfectants, and went to work. As he worked, he said something to the woman. She went away. A moment later the anchor was up and the motor was humming. We were moving out into the ocean.

The man turned to me suddenly, smiled, said, "Ferdinand." He stuck out his hand. I shook it.

"How is he?" I asked.

"Oh, he is good. Got good skin."

"Haven't I always said I have good skin, Hap?"

"Always," I said.

"One wound pretty good in the stomach," said Ferdinand. "But it is not so deep." He pulled a large needle and thick thread from the box.

"Oh shit," Leonard said.

"Hold his head," Ferdinand said.

"You don't have to do that," Leonard said. "Just sew."

Ferdinand started right in. After the first pass, Leonard said, "Hold my goddamn head, Hap. Hold my legs. Sit on me. Do something."

I held him as best I could, and Ferdinand made eight stitches.

12

Time flies when you're having a big time.

I don't know exactly when I fell asleep, but I awoke lying on the cabin floor by the bunk where Leonard lay. The woman was asleep on the bunk across the way. I barely remembered us going inside the cabin. Nothing like a good fight and a knifing of your best friend before dinner.

'Course, we might not get any dinner.

I got up, went out of the cabin, onto the deck. It was dark and the moon was up. The sea was a giant basin filled with ink. The boat lifted up and down like a carnival ride. I had never been so sick of water in all my life.

The old man was up top at the controls. I climbed up there and he turned and grinned at me.

"You sleep a little?" he said.

"Yes sir," I said. "Thank you. Thank you very much."

I could see a string of lights out in the distance, along the shoreline. They looked like lightning bugs pinned to a display board coated with black velvet.

"I didn't even know I was sleepy," I said.

"It is fear, my friend. I do not say you are a coward. But we all have fear. It exhausts."

"Been there before," I said. "How bad is he really cut?"

"Not so bad. Not good. Not bad. No cut is good. It did not go deep."

"I appreciate your help. Can I ask why you helped?"

"Why not? I do not like many men on two. Though, you two do pretty good. I think they not have the machete, the knife, you might have been all right."

"You saw it all?"

"From my boat. I was coming in, I saw it. I pulled to the dock. I've seen them do that before. Take money from tourists. They try and rob me once."

"How'd that work out?"

"They did not have a knife. I did not have a knife. But I am strong."

"They're really police?"

"I recognized them. Cozumel. They come here, do what they like, go back across the water."

"Won't they know who you are?"

"I do not think so."

"Well, I hope not. Are you out here to hide from them? I mean, out this late. It must have been some hours now."

"It has been a few hours. I went out to sea some. To fish."

"You went fishing?"

"It is what I do."

"Catch anything?"

"No. That is sometimes what I do. Catch nothing."

The lights of the shore grew closer. I started to say something about having a room rented in Playa del Carmen, but then decided to hell with it. It didn't matter.

As we neared the lights, Beatrice came up the ladder.

Other than the fighting chair where Ferdinand sat, there were a couple of deck chairs up there. Beatrice took one of them, and I took the other.

She said, "Your friend is sleeping good. I believe he will be okay."

"Thanks to you two."

She made a kind of grunting noise. "My father, he is always helping someone. He gets no help from anyone else, but he is always helping someone."

"That is what it is about, Beatrice," the old man said. "Is that not the way of God?"

"If it is, let him do it."

"Beatrice!" Ferdinand said.

She sat quietly for a while. She said, "I'm sorry." Then to me: "I fear for my father. The police, they are very corrupt here in Mexico. If they know what he did, he could be imprisoned. Hurt. Here, the police, they do as they please."

We cruised the water for what seemed like a long time, and though the lights came closer, they did not come close enough fast enough. It seemed as if we were perched on the lip of forever, unable to move forward.

Finally we arrived at the dock in Playa del Carmen. A young, shaggy-haired boy, maybe twelve, in blue jeans and a dirty Disney T-shirt with Mickey's head faded into nothing, ran out to the boat and climbed on board. He started when he saw me, but Beatrice spoke to him and Ferdinand laughed.

"He has been taught that all Americans are dangerous," said Ferdinand. "His name is José and he works a little for me. He waits for the boat to come in and helps me carry the fish and do little chores. Tonight, I have no fish. Just you two. You are my fish. Go ashore. I will lock up the boat. José and his brothers will stay with the boat."

"What brothers?" I asked.

"They will be along. You best look after your friend. Beatrice will help you."

Beatrice and I went inside the cabin and stirred Leonard. He groaned when we woke him. We helped him up. He tried not to act like someone in pain, but he couldn't help it. I said, "Maybe he needs a doctor."

"That could be," Beatrice said. "I have some antibiotics. I can give him those. It will be a while before we are where I can get them."

I considered this. I asked Leonard what he thought.

"Well," he said. "I've felt better. But I've had a lot worse. I think if I get some antibiotics, some rest, I'll be all right."

Beatrice helped me take Leonard off the boat and onto the dock. I had no idea what was going to happen from there. Neither she nor her father owed us anything. They could have just turned us loose in the night. Fact was, they had put themselves in considerable jeopardy to aid us. But I was relieved when Beatrice said, "We'll take your friend to our home for tonight. I want you and him to leave tomorrow. Do you understand that?"

"Sure," I said.

"I am sorry for your friend, but we do not need enemies. My father makes enemies often."

"I bet he makes friends often too," I said.

"Enemies seem a little more determined than friends," she said. "Friends have a way of going away when you need them."

"That isn't my experience," I said. "It depends on who you call friend."

She had one of Leonard's arms draped over her shoulder, and I had the other. He was groaning as we walked along.

I followed Beatrice's lead. We ended up out back of

a stucco building where there were cars sitting in a dark lot near a sign painted on the side of the building. The sign was for some kind of Mexican pastry and the moon made it shiny and white and surreal there in the night.

Beatrice unlocked an old white van and we got inside. The interior was well worn, seats ripped up, patches of cloth hanging from the ceiling. The van had no back seat and was empty of possessions, except for some tow sacks in the back. We placed Leonard on those. I made as comfortable a pillow as I could for him out of a spare sack. He said, "I lost my goddamn hat."

"Just goes to show," I said, "the day hasn't been a total loss. But we've discussed what happened to the hat."

"We have?"

"You weren't feeling too good at the time, but yes, we discussed it. One of our muggers stepped through it."

"Oh yeah. I remember."

I climbed in the passenger's seat and Beatrice started the van. I said, "What about Ferdinand? He said he was coming."

"He always says that, but he does not come. He stays with the boat with José and his brothers. I think he likes it that way. He loves that boat. If he were coming, he would have come."

The van coughed and sputtered and rolled forward with a protesting lurch, banged into a couple of potholes, crunched gravel, and off we went.

We drove along bad roads for an hour or so. It had grown very dark because clouds had bagged the moon. There was just the van's headlights on the road, and a little glow from the dash light that shone against Beatrice's face and gave it a ghostly appearance and made her little silver earrings float about her ears like spectral fish swimming in the ether.

We talked a little, but nothing to take note of. We just

rode on into the night until we came to some sparsely wooded hills that swelled on either side of the road, and we were swallowed by them. Somewhere along there, without meaning to, due to the rocking of the van, the kind of day I had had, I drifted off to sleep, and it was the dying of the motor that brought me awake.

It was a simple house, part adobe, part thatch, just like you see in the movies about Mexico. There were scrubby trees in the yard and an old white Ford without tires or wheels sitting out to the side of the house. Prickly pear had grown up all around it and the moon was out from behind the clouds again and I could see the car was stuffed with all manner of junk.

Beatrice helped me wake Leonard and get him into the house. I held Leonard up while she lit lamps. I didn't see an electric light or refrigerator. The house was very small. Three rooms. Two of the rooms were bedrooms, the other was a kitchen of sorts with an old wooden stove. After we got Leonard stretched out on a bed in one of the bedrooms, slipped off his shoes, she took me outside and showed me where the outdoor convenience was. It was a leaning rectangle of graying slats with a tin roof and it smelled just like what was under it. Beatrice seemed a little embarrassed by it all.

We went back inside and she got a large jar of pills and brought them out. "Antibiotics," she said.

"Jesus, that's certainly the economy version," I said.

"You can buy them like that here. Not like in the States."

"Do you go to the States often?"

"Not anymore," she said. "I lived there once. I studied archaeology at the University of Texas. Austin."

"I've always been interested in archaeology."

She gave me a curious eyeballing.

"Seriously," I said, and told her about having done some digs here and there when I was young, Caddo Indian stuff in East Texas mostly. I had been the shovel boy for a nice amateur archaeologist named Sam Whiteside. She talked about going to the University of Texas, then the University of Mexico, and how she had graduated with a degree in anthropology and archaeology.

She got some water and the pills and took them to Leonard. He was sweating slightly and had a fever. He was only partially awake.

"These," she said, shaking the jar of pills, "should get the infection down. He has not lost much blood. Tomorrow, he rests some, eats, then you go."

"Okay," I said, trying not to think too far ahead.

"We'll give him the pills now," she said.

"But not all of them?"

She smiled. "Not all of them. Just a few."

"Leonard," I said, waking him. "Time to take your medicine."

I supported his head on my arm while Beatrice gave him the pills and held the glass so he could sip water. When that was finished, I lowered Leonard back onto the bed and he went to sleep immediately. Beatrice blew out the light and we went out of there.

In the kitchen she lit the lamps and poured some water from a pitcher into a basin, gave me a bar of lye soap. I used it to wash my face and hands. When I was finished, she handed me a towel.

"We do not have many conveniences," she said. "I had nice things in the States, but here my father is very poor and he lives as he has always lived."

"That's quite all right," I said. "I thank you for helping us."

She opened a metal box on a shelf and took out a loaf of long, brown, home-baked bread. She split it down

the middle, made slices from that. She removed a big
cake of flaking cheese from the storage box, cut slabs
from it, put them on the bread. She poured wine from
a bottle into two fruit jars and gave me one of the jars.
I don't really like wine, but I wasn't about to be rude.
Not after all she and her father had done for us.

We sat in some old but comfortable chairs at a cheap
table supported by wobbly aluminum legs and ate our
bread and cheese and drank our wine.

The bread was full of flavor, and the cheese was sharp.
I even found I liked the wine. At that point, however,
having not eaten in some hours, I think I might have enjoyed a steaming slice of dog shit on a roof shingle.

As we ate, we talked. "I earned my degree," she said,
"but I never used it. I came back here when my mother
died to take care of my father. I have been here ever
since."

"Your father looks like a capable man to me," I said.

"In many ways he is, but he cannot take care of himself at home."

"Maybe he can," I said.

She smiled at me. It was a lovely smile. "You don't
understand what's expected of me."

"By your father?"

"By my past. I have been raised to do the woman's
work."

"You went to the university. That's certainly a mod-
ern enough approach. Does your father expect it of you?
Staying home, I mean?"

"No. But I expect it. I feel I'm failing if I do not do
it. I know I do not have to, yet I do."

"Maybe you should change your thinking."

"My thinking is changed, but my doing is the same."

I smiled at her. "That's one way to put it. Do you
work on the fishing boat?"

She nodded. "And do other things. I go on the boat to keep from staying here. No one lives near here. There is nothing to do. I do not like the boat, but I have my father there, and I can keep busy with the baiting, the cleaning of the fish."

"I assume you sell the fish."

"Yes. What do you do? Are you on vacation?"

"I'm a security guard at a chicken plant."

She grinned wide, and she looked very beautiful when she did that. It gave her deep dimples. Her eyes were bright in the lamplight. I loved the way she spoke English, the way her accent curled around the words and made them sexy.

We talked for a long time. She poured more wine. I meant not to drink it, but I was geared up and nervous. By the time I finished the second jar of wine, I was beginning to feel a little sleepy.

She told me about her life and her disappointments, and they were all tied to tradition and how her mother had lived and how she had tried to break away from it, but couldn't. It had stayed with her like a disease. She loved her mother and what she had done, but didn't feel it was for her—and yet, here she was, in many ways taking her mother's place. A woman over thirty and not getting younger and feeling she was missing out on the world.

"There is never any money," she said. "My father cares little for money. He works. He makes enough to feed us, to get oil for his lamps, a few items here and there. He wants nothing else. He sells his fish too cheap. He does not have money, he does without. It does not bother him."

"But it bothers you."

"I do not ask to be rich, but I would like to have nice clothes. Some things. Is that so bad?"

"No," I said. "It isn't. Fact is, I haven't had all that much myself. It's my fault. You can want too much, but you can want too little as well. I think I've wanted too little. Your father, he seems content, and that's fine. But it's all right you want something more. I think he could do without you, he had to. He seems independent."

She smiled at me, reached to take my glass, touched my hand. She leaned forward, stared at me. "Would you kiss me?"

It didn't seem like a chore. "Yes I would," I said, and did. I liked it so much, I did it again. I don't know exactly how it happened, but the next moment she was out of her chair and in my lap, and we were kissing deeply. She smelled good, her hair was soft, and her lips were sweet.

Still, part of me felt bad about the whole thing. Sort of like I was cheating on Brett. But Brett had gone her own way. I had no reason to feel guilt. No reason at all.

Another part of me felt as if I were taking advantage of a lonely woman who had had too much wine, but that part wasn't speaking too loudly. Hell, *I* had had too much wine.

I kissed her deeply. She ran her hand between my legs and took hold of me and squeezed, and soon I had her in my arms and was carrying her to the empty bedroom. I laid her on the bed and helped her undress, pulling her shoes off, her jeans, her sweatshirt over her head, unfastening her bra and removing her panties.

I stood by the bed and removed my clothes and removed my wallet and took out a prophylactic and gave it to her. She laid it beside her. I climbed onto the bed. She stroked me and finally took the rubber from the package and slipped it over me, then she spread her legs and took hold of her knees and pulled them up so that they were damn near touching her ears.

I entered into her, and in spite of the prophylactic, it felt so good, and it had been so long, I almost came on the spot. It was tempting to just go ahead and let it go, but I fought being selfish. I did the times tables for a while, till they got beyond me, then I tried to remember how to cook a couple of Mexican dishes and thought about the theme songs from favorite TV shows, finally got hold of myself. Then I was relaxed, making love, keeping control on my needs, administering to hers. She knew just how to coax me along, knew what to whisper in my ear, where to put her fingers, how to touch me.

We did it in that position for a while, then she rolled over and I took her from the rear.

Finally, to both our satisfaction, we finished in the traditional position, her letting go first, then me.

It wasn't as wild as it was with Brett, who could do more tricks with a six-inch dick than a monkey could with a hundred feet of grapevine, but Beatrice's lovemaking was slyer than Brett's, calculated as if by script.

She was certainly a woman of experience, and it was exactly what I needed, and from all observation, what she needed as well. As that ol' Merle Haggard song goes, "It ain't love, but it ain't bad."

We lay together and I thought about the day. I had been on a cruise, off a cruise, seen famous ruins, been in a fight. My best friend had been knifed, we had been saved by a wild old Mexican with a machete who turned out to be very nice and had a lovely daughter, and Leonard's awful hat had been destroyed. The lovely daughter had fed me and fucked me, and now I lay me down to sleep.

I wondered what Brett was doing.

Maybe what I had been doing.

Wrong approach.

I closed my eyes.

I pulled Beatrice close.

And wondered again what Brett was doing.

No future in that.

Finally, I slept.

13

NEXT MORNING I ROSE while Beatrice slept, dressed, went in to check on Leonard. He opened his eyes when I walked into the room.

"Morning," I said.

"Morning. My, you look happy. Been poundin' the possum, ain't you?"

"Now that you mention it, yes."

"I can always tell. You have that smug look and the eyes get hooded, like Robert Mitchum."

I sat on the edge of the bed. I said, "Now what?"

"Well, now that you've had what you need, have taken advantage of a poor peasant girl—"

"Hah."

"—I don't think we want to stay here."

"Very good. But that isn't exactly a plan. How're you feeling?"

"Like I've been wiped, flushed, and I'm on my way out to sea. I'm bored enough to collect farts and name them, yet I don't feel like I could do much. I'm lucky I had good stomach muscles, or I'd be dead."

"You're lucky he had a short knife," I said. "Your stomach muscles aren't that good."

"And yours aren't good at all."

"What I have are table muscles. They're more subtle. Look, I'll see if Beatrice will take us into town. Maybe we can make a phone call there."

"How would we get out of here? Get back to the U.S. Pontoon boat?"

"I haven't a clue. Question is, are you up to it?"

Leonard tried to rise, said, "You know what? I'm not up to it."

"Then we better not arrange a way out yet. You don't need to travel, you feel that bad."

"You don't hear me fighting with you."

"Then you are hurt," I said. "I've never known you to give in to me that easy."

"You got a point, bucko."

"Lie down. I'll see I can rustle you up some breakfast."

I left out of there, discovered Beatrice was up and moving toward the kitchen. I followed. She smiled at me.

"Last night was very good," she said.

"Yes it was."

"It meant something to me, but I do not want you to think it meant everything. Do you understand?"

"I do."

"Good. Are you hungry?"

"I am. And so is Leonard."

"How is he?"

"Better, but not up to snuff. I know you want us to leave out, Beatrice. And we will. But maybe another day or two for Leonard to rest."

Suddenly she became very hard. "One more day. No more than that."

"Fine," I said. "One more day."

She put some grounds in a pot and started coffee. It was so dark and rich with aroma it made my nose hairs quiver. I had a feeling it wasn't decaf. She located some more bread and cheese and took it to Leonard. We sat in the room with him and ate the same. Beatrice brought us cups of coffee. After two cups I felt as if I had been blackjacked and ass-kicked.

In spite of the food and coffee, Leonard drifted back to sleep. Beatrice smiled at me. She wiggled her finger for me to come, stood up, and went out of the room.

We went back to her bedroom and went to bed. We made love one more time. I was lucky she wasn't like Brett. I wouldn't have had enough rubbers.

At least it had been that way for a while.

After we lay together for a while, Beatrice led me out on the back porch and showed me how a shower was set up there with a pull chain. The water was in a big tin reservoir. It was put there by the rain and sometimes brought in from outside, but there was only so much water, she said, so we showered together. Which wasn't something I considered a drawback.

As I soaped her up in the pink morning light her breasts, damp with the water from the homemade shower, were dark and slick under my touch, and the thick nipples were tantalizing. I liked the way the soap foamed over them and the way the water plastered her hair to her head, which in the light of day I could see held streaks of gray. I liked the way the water beaded in her pubic hair. Her eyes were deep and dark, her face was full of an expression that showed me there was plenty to like and a lot that was hard to understand. She was a real mystery. I liked that. I liked it so much I kissed her.

*   *   *

About two that afternoon I helped Leonard make it out to the outdoor convenience, stood by outside while he finished, trying to stand far enough away I didn't have to hear the usual bathroom sounds.

"It's great to have a valet," Leonard called through the toilet walls.

"Yeah, well, just don't ask me to wipe your ass for you."

"Hap?"

"What?"

"There's a Mexican catalogue in here."

"It's Mexico, you moron."

"I mean, that's what you wipe your ass with. Pages from it."

"Ouch."

Back in the house, Beatrice, dressed in a simple white cotton dress with red and purple flowers stitched on it, searched through her shelf of books, found Leonard a book in English, Andrew Vachss's *Dead and Gone*, left it with him along with a bottle of water, bread and cheese, and a cup of coffee.

She and I drove into town so I could try and make some kind of arrangements to get home. As we drove along with the sand blowing up and making clouds on the road, she said, "I was supposed to be at the boat this morning, to help."

"What are you going to tell your father?"

"I will not tell him that I was servicing you."

"I hear that. Hey. Wasn't I servicing you too?"

"You were. You did good."

"Great. Good dog. Want me to fetch your slippers?"

Beatrice laughed her musical laugh.

"Will he be mad?" I asked.

"No. He does not make me work on the boat. It is as I said last night. I feel obligated."

"Thanks for going against your obligation this morning."

"That is all right. Even the obligated must have, how do you say it, ashes hauled?"

"Close enough. But, you know, I hate it for your father. I mean, he helps us out, then we mess up his schedule. I make love to his daughter."

"He likes to take José out. José goes with him often. José or his brothers. He enjoys being able to give them a little money. They are even poorer than we are. Father catches quite a few fish. But if he caught all the fish in the ocean, he would only make so much money. It is not a rich life, the life of a fisherman."

"I hear that."

In town we stopped at a little café near the dock. Outside the café the smell was briny and strong of fish. Inside the café there was the smell of cooking fish, and that unique smell of hot sauces and fresh tortillas.

I used some of the money I had to treat Beatrice to lunch, reminded myself to stop by later and get something for Leonard.

We had spicy fish with beans and rice and tortillas. As we ate, I halfway expected one of the cops from across the bay to come in, but that was probably just fearful thinking. Even though the towns of Playa del Carmen and Cozumel were separated only by water, it was enough water unless the renegade cops made regular pilgrimages here.

When we finished, Beatrice had coffee while I found a pay phone that worked near the restaurant and called John's number using my calling card. I got the answering machine. I left a message outlining briefly what had happened. Where we were.

I called Charlie.

"Yes."

"Hey, Hap. You gettin' any cruise ship pussy?"

"No. Actually I'm in Playa del Carmen, Mexico."

"Hey, getting any señorita pussy?"

"Actually, yes."

"Female chihuahuas don't count."

"You're just as funny as clown shoes."

"Hey, I know it."

"Listen. I got a little problem."

"Oh, shit."

"No. Nothing like that. Not the usual."

"Anybody dead?"

"Not yet."

I gave him the shortened version of events.

"Damn. Is Leonard bad?"

"Not bad, but hell, he took a knife. No little thing. It could have been a lot worse. It's a small cut, not too deep. Which is a good thing. This isn't exactly a medical Mecca here."

"You guys. You're somethin'. You could fuck up a wet dream. What do you need?"

"Well, mainly I wanted you to know what happened to us. And I think I'm going to need some money wired until I can get to my money on board the ship. Then I can pay you back."

"How much you need?"

"Well, we'll have to arrange for plane tickets. Stuff like that. I've got some money. But, since I'm not certain how long Leonard's going to have to recoup, if we're going to have to take a hotel or not, maybe a couple thousand. Three would be better."

"Shit. Ask for ten. Same thing."

"I know, Charlie. Maybe you could loan me some, a little from Marvin—"

"—Marvin's in a fuckin' wheelchair. What's he gonna do? Run a little soapbox derby for extra bucks?"

"You know my deal. I'm actually good for it for once. And besides, even when I'm not good for it, I pay it back, don't I?"

Charlie sighed. "I can ask."

"Brett might loan you a little for me. Between the three of you, you might could scrape it up. Shit, man. A thousand would probably do it, we had to. Oh, and John, of course. He's probably got the whole thing."

"Why didn't you call him?"

"I did. He wasn't home."

"So I was second choice?"

"Pretty much."

"Look. I'll see what I can do. Give me John's phone number."

I gave it to him.

"You know Brett's?"

"I do."

"I wouldn't count on much there. I'm just being wistful. John's probably the best bet."

"All right. Who else?"

"I think that's about all the people who like me. And some of them are a mixed bag. There's a lawyer friend named Veil, but I have no idea where he is these days. And besides, I'm not sure he and Leonard truly like one another."

"I know Veil," Charlie said.

"You do?" I said.

"Everyone knows Veil. You got a number I can call you?"

"No. The lady we're staying with doesn't have a phone."

"She the one you're doing the hole punch with?"

"That's an indelicate way of putting it. But yes. We'll

only be there today, though. Tomorrow, we have to head out."

"Didn't turn out so good, huh? Bad in the sack?"

"She was fine."

"Hell, I meant you."

"I was quite good, actually. She told me so."

"Now there's something you can depend on."

"Charlie, I don't know where to wire the money. I guess what I'll do is call you back tomorrow, see if you could raise it, then I'll let you know where to send it. I get the money I can book a plane flight."

"Haven't you got a credit card?"

"I do. But it's one of those that has a low credit limit."

"A kiddie card."

"Pretty much. Something like three hundred dollars. I might even have enough with that and my cash and Leonard's to put together two plane flights, but if we need to eat, anything goes wrong, well, we'd be screwed. Besides, I need to slip these people a little something. They didn't ask, but the old man literally saved our lives. He patched Leonard up good and just in time. Without him and the antibiotics his daughter gave us, Leonard might be deceased."

"All right, Hap. Give me a call tomorrow."

"Done deal," I said.

I went back to the café and joined Beatrice for coffee. The coffee was rich and black and almost took my breath away. Same as Beatrice's eyes.

"When does your father come in?"

"Usually midday. And then he goes back. He used to stay on the boat all day. But now he fishes very early, comes back, goes out again late. He does not go too far. He does not have to. He seems to know where the fish are. This is one of the places he sells the fish to, this café. Perhaps the fish we ate is one he caught."

"Doesn't it bother you to eat a fish you know personally?"

"Not at all."

"That seems inconsiderate."

"Fuck the fish," she said.

She saw me glancing at her little finger, the one with the tip missing.

"You wonder what happened?"

"Yeah. I guess so."

"Fishing line. A shark was caught. He jerked, the line tangled. It took off the tip of my finger."

"I didn't mean to stare."

"It is all right."

We wandered around Playa del Carmen, looking at the tourist shops. Actually, after one shop I was pretty much worn out. The rest were the same ol' same ol', but I put up with it because Beatrice seemed to think she was showing me a good time.

She suggested a ferry over to Cozumel, but I wanted to be available when her father showed and I didn't want to give those cops the chance to see me again. I told her so.

"Of course," she said. "I wasn't thinking."

All I could think about was Leonard back at their home, wounded, with nothing but bread and cheese to eat. I ought to get back there, and maybe it would be best to get him closer to town right away, one of the hotels. I might even be able to find a doctor, provided Charlie could rouse enough money.

I said, "Since you need us out tomorrow, we could walk around and see if I can find a hotel for me and Leonard. We actually had a room rented, but we didn't show last night. We might can get a room there again."

She didn't hesitate. "Very well."

We ended up at a different, cheaper, but nicer hotel. It was white stucco with a large palm near the front and a sign that translated something like the House of Siesta. Out front was a medium-sized yellow dog that looked croaked. It lay in the hot sun like a flapjack on a griddle. When we stepped over the dog, it wagged its tail, just to let us know it didn't need burying.

Inside, Beatrice spoke Spanish to the man behind the desk. He had rooms.

"Shall I set you up?" she said.

I had been watching a couple of very large cockroaches practice sumo style shoving in the corner of the room. Kind of made me feel homesick, actually.

"Yes. Make it two nights. I want to give Leonard a little time to rest, time for the money to get here."

She talked to the desk clerk. I gave him my charge card. Signed some papers. When he gave me back my card, Beatrice said, "Tonight, you two stay with us. I arranged for you a night after that. That is enough, is it not?"

I was surprised after what she had told me about wanting Leonard and me out, but I said, "Should be. If not, I can extend it. It doesn't look as if people are knocking the doors off this place to get in."

"It's nicer than our home," Beatrice said.

I felt bad, but didn't know what to say, so let it go.

As we left the hotel, I said, "Why are you letting us stay tonight? I had the feeling you needed us out."

"You are why. I thought maybe we do tonight what we did last night. As for why I want you out, well, I have personal reasons. They are not your fault."

"I can live with that," I said.

We wandered around for a while, but her father didn't

show at the dock. We finally went back to the café and bought some coffee and sat at a table and talked.

"Have you ever wanted something so bad, and you had it in your hand, and you let it slip away," Beatrice said. "Just one decision, and everything changed."

"Beatrice, it's the story of my life."

"I had my chance in the States. But I came back here to be a Mexican woman in the tradition of my mother. Why? I know better. Why did I do that?"

"Perhaps you were worried about your father?"

"I like to think so. I told you that last night. But it is more. It is like I am imprinted, and I keep doing the same thing. I cannot go backward now, not easily. I have squandered so much, so much time. I would like the big score, you know?"

"I know. I've tried that myself. It can happen, the big score. Win the lottery. Gamble and hit the jackpot. But most likely you don't win the lottery, you don't hit the jackpot. Slow and steady wins the race."

"I am nearly thirty-five, and I have not begun my race. I ran it for a while, but in the wrong direction. Correct that. I ran in the right direction, but like an idiot I turned and came back the way I had run. Now I am at the starting line again. And I am tired, Hap."

"I'm not trying to get into your life. I don't know your life that well, Beatrice. But why not go back to the States? You've got the education. There are opportunities there. You said your father doesn't expect you to be here. He'd understand. He'd want the best for you."

"Too hard," she said. "I would have to get more education to actually get a good job in archaeology. That takes money. I do not have money."

"Work and earn money. Then take the courses you need."

"Work at what?"

"You have enough education to get a job. At a small museum maybe."

"It takes too long. I need the money right now, so I can take the classes. So I can have freedom. I am sick of having nothing, Hap. Physically sick."

"Maybe we want too damn much," I said.

"That could be," Beatrice said. "But you know what? I want it just the same."

14

LATE THAT AFTERNOON the old man's boat came in. We were at the dock waiting. When the boat arrived and was tied at the dock, the kid, José, jumped off, Spanish tumbling out his mouth so fast you could almost see the words.

"It is Father," Beatrice said. "He has been hurt."

We both rushed to the boat, climbed on board.

Ferdinand was lying on the bed in the boat cabin. His leg was bound up in white cloth and there was a lot of blood.

He and Beatrice spoke to one another in Spanish. When they finished, she sat beside him on the bed. I leaned against the door frame. The old man smiled at me.

"Señor. How are you today?"

"I'm good. But you're not. What happened?"

"Stupid accident. I do this all my life, and now I do this stupid thing. I hooked a small shark. I brought it in, and in the process of hitting it in the head, it came off the hook and wiggled on the deck and bit my lower leg. It is not bad. It was a very little shark."

"He cannot walk," Beatrice said. "I consider that bad."

"No, señor. It is not bad."

"Bad enough. I hope you doctored it as well as you doctored my friend."

"I stitched it up myself."

Beatrice leaned over and looked at the bloody bandage. She started removing it.

"It is fine," said the old man.

Beatrice let out her breath. "It is not fine. My heavens, Father. It is terrible. You need to see a doctor."

Ferdinand spoke to her in Spanish.

She looked at me. "He says he cannot afford a doctor."

"Do you know where one is?"

"Yes. "

"Then let's get him there."

José had come back onto the boat. He looked in at the old man, his eyes wide. The old man spoke to him. The boy immediately began to unload their catch.

"José and his brothers will help sell it in the marketplace. Father will give them nearly half of it. They do not deserve half of it. Only the boy went out."

"He works hard," said Ferdinand. "His family is poor."

Beatrice barked a laugh. It wasn't a happy laugh.

"Father, you are something. Come, let us get you up from there."

The doctor wasn't home. I sat on the doctor's porch with Ferdinand while Beatrice went to find him. It was nearly dark when she finally came back, an old man plodding along beside her.

He looked like something out of a Humphrey Bogart movie. He wore a white linen suit that looked as if he had slept in it. Scuffed black shoes run-down on the sides and a shirt that had been last washed during the Mexican Revolution, and then only because he had been caught out in the rain. He had salt-and-pepper hair and the front of it hung down on his forehead as if it were too ill to consider being combed.

I heard him call Ferdinand by name, then the rest of it was in Spanish, which left me out. They apparently knew each other well.

I helped the old man up. He was stiffer than before. As the doctor came to help me, I could smell liquor on his breath.

We got Ferdinand inside the house. There were clothes piled up and a couple of men's magazines on the couch with naked señoritas on the cover. One was open to a centerfold and there was a German shepherd in the picture with a lady one could no longer describe as young. In fact, she looked as if she might have been more at home with a horse.

The doctor paused long enough to flip the magazine closed and toss it off the couch.

I glanced at Beatrice. She looked at me and shook her head. We sat Ferdinand on the couch. The doctor disappeared into the other room.

Ferdinand said, "They are not his magazines. He has a very crazy son. He is my friend's shame. He lives here with his father."

"The question is," I said, "does the son have a German shepherd?"

"I do not think so."

The doctor came back carrying a bag. He pulled up a chair in front of the couch, sat in it, carefully lifted the old man's leg, placed the foot on the chair in front of him and began removing the bandages.

The injury was pretty bad. You could see where the old man had poured some kind of red stuff over the wound, and it wasn't bleeding badly, just sort of oozing, but it was too deep and too wide for stitches, though the old man had tried.

The doctor clucked over it for a moment. He got a bottle of whiskey out of his bag and gave it to Ferdinand. Ferdinand unscrewed the cap, took a snort. The doctor took the bottle back, took a snort himself. He offered us some. Beatrice and I declined.

The doctor went away, came back with a pan of water. He went to work on the leg, cleaning it, snipping away the thread where the old man had tried to sew what couldn't be sewed.

I went out on the front porch. The smell of the wound bothered me. I had smelled far too many wounds in my lifetime. Beatrice came with me.

She said, "He will be out of work now."

"What about the kid, José? Or his brothers? Can't they work for him? Help you out."

"They would expect to be paid."

"If you catch fish, pay them. If you don't—"

She laughed. "It is so easy for you, is it not. Being an American. There is always money."

"I don't know what you think you know, honey, but one thing is for damn certain, I haven't got any money. Leonard and I own a dime and we let each other carry it from time to time, but heaven forbid we should spend it."

Beatrice shook her head. "My father owes money, you see. He has to make it back. He will pay the doctor from his catch. Give him fish. We need every fish to make every peso we can. Not only to live, but to pay back his debt."

"He borrowed money?"

She looked at me with those beautiful, soulful dark eyes.

"He borrowed for me . . . It is not your business, Hap."

"Very well," I said.

She studied me for a moment, as if trying to make

certain I wasn't going to wrestle it out of her. When she decided I wasn't, she told me anyway.

"He borrowed from a man who adds much interest. He borrowed so that I could go to the United States, to the university. He has been paying it off all along. And I, well, I did nothing with my time there."

"You chose to come back. You could have done something with your education if you wanted."

"Let me put it this way. One night I am in the U.S., and I am out with friends, and they order fish. And I am looking at the fish, and thinking, this is what my father does, and he is doing it every day so I can be here. I decided to come home, help him earn the money back. This was more important. I knew he would never pay it off. The debt would be there. It was right for me to assume the debt."

"What about what you told me before? Being like your mother. Or feeling obligated to be that way."

"That is part of it too, Hap. If I were smart, I would have got a job and helped pay off the debt. My degree would have helped do that. Instead, I come back and live like a peasant to pay off this big loan by helping him fish. What kind of thinking is that, if it is not the thinking of someone who believes they are trying too hard, and wrongly, to rise above their station."

"If you'll forgive me, Beatrice. It's stupid thinking."

"I know. But I do it just the same. Let me tell you why I want you to leave tomorrow. My father has a charter. A big important charter. Men who want to fish. They have agreed to go out three days. They will pay a lot for this. Far more than the cost to fish. They are rich Americans and my father has guaranteed them each a trophy fish. There is a place where there are plenty of great fish. My father knows it. If the fish are not there, we do not make as much. And I must be very kind to one of these men."

"I don't think I like the sound of that."

"I am not yours, Hap."

"I didn't mean it that way. I don't like the idea of any woman having to be nicer to a man than she wants to be."

"I have met this man. He is not my favorite. But this money, it could pay off our debt to this other man I told you about."

I was liking the sound of it less and less. But Beatrice was right. It was not my problem. And she was not my woman.

"What happens if you don't find the fish?"

"This man my father owes. He is a man with much pride. More pride than the need for money. He can be unpleasant."

"Jesus, Beatrice. Your father is in to a loan shark?"

"He is more than a shark. He is a school of sharks. One time a man owed him and did not pay, and this shark, Juan Miguel, he had the man killed, the body skinned, boiled, and sold his skeleton to a medical school."

"That sounds like a story to me, Beatrice."

"This is Mexico, Hap. Stories like that are real here. The final word is this. We owe him money. We are behind in our payments. He has threatened my father. He and his thugs."

"Your father doesn't seem worried."

"He is worried. But he keeps it to himself. He will seem even more congenial now than before. It is his way of dealing with disaster. Tomorrow he will lose the big charter because of this, and then there will be no way to pay the money."

"My God, how much could he owe?"

"In American money, it would be eighty thousand dollars."

"Christ. A fishing trip, even if these guys catch ten trophy fish apiece, won't pay for that."

"But it will keep him at bay. We have managed to pay some of the debt already."

"He loaned a fishing peasant eighty thousand dollars? He's an old man. How would he think he'd ever pay that off?"

"The debt is his, then it passes to me. He pays what he can, and I continue to pay throughout my life. With interest, of course."

"You should have stayed in the U.S."

"Then they take it out on my father."

"Then he should have come to stay with you."

"It is his debt, and he feels obligated to pay it. It is not like for you, Hap. He could not just go to a bank and get a loan."

"Hon, I couldn't get a bank to loan me the time of day."

She studied me carefully, to make sure I was serious. She sighed abruptly and looked off toward the ocean. I had the uncomfortable feeling she might be waiting for me to offer her money.

I said, "Seems to me it would still be worth sharing with José and his brothers. That would be the best way, wouldn't it? Have them help you fish, pay as you go."

"My father does not want to give away his place to fish. José and his brothers, they are good boys, but they would tell others. They work for whoever they have to work for. I do not blame them. But this place, my father needs to keep it secret."

"If it's so full of fish, why does he often go without fish? Today he didn't come back with fish. Except the shark that bit him."

Beatrice didn't answer.

"Listen, Beatrice. I'm just an ol' East Texas boy, but I'm not dumb. And I mean no disrespect, but what you're telling me, it doesn't add up. I hate to be one to talk about welshing on a debt, but in this case, where your life is in danger, why don't you just run for it. Go to the States and forget it. Pay it back later if you feel you owe it. When you can."

"You cannot run from Juan Miguel. Don't worry, Hap. I have told you more than I should. Really, this is not your business."

It never is, I thought.

We walked back into the main part of town and ordered some food for Leonard. They wrapped it in brown paper and put it in a sack. I went back to the doctor's house. The doctor loaned the old man a pair of crutches, and he used them to go with us back to his boat.

Beatrice and I helped him secure it, then we made our way to their car, and Beatrice drove us to their place.

On the way, the old man talked very pleasantly to me. You would have thought nothing had happened to him. That this injury didn't matter. He acted like someone eccentric and wealthy who didn't worry about money.

Beatrice, on the other hand, was quiet. A cloud seemed to have descended over her. Or perhaps I should say a darker cloud. From the moment I met her there hung about her a grimy aura of disappointment, as if all her ambitions were living things that she had seen slaughtered.

At their place I checked on Leonard first thing. He said, "It's about time you came back. Hell, I'm bored. I read the Vachss book. Great. I got up enough energy to look for more books I wanted to read, but there wasn't much in English that interested me. Where's Beatrice? The old man? What's his name?"

"Ferdinand. By the way. He had an accident."

"Accident? What kind of accident?"

I told Leonard all about it. Gave him the details of the day.

"I'll be damned. Where is he?"

"With Beatrice in the kitchen. Fixing some food. I brought you some. I thought we'd be back a lot earlier. Sorry. Hope you weren't too hungry. I was going to get you some vanilla cremes or wafers, but couldn't find any. Actually, I didn't look that hard."

"Gee, thanks."

I sat down on the edge of the bed and handed Leonard the grease-stained sack. Inside were burritos and tacos.

"Think you got enough?" Leonard said, peeking into the sack.

"I figured you'd be hungry."

"You're right. I ate the bread and cheese right away. Got bored. This smells great . . . What about us going home? You made a call, right?"

"Right. Go ahead, eat."

"Something's wrong? It always is, so why wouldn't it be now."

"I didn't say that."

While he ate, I said, "You know, I heard a joke the other day at the chicken plant."

"Oh no. I don't want to hear it. Your jokes suck, Hap. And that means things aren't going well. You always try and soothe me with a joke. It only makes it worse. So just cut to the chase."

"I didn't say I had bad news."

"But you do. I know you well enough to know something's come up."

"All right. I have some bad news."

"I knew it."

"Well, considering I have some bad news, you might want to hear my joke."

"Just skip the joke and go straight to the news."

"Then you'll never hear this great cowboy and Indian joke."

"I can see now you're going to tell the joke. No matter what I say or do, short of killing you, you're going to tell me this goddamn joke. Am I right?"

"I heard it from a fella out at the chicken plant."

"You said that. How bad is the news on the other side of it?"

"Not that bad."

"Oh, for heaven's sake. Go ahead . . . Wait. Why me, man? Can't you just save these for someone who cares? I hate jokes. You always do this when I'm sick or injured. Which, come to think of it, when I'm around you, is pretty frequent. I got to tell you, Hap. I been thinkin' I want to put my feet up some. Know what I'm saying?"

"You want to put your feet up."

"I mean, I love you, brother, but there's something about us, when we mix together, it makes shit. Know what I'm sayin'?"

"I do."

"Maybe we could call one another, have lunch, go to a movie. Double-date. Me and John. You and whoever . . . But man, we plan something big together, I seem to always get shot, knifed, beat, et cetera. And come to think of it, you look pretty good. You aren't cut up or banged up."

"I got a few bumps. And hey, I been on the bad end before. Don't make yourself too special. Now the joke. There's this cowboy—"

"Shit. Go for it."

"—and he's captured by Indians. The chief says, It's

the custom of our tribe to give the condemned man three days of granted wishes. Stuff besides 'I want to go home.' That kind of thing."

"This sucks already. You can't tell a joke to save your life."

"So, the chief says, Cowboy, you got three days and a wish a day. Use them wisely. What do you want first? Cowboy says, Let me talk to my horse.

"Cowboy calls his horse over, whispers in the horse's ear, horse thunders off, and just before sundown the horse shows up with a beautiful redhead on its back."

"Man or woman?"

"In my story it's a woman. Has to be for the story to work. You'll see."

"All right."

"Cowboy takes the redhead into the tent and they make love, he puts her on the horse, and the horse thunders off, taking the redhead back to town. Or wherever.

"Next day. Oh yeah. The horse has come back. That's important."

Leonard sighed.

"Chief says, This is your second day, your second wish. What'll it be? Cowboy says, Let me talk to my horse. He whispers in the horse's ear, and off thunders the horse.

"Near dark, horse shows up with a beautiful blonde on its back. Cowboy and the blonde go into the tent where he's held captive, and make love. He puts the blonde on the horse, and the horse takes her away."

"Don't forget the horse comes back again . . . Am I right?"

"Yeah. The horse comes back. So, the horse is back, and it's the last day, and the chief says, Pick this wish wisely, cowboy, because it's your last.

"The cowboy sighs, says, Let me talk to my horse. He calls the horse over and grabs it by the ears and puts his face close to the horse's face. He says to the horse, Listen, stupid. Read my lips. POSSE. POSSE."

I paused.

"Yeah," Leonard said. "So."

"Think about it . . ."

"Oh, I get it. Now isn't that funny. The horse thought he was saying pussy. You heteros are just full of fuckin' fun. Hap, I want to go home. Tell me what happened with the phone call."

I told him.

"You got us a room in town, though, right?"

"That's right."

"So the worst is a little delay?"

"Well, yes. But . . ."

"Oh, shit. No."

"Don't panic."

"Don't hesitate."

"I'm supposed to call Charlie tomorrow. He's setting things up. But way I see it, Ferdinand saved our lives. You're out of it anyway. Why don't I sort of help them out on the boat."

"You can't even float a paper boat, Hap, let alone go out on the ocean and fish. Didn't you learn anything from our short cruise?"

"Yeah, don't insult the guy at the ship's restaurant. You're blaming me, but think about who really got us into this mess."

"It was your idea to go on a cruise."

"Actually, it was John's."

"You're right. When we get home we'll kill him."

"I bet he's watching that *Kung Fu* thing right now."

"Could be. Or he's taping it. Him and Charlie probably call each other up and talk about the characters."

"You see, Leonard, way I see it is, I can at least volunteer to be a deckhand till the old man gets better. It's a bad wound, worse than yours, but he can probably get around in a few days. Beatrice and I can take care of business till then. And there's another thing."

"There always is."

"Ferdinand owes some money."

"Define 'owes some money.'"

"I think I should help you to the outdoor convenience."

"I didn't ask to go."

"I think you should go anyway."

"Well, actually, I do need to go."

"Good, that way I can tell you in private."

Leonard rolled to the side of the bed. "Hell, I can walk by myself. I feel a lot better."

"But you'll humor me."

"If I must."

Leonard put on his shoes. I put my arm around him and helped him outside. It was fairly dark and the moon was up and it was a fragmented moon. Clouds scuttled across the sky and in the distance I saw sheet lightning rage across the horizon. You could smell rain in the air, but it was still some distance away.

As we walked, I told Leonard the story Beatrice told me. He went inside the outhouse, and I stood outside, leaning on it, talking to him, finishing up my story through a split in the walls.

"Let me see," Leonard said. "She went to the States, and her father provided the money with a bad loan. She got a degree, but then felt sorry for her father. She was being driven by an inner force to return and do traditional Mexican woman things. And now she's in a tight spot with someone named Juan Miguel who might kill her and sell her bones to research, and she's going to pay a big chunk of the money by sponsoring a three-day fishing trip to a secret place where fish live, but the old man doesn't seem to go there on a regular basis even if he is living on crumbs and owes a gangster thousands of dollars. Duh."

"Maybe it's just worth more to him to go there when he's got rich tourists. It could be like that."

"And when I come out of this outhouse I could be white, bowlegged, and have a vagina, but it isn't likely. Bottom line is, you're gonna help her, aren't you. And, of course, you would like me to help."

"That sounds about right. Hurry up, man, it stinks."

"You think it's rough out there, you ought to be in here."

"What d'you say, Leonard? Shall we help?"

"I say when it comes to women you are so goddamn dumb as to make a box of tenpenny nails seem high on the IQ scale."

"You think she trained a shark to attack her father so she could get me on their boat and make a work slave of me?"

"No. It's broader than that. Damn. This catalogue is not a good idea. Maybe they could at least spring for some toilet paper. I think I ripped myself."

A moment later Leonard came out of the outhouse. I put my arm around him and started helping him back to the house, even though he didn't need the help. We went slowly so we could continue talking.

"You will wash your hands at the house, won't you?" I said.

"Just the one I wipe with. Which, by the way, is the one I have around your shoulder right now."

There was one little sad tree in the yard, and we went over to that. It was only a little taller than we were. Its limbs were gray and scaly, like a snake shedding its skin; they were spread out wide, like gapped fingers in the moonlight.

Leonard leaned against the tree's bent trunk. He said,

"As your queer friend, I don't have the same blind side to women you do. A queer can look at things head-on, my honky. Least as far as men and women go."

"How is Beatrice, a woman I just met, giving me the screw? Outside of the actual screw, I mean."

"She's one of life's victims. Woe is me. Everything happens to her. I think her father, nice man that he is, may not have his head on just right either. Call it a hunch.

"Look. Don't get me wrong. I'm glad she and her father helped us, but I say tomorrow morning we head into town and get that hotel room and plan our way out of here."

"Well, she hasn't exactly asked me to help. Maybe she doesn't even want me to help. She even told me she wants me and you out of here tomorrow. Probably because all of this coming down. But I think with her father on crutches, she might need some help. That's all I think there is to it."

"If she doesn't want you to help, then don't. Don't force it."

"I just hate to see anyone bullied."

"I promise you, this whole business she's telling you, it's got a light coating of slime on it. Maybe she doesn't intend for you to get involved. Maybe she knows the whole thing sucks the big old donkey dick. I don't know. But it's not our business. So let's just walk away."

I stood quiet for a moment. I looked at Leonard leaning against the tree. He wouldn't be much help anyway. Not by tomorrow. Did I really need to run off and help Beatrice and her father pay a debt that wasn't mine? She wasn't even my woman. Not really. She had said so herself.

"You know what, Leonard? I'm gonna fool you. I'm gonna do just what you say. For once. You're right. This isn't our problem."

15

EARLY NEXT MORNING it was very humid and I awoke sweaty. I had been given a pallet on the floor in the room where Leonard slept in the bed. Beatrice had slept on a pallet in the kitchen, and the old man had slept in her bed.

In the middle of the night I awoke to see her standing at the open doorway of the room where Leonard and I slept. She wore a thin white thigh-high nightgown. Her legs were dark and sexy in the shadows. She smiled when she realized I was looking at her. I could smell her perfume from where I lay. It smelled dry and earthy.

I got up, she took my hand. We went to her pallet in the kitchen. Beatrice was soft and sweet and I only thought of Brett a little.

Before daylight, I returned to the room where Leonard lay wide awake.

"You're so bad," he said.

"You said it," I said, and lay down on my pallet and went to sleep.

It wasn't a good sleep. When I awoke I was exhausted and my bones felt as if they had been sawed up, put in a blender, then poured back into my body. I was sweaty.

I rose and wrapped up my blankets and pillow and put them on the bed next to Leonard. Who, of course, was snoring like a man who had just won the lottery.

I slowly moved my body, heard my knees and ankles and hips pop. I got up and limped about. I didn't find Beatrice.

The old man was in the kitchen. He was on his crutches by the stove. The kitchen smelled of coffee and something baking. The aroma filled my head and made my stomach growl.

"I am baking some bread for breakfast," Ferdinand said. "I have some butter. We can eat it together. Maybe your friend will be hungry then. Is he doing better?"

"Much better, thanks to you. He ought to be up and around today."

"It was not too bad a wound. He lost some blood. That was the most of it. The blood. I wish I had a steak to feed him. Steak is good when you lose blood. I know a man down the road who owes me a goat. Perhaps later we can get him to give me the goat and we can butcher it and cook it. It is not a steak, but it is meat."

"Perhaps," I said. "Where is Beatrice?"

"She has gone into the town," Ferdinand said. Like Beatrice, I loved hearing him talk. It was musical even when he spoke English. He spoke nearly perfect English. But the way he emphasized or accented certain words made it sound so unique. I liked the way he looked too. The way I would have thought Hemingway's Santiago must have looked in *The Old Man and the Sea.*

"She said she will come back for you," Ferdinand said.

I was thinking about the boat gig she told me about. What had happened to that? I couldn't help myself, I said, "Not to meddle, but didn't she tell me she had an important job that the two of you were to do today?"

"You are right. We are supposed to do a job. I have

told her I cannot. Even though we must and it is important. We cannot. She has gone to tell the men we cannot and that we must delay the job if they will delay. Otherwise, no job. Did she tell you the job?"

"Very little," I said.

"I would like to do the job. It pays well, but I cannot. This is the first time in twenty-five years I have been injured that I do not fix it myself. Like I fix your friend."

"You did a good job."

"I am too old. I cannot fix myself. I cannot deal with it the way I once did."

"No reason to."

"I do a lot of things, allow a lot of things now that I would not allow before. I am nowhere the man I once was."

The old man's gaze took a position over my shoulder. I turned and saw Leonard shuffling in. He found a chair and sat.

Leonard said, "I don't know if I thanked you properly or not, sir. But thank you. You did us both a great favor. You're good with that machete."

"The machete was part of my life growing up. For work, for play, and for fighting."

"Play?" Leonard asked.

"Play fighting. We fought using the flat of the blade. The art of machete fighting is nearly lost, my friend."

"I can see that," Leonard said.

The old man smiled.

When the bread was done it came out flat and blackened in spots. We put some real butter on it and had coffee. It wasn't a gourmet meal, but it wasn't bad either.

We sat around the table and talked about this and that, the weather, life, women. I didn't mention Beatrice, of course, but from the way the old man looked at me, it was obvious he knew what his daughter and I had been doing. Once he stared at me long enough and hard enough I added too much sugar to my coffee.

When we finished all of that coffee, he brewed us more and we drank that, and by noon he had found a bottle of wine and was drinking heavily from that.

Neither Leonard nor I touched the wine.

About two o'clock Ferdinand passed out in his chair and Leonard and I put him in his bed, took off his shoes, and propped a pillow under his head.

"I like the old bastard," Leonard said. "He tells good stories."

"He's worried," I said. "He's trying to put his mind on other things."

"There you go worrying about other people's problems again."

"You said you like him."

"I said I like him. I didn't say I wanted to raise him. We get home, I'll buy you your own old man. Better yet, you can take care of me. Hold my balls up while I wash."

"That'll be the day."

We went back to the kitchen and got the last of the coffee. We had already gone through two pots, and now, with another cup of coffee poured up, I felt as if I might be able to levitate, in an agitated sort of way, of course.

There were a couple of chairs on the front porch, so we went out there and sipped our coffee. It was hot outside and the coffee made us sweat twice as bad.

We hadn't been out there long when we saw a dust cloud coming from the south, a red clay swirl against a bright hot sky. Pretty soon, out of the cloud, came Beatrice in the van. When she braked to a stop, the dust continued on, as if it had disgorged her. It passed over the house and made us duck our heads and cough. When I looked up there was a coating of it over what remained of my coffee. I leaned out of my chair, past the edge of the porch, and poured it in the dirt.

Beatrice practically leaped from the car. Her hair was up. She wore jeans and an oversized red shirt with white deck shoes. There was a sweat line around her neck and sweat blooms under her arms. She saw us on the porch, sauntered over a little too casually.

"How are you this morning?" she asked.

We both answered in the affirmative.

"And you?" I said.

"Well enough. Are you ready to go into town?"

"I suppose we are. Maybe you could show us a store or two where we can buy a few things. We left some stuff at the other hotel, but we haven't the inclination to go back for it."

"Some bellhop is wearing Hap's new underwear right now," Leonard said.

"I will just check on my father, wash a little, change clothes, then we will go."

She rushed inside quickly, as if she might burst into tears at any moment. I started to follow. Leonard took hold of my arm.

"Leave it be, buddy. It's not your problem. You can't solve everyone's problems. Look at it this way. You can't even solve your own."

"Point," I said. "Damn good point."

A little later, when Beatrice had herself together, looking fresh in a blue blouse, she drove Leonard and me into town, to the hotel where I had rented us a room.

After Beatrice had gone up with us to see our room, which though not fancy was nice, I walked her back to her car.

She opened the door, said, "You have been very kind."

"I have to say the same."

"I have been loving, have I not?"

"You have."

"No complaints?"

"No complaints," I said. "You'll give our best to your father?"

"Of course," she said.

She got in the car, pulled the door to. The window was open, she leaned out of it.

"I think, in another time, things could have been different," she said.

I wasn't sure I wanted them to be that different. I liked her, but I didn't love her. I loved Brett, goddamn me.

Still, I couldn't help myself. "How did it go?"

"Go?"

"You know. With the men who wanted to rent your boat?"

"You don't want to know," she said, and I saw a tear well up in her eye. I started to push it, remembered Leonard's advice.

"Whatever you say," I said.

"Goodbye, Hap. "

"Goodbye, Beatrice."

She drove away, and I thought that was the end of it.

16

I WAS IN THE HOTEL ROOM, taking off my shoes, getting ready to lie back on my bed and rest a bit, when Leonard, who was already reclining on the other bed, said, "You know what we should do, Hap?"

"I hope you're not going to suggest anything sexual."

"Nope. I didn't bring any of my devices with me. But, now that you mention it, we could catch a mouse and grease him up, let him run up our ass. That might be fun."

"We don't have a mouse."

"There are little black turds next to that hole in the wall to the left of the electric socket by the TV set. So that tells me there are mice."

"Now you've piqued my excitement. But alas, we've nothing to grease the mouse with."

"You're right. And who's to say we can catch one? They're pretty fast, you know."

"All right, I bite. What should we do?"

"Stay."

"Stay? I thought you wanted to go."

"I wanted to get you away from that woman. Women make your head mushy. I tell you, she's a manipulator."

"Not much of one. She dumped us off and went home."

"It would have been just a matter of time, Hap. What we ought to do is just go ahead and turn this into a vacation. Have Charlie wire us some money just like you planned. But we do it a little different. We can get a flight out of Cancun in a couple weeks, be home a few days before we're supposed to go back to work."

"Don't you want to see John?"

"Of course. I love him. But this is our chance for a vacation. We've never really had one. Not a real one. Not a good one. Things we do tend to go wrong. This could be different."

"We've already been abandoned by our own cruise ship."

"Yeah. Well, you're right."

"Cruise ships are noted for their hospitality. Their ability to deal with cantankerous assholes. Yet, somehow, you found a way to piss them off."

"It was just that one guy."

"You've been in a fight. You've been knifed. That's not quite as good as being shot, but it ought to count for something. And your hat was destroyed."

"True. You're right. It's not a totally different kind of trip for us, is it? There's some of the old charm still there. But the rest of it, we can make it uneventful. We get up late. We eat late. We wander around town. Maybe go fishing. Get out on the water."

"I don't like water. I've seen all of it I want to see."

"We could see the sights. I wouldn't even mind going back to Tulum. Wouldn't it be nice just to hang? Nobody trying to kill us. No one beating on us. It could be rejuvenating."

"People do try to hurt us a lot, don't they?"

"On the nosey. Maybe that should tell us something."

"What?"

"I'm not sure. I think we irritate people."

"We? You got a mouse in your pocket?"

"If I did, we'd be in business. A dry mouse, but in business . . . But tell me, Hap. Doesn't that sound like a pretty damn good idea?"

"A dry mouse?"

"A real vacation."

"You know, it doesn't sound too bad at that."

Early the next morning I went downstairs and expanded our stay at the hotel to a week. I put it on the charge card, knowing full well I was working on the edge. It might not take more than a couple of pennies for it to be full.

I didn't want to use the hotel phone, because the prices were jacked up, so I walked down the street to the same pay phone I had called from before, dialed Charlie to let him know our plans. He seemed bored to hear I was calling. When I told him what we had in mind he wasn't bored any longer.

He had already raised some money, and was surprised we were staying. So was I, but I was glad to break him out of his boredom. I consider it a kind of special accomplishment to rattle Charlie.

I told him Leonard wanted a real vacation and I felt like I owed it to him. So far, this one hadn't been as bad as our other outings.

Charlie agreed that it hadn't been as bad as it sometimes gets. He also agreed to wire us the money, tell John we were all right, and explain our plans.

On my way back to the hotel I was surprised to see Beatrice sitting in her car out front. When she saw me walking up, she got out, leaned on the hood.

The jeans she was wearing were so tight they must have made her ankles swell. She had on a halter top that was working overtime to hold her breasts in. The sun struck her black hair and made it the color of a raven's wing. There were little brown freckles on her shoulders I hadn't noticed before, but now, out in the full sunlight, they showed clearly. I liked them.

I said, "Don't tell me this is a coincidence."

"I was trying to decide if I wanted to go in and ring your room. I did not expect you to be out so early."

"I had a phone call to make."

"You are not leaving already?"

"That seems like a funny question. You know I was supposed to."

"Yes."

"Leonard and I changed our minds. We're going to stick a few days."

"Good. Good. I need to talk to you."

"We can go upstairs," I said.

Leonard greeted Beatrice with as much enthusiasm as his suspicious mind could muster, and we all went downstairs together and over to a little café for breakfast. The café was fairly crowded and there was the sound of European and American voices all over the place. A cruise ship had most likely sent in its passengers on a tender. We found a table in the corner, ordered coffee and food, waited a long time for it.

While we waited, Beatrice said, "I have had a situation arise."

"Oh?" said Leonard. "Really?"

I gave him a hard look. He gave me back a dreamy smile.

Smug sonofabitch.

"You have problems with me?" Beatrice said.

"I just don't like to be fed shit and told it's tapioca," Leonard said. "My buddy, Hap, he don't mind some shit for tapioca. He even gets to like it now and then."

"I do not understand," Beatrice said.

"Look, I'm not trying to be offensive," Leonard said.

"You are doing a very good job of it," she said.

"All right. Take it like you want to take it. But I think you can smell a sap good as a shark can smell blood. I think you've got a scam going and you're playing him into it, which means you're playing me into it. It happens to him, it happens to me."

"You think that, Hap?" Beatrice asked.

"He's right more than he's wrong," I said.

Beatrice hung her head and stared at the table. She looked soft and cute and childlike. I wanted to reach across the table and slap Leonard.

"Well," Beatrice said, "I did not set out to ask you for anything. I met you by accident, you must admit that. My father and I did help you in your time of need."

"So now you need help?" Leonard said.

"I do."

"You and about three million other women Hap knows. Not to mention guys, pets, et cetera."

"Ah ha," I said. "You rescued an armadillo once."

"I admit it," Leonard said. "That was another fine mess you got me into, if you'll recall."

He was right. There was nothing to say.

Our food arrived. We drank coffee and ate, waiting for Beatrice to drop the next shoe. Hopefully a very small shoe, like a flip-flop maybe. But no, that would be too easy. I figured it would be a boot. Steel-toed. Very heavy.

She ate and we paid up and left.

Outside she said, "Hap, can we talk?"

"Alone, you mean?" Leonard said.

"Yes," she said.

"That figures," Leonard said. "He's no good alone, lady. But then you know that, don't you? Don't ask him to do anything you wouldn't ask me to do, because you ask him, you're asking me."

"It does not have to be that way," Beatrice said.

"Yes it does," Leonard said, and walked away. He called back: "I'll be at the hotel. Crying."

"Will he really?" Beatrice said.

"In a manner of speaking," I said. "Come on, let's walk and talk."

We went along the shoreline on a concrete walk. The sea was bright green, as if lit from below by an emerald light. In the distance I could see the brown line that was Cozumel and against that the horizon. The ocean stank of oil and dead fish and up close to shore there were plastic wrappers and aluminum cans washing against the blinding white sand.

"Now that Father is injured, he cannot do any more than drive the boat."

"What about you?"

"I am company."

"Ah. Company. To this man you told me about."

"Yes. This rich American and his friends. They are here in Mexico for a short time. This one who arranged it all. He wanted to fish the other day. When my father could not go out, he was ready to cancel. We would lose all the money. I tried to convince him with words to wait. To give Father just a couple of days. He could be on the boat then. He didn't want to listen. So I convinced him with something besides words."

"You slept with him?"

"If this man I slept with is a pig, the one Father owes is a butcher . . . It is not for me, Hap. It is for my father.

If I don't make the money, the men my father owes will kill him. They may kill me."

"What are you asking, Beatrice?"

"Help me. Just for a day or two. Please."

Leonard said, "Once more into the breach."

We were sitting at the café again, just me and him, having coffee. Leonard was feeling pretty good. His appetite was back.

"You know she's just jerkin' you?" he said.

"Yep. I know."

Leonard sipped his coffee. "I don't care she slept with this guy. That's her choice. I don't see that as something pathetic. You aren't jealous, are you?"

"We aren't in love, if that's what you mean. But it hurts my pride some. She slept with me, then she slept with the other guy to make sure he went fishing. Worse yet, she has a hotel room and is staying in town tonight. I doubt it's just because she wants to be close to the sea."

"More favors?" Leonard asked.

"I suppose."

"Maybe he was just a better lay. I bet that was it."

"Thanks for being concerned with my pride."

"Don't mention it . . . So we're going to be conned into being sailors."

"You can con me all you want, and I'm no sailor. Actually, I think she wants us to bait hooks, that kind of thing."

"Believe it or not, that takes skill."

"Aren't you the one said you wanted to go fishing?"

"Yeah, but I wanted someone else to bait my hook."

Next morning, Leonard and I arose early and couldn't find anything open to have breakfast, so we walked on over to where Ferdinand's boat was docked. Ferdinand's boat was being loaded with bait by José.

"I thought we were the crew," Leonard said.

"When it leaves dock, we are."

I climbed on board. I found Ferdinand on crutches. "Where is Beatrice?" he asked.

"That is what we were wondering, señor."

About that time a large man and two other men came up the dock and climbed on board the boat.

One of the men was about thirty-five, tall and stocky with close-cut blond hair and burning blue eyes. He wore a loose blue shirt and tan khaki slacks and white deck shoes.

Right off I thought he was an asshole. I also thought he was the guy Beatrice had screwed to maintain the fishing charter. He looked too damn smug and in charge to be anyone else. The guys with him were both about his age and were dressed similarly. One was thin and had dark brown hair and a mole on the side of his face that could have been painted with eyes, mouth, and nose, and passed off as a Siamese twin.

The other guy was a handsome, average-sized black man. I watched to see if Leonard checked him out.

He did.

Blondie said, "We goin' or what?"

Ferdinand smiled, straining at it I'm sure. He said, "Yes. We are waiting on Beatrice."

"Beatrice," he said. "She's not here?"

"Ferdinand just said that to see if you'd ask if she's really here," I said.

"Yeah," Leonard said. "She's hid. We're all going to start searching the boat for her in a minute. Whoever finds her gets a gummy bear."

"And who are you two?"

I wanted to tell him I was the guy that was going to

throw him off the boat, but it wasn't my boat and I was here to help, not make matters worse.

"A friend," I said.

"And him?" Blondie said, nodding at Leonard.

"I jes do duh coffee and put fishes on duh hooks," Leonard said. "I's known as Unca Leonard."

"That's funny," Blondie said.

"Why thank ya, suh. I's got me uh liddle niggra minstrel act I's been workin' on."

The black guy laughed. Mole Face was smiling. José finished loading bait, then, sensing tension, disappeared like morning fog.

"Look," I said. "We'll go back to the hotel and see what's up."

"I'll go with you," Blondie said. "I left her early this morning so I could run some errands. She's supposed to be here. I'm gonna give her a piece of my mind."

"I wouldn't give her too much," I said.

"Yeah, and why's that?"

"Because I might not like it."

"And I don't know you got mind to spare," Leonard said. "I think you use most of it just getting up in the morning."

Blondie snorted, looked at Leonard. "Lost the minstrel act, didn't you?"

The veins on the sides of Leonard's neck expanded.

"Whoa," the handsome black guy said. "It's cool. It's cool. Let's not get off on the wrong foot. We're down here to fish."

"Yeah, and this charter hasn't been nothing but a problem," Blondie said. "I'm ready to chuck the whole thing."

"Hey," Mole Face said. "You got some poontang out of it, didn't you . . . Oh, sorry, old man. I forgot she was your daughter."

Ferdinand didn't say anything. He just looked stunned.

I put my hand on his shoulder. "It's all right. Me and Leonard will go check on her."

He nodded.

We climbed off the boat. Me, Leonard, and the blond asshole.

"You don't have to come," I said to Blondie.

"Yeah, but I want to," he said. "I left her this morning, I told her to hurry along. One thing I hate's a woman that doesn't do as she's told."

"You asswipe," Leonard said. "I've got a mind to knock your nose on the other side of your head."

"Don't push it, buddy," Blondie said.

Leonard laughed. It actually scared me, and I love him. I figured Blondie, if he had a couple of brain cells left, must have felt his stool go loose.

At that very moment Beatrice came rushing up, breathless. Boy, was Blondie glad to see her. I saw a bit of color come back to his face.

Beatrice was holding her side, showing she had been hurrying. Her hair hung wet around her face. She had on a shorty towel robe, flip-flops, and was carrying a large yellow plastic bag. She saw us staring at her.

"What?" she said.

"You're making us wait," Blondie said.

"I'm sorry, Billy," she said. "Really."

She almost started to cry. I noticed she had a bit of a black eye.

I took hold of her arm, nodded at the eye, said, "He do that?"

"Wha . . . Oh, no. I slept on my hand or something. I am fine."

"She bumped her head on the headboard last night," Billy said. "When I was putting it to her from behind."

Beatrice felt me tense. She said, "Please, Hap. Please. I'm not bothered, you shouldn't be."

I let my breath out slowly. "All right."

"You're not needed here," Billy said. "In fact, why don't you and your man here stick to shore."

"I need them along," Beatrice said. "They'll bait the hooks."

I knew then why she had really wanted us along. She was afraid of this joker.

Billy looked at Leonard. "Now you've nothing to say?"

"I was concentratin'," Leonard said. "Tryin' to decide how hard I'd have to pull your head for it to come off."

Billy tried not to show he was bothered, but his bobbing Adam's apple betrayed him and the Elvis sneer he manufactured trembled. "Come on," he said. "Let's fish."

17

As we boarded the boat behind Beatrice and Billy, Leonard said, "What I suggest is we finish out the day, I whip his ass. If he still wants some, you can have him."

"We'll flip for first later."

Beatrice took us aside, said, "Father will show you how to bait the hooks. It is hard at first, but when you have baited a few, it will be easy."

We set the boat free of the dock and chugged out into deeper water. The day was hot, the sky blue, spotted with clouds as white as Santa's whiskers. The diesel exhaust, combined with the motion of the boat, the heat, made me feel ill. Within fifteen minutes I was vomiting over the side. Pretty soon thereafter, Leonard was doing the same.

Billy was sitting in the fighting chair, drinking a cold beer he'd pulled from the ice chest. He laughed. "Couple old sea salts."

As we hung over the side of the boat, Leonard said, "I'm mortified."

"Did you bring the seasickness pills?"

Leonard shook his head. "Afraid not."

*   *   *

It was a long day. I had only thought it was hot. Now it turned hot. The sardines in the big plastic buckets smelled ripe as disease.

Ferdinand showed us how to bait the sardines on hooks. It was harder than it looked. But after only a few fish came off the hooks and I had poked only five or six holes in my hand, and Leonard had managed to rediscover his East Texas heritage by teaching everyone on the boat all the curse words known to humanity in English, we had it going.

A little fishing was done en route, but nothing was caught. We moved out into deeper water. The sea was bobbing and rolling at first, but as we went out farther it became more violent. Not stormy, just active. The diesel smoke that had made us sick before was worse now, and the waves were enormous.

Leonard and I went back to tossing our guts over the side, then dry heaving.

Billy loved our predicament. He had a strong stomach, so therefore he thought he was a strong man. He gave the rod to the black guy, whose name was Landis, and stood near us with his beer, slurping it.

"What you boys need is a big old bowl of greasy chili."

"You motherfucker," Leonard said. "I didn't feel so bad, I'd stick that bottle up your ass, see if it would help you float."

Billy moved on. The boat chugged on.

Out where it was deep, the waves rose up around us in blue-green mountains, then dropped away, as if swallowed by an earthquake. The little boat rode up the waves, and down the other side, then the mountains appeared again.

I had only thought the cruise ship we were on was small and scary. All I could think about was one of those waves crashing on top of us, carrying us down into that bottomless water.

In time we got used to it enough we could work baiting the hooks. Landis fished for an hour and got bites, the bites took his bait and we rebaited, but no luck.

The guy with the mole on his face took a turn. His name was Jason. He sat down in the chair and slipped on the waist and shoulder straps.

I baited his hook and he sat with the butt of the rod in the swivel and waited. He fished for almost an hour, then there was a click on the rod and the line began to sing like electricity charging through a wire.

"I got something," he said.

"No shit," Billy said. "Hold on to him."

I looked out at the water. The line had gone taut. Jason tightened the drag, jerked back on the rod. The rod bent slightly.

"Now I've got him," Jason said.

"You've got him when he's on the boat," Billy said.

The fish cut to the right and the line moved with him. Jason hit him again, burying the hook. He said, "He's not too big. He's nothing."

Jason rapidly cranked the fish on deck. It was a barracuda.

Ferdinand came out of the cabin on crutches. He had one hand dangling off the crutches and in it he held a sawed-off baseball bat. He lifted one crutch from under his arm and laid it on the ground and leaned forward and used the bat to whack the flopping barracuda on the head.

Ferdinand had a pair of shears in his back pocket. He dropped the ball bat, pulled them out, managed himself to a squatting position, put the barracuda's head between the blades, and snapped down hard. The head nearly popped off. Ferdinand snapped down again, and this time the head came loose. He cut the line that held the barracuda to the rod, tossed the barracuda's head into the ocean.

He crutched into the cabin, came out with a metal box. He opened it, and quickly, expertly, he tied a large hook to the cut line.

"Bait it," he said.

I reached into the bucket of stinking fish and did just that.

Ferdinand took a large knife from the box, cut the barracuda open, and dumped its guts into the water. He put the barracuda into a large ice chest just inside the door to the cabin.

Jason said, "That's my fish and that's just about my hour."

"You're next, Billy," Landis said.

"A barracuda," Billy said, "that's no kind of fish."

"Sometimes the barracuda is all the fish you hit," Ferdinand said. "Barracuda are good to eat. I can sell them to the restaurants. There are people who like to eat them, thinking they are eating a very dangerous fish. They are not really that dangerous."

"Well, if he'd wanted to mount him he'd have been shit out of luck, wouldn't he?" Billy said. "Way you snapped it up and cut off its head. What if we don't want to sell it to a restaurant? Maybe Jason here wants him on his wall."

"No," Jason said. "No problem. Go ahead. Take your turn."

"When I catch my fish, I want him on the wall. So don't fuck with him. You hear, old man?"

"I hear," Ferdinand said.

"Let's let the lady fish," Billy said.

"That is all right," Beatrice said. "I see enough fish."

"No," Billy said. "I insist."

Beatrice looked at him, said, "Very well."

"You don't want to fish, don't fish," I said.

"No, it is all right," she said.

Beatrice took off the short cloth robe. Underneath she was nearly wearing a bathing suit. There was almost enough cloth there to hide a quarter if someone shaved it around the edges with a pocketknife. The suit was black, one of those things with a string that went up her ass and covered nothing. The top just managed to fit over her nipples. I could tell she didn't wear that sort of thing regularly. The skin on her buttocks and around her breasts was lighter than the rest of her, which was deeply tanned. Her pubic hair, which had not been waxed or shaved, escaped at the edges like little black tentacles waving to the public. What cloth was there clung to her snugly and showed the shape of what the old romance novels called her womanhood.

Though Beatrice was probably new to that kind of bathing suit, she wore it naturally, as if unbothered by scrutiny, but I thought I saw in her eyes a look I had seen before.

Late at night, while driving, a cat had darted in front of my car, and I'd hit it. When I got out to see if there was hope, the cat had looked up at me, dying, its eyes hot and savage, terrified in the glow of my flashlight. Even out there in the brutal sunshine, Beatrice's eyes looked that way.

My guess was Billy had bought that little get-up for her and expected her to wear it, and she was doing just that.

I looked at Ferdinand out of the corner of my eye. I could tell from the look on his face he wasn't happy. That kind of bathing suit wasn't exactly the sort of thing a daughter wore around her father.

I baited Beatrice's hook.

She thanked me, seated herself in the fighting chair, strapped in, and cast. She was very good at it. The line went far out and into the rolling water. She put the butt of the rod in the swivel. She took a beer from Jason and sipped it. Billy stood by her chair for a while; then, bored, he got another beer and sat on one of the benches built into the side of the boat.

It was sticky and the bobbing of the boat no longer made me sick. It rocked me pleasantly. I watched Beatrice for a while as she reached inside her yellow bag beside the fighting chair, took out suntan lotion and began to apply it. I observed carefully as she rubbed it on the tops of her feet, up her ankles, all along her legs, and finally her flat stomach and the tops of her breasts. I felt the boss change positions in my pants.

She finished that, took large sunglasses from her bag and put them on, picked up her beer again and sipped it. I began to feel sleepy. I sat against the side of the boat, leaned against one of the benches, drifted off, thought of home, and Brett.

Brett wasn't as young as Beatrice. Or quite as firm. Or as brown. But God almighty she had it going. I missed her. I wished she missed me too. I wished I was ten years younger, handsome, had five million dollars and three more inches on my dick and my hair wasn't thinning. While I was at it, I threw in wishing for a pastrami sandwich on rye and immortality.

Of course, wishes are wishes. As my dad used to say, wish in one hand and shit in the other and see which one fills up first. The same can be applied to prayer. Shit in one hand and pray in the other. Within moments you can determine the real power of prayer.

I was awakened by the singing of the line. I sat up to see Beatrice drop her beer foaming onto the deck, reach out, and take the rod from the swivel.

"You got something," Billy said.

"No shit," Leonard said.

The line went tight and Beatrice jerked the rod, hit the fish, and it jumped. It was long and enormous. A sailfish.

"Goddamn," Billy said. "Look at that. That's record size. Don't you lose him. Hit him again."

And she did. The line went even tighter. Beatrice was pulled forward against the straps of the fighting chair. I could see one of her nipples peeking over the top of her bikini. It looked brown and friendly.

Beatrice tightened the drag. The line veered to the right, wide. Then back to the left, like a thin saw cutting lumber.

"Loosen the goddamn drag," Billy said.

"It's all right," Beatrice said.

"I know fishing. Loosen the drag."

"So do I," said Beatrice. "My father owns a fishing boat."

"Don't you talk back to me."

"Sorry," Beatrice said, and loosened the drag.

I was suddenly up and standing next to Billy.

"You keep talking to the lady like that, and you'll be swimming home," I said.

"Lady?" Billy said. "Look at those tits and ass hanging out. You call that a lady?"

At that moment I tensed to hit him, but Leonard took hold of my arm.

"It's their show," he said softly. "For the moment."

I took a breath, stepped away back to the bench, and sat down.

All right, I told myself. This is her game. Let her play it. She wants it like this. She knows what she's doing. It sucks. But it's her game.

Ferdinand worked the controls, reversed the boat and slowed the speed, gave the big fish room to run.

"I have one on my wall that's a record," Billy said. "And it's not near big as that one. I've never seen one that big. And a goddamn woman hooks it. Don't you lose it. You hear?"

"Yes, Billy," Beatrice said.

Acid boiled around in my stomach. I looked at Ferdinand. He was stoic. My admiration for him was fading. Surely he knew the score. He must, or he wouldn't let this shit go on. And if he knew the score, then that meant he wanted Beatrice to do what she was doing.

Leonard sat down beside me.

"Just be cool," Leonard said.

The rod was bending. Billy said, "Loosen the goddamn drag."

"It will hold," she said.

"Loosen it."

She did. The line sang, vibrated like a violin string. The fish went wide to starboard.

"Look at that cocksucker run," Jason said.

The fish leaped.

I've never seen anything so incredible. Up it went. The sunlight hit the fish and it was many colors. Red and blue and gunmetal gray. Its veins appeared to stand out under its flesh. Nothing like it would look the moment it hit the deck, dying. Its color would fade. It would fade even more on the trip to shore. It would lose all of its real color in the taxidermist's shop. It would end up dead and mounted on someone's wall over their couch. A living, twisting, multicolored piece of magnificence turned to a hard, leathery, listless shadow of its former self.

The fish struck the water and disappeared.

The line slacked. The pole began to straighten.

"Hit him again," Billy said.

She did. With a pull and a grunt. Then she hit him again.

Sweat pops were coating her forehead now, running down her chin and chest. The bathing suit was damp with it. A convention of sweat beads gathered in her belly button and made the bits of exposed pubic hair limp. The muscles in her legs and arms coiled and knotted, as if being braided from the inside. She pressed her little feet hard against the footrests.

"It's too big for her," Landis said.

"No," Billy said. "She can land it. It's the biggest fucking sailfish I've ever seen. It's a goddamn dinosaur."

Beatrice worked the line, the drag. It was obvious she knew what she was doing, probably better than Billy, but it was just too much fish. It might have been too much fish for anybody.

Billy poured a cold beer down her back.

"Chill out and hang in," he said.

I looked at Leonard. "Let me just knock a tooth out."

"Not yet. Don't fuck her game for your pleasure."

Beatrice hit the big fish again, solid, and it leaped. Pinned itself against the sky like a brooch on heaven's chest. Hung there for what seemed way too long to be natural. Then, finally, even it was overcome by the laws of gravity, and down it went, slicing into the water.

"It's like a goddamn submarine," Jason said.

The line went solid again, jerked Beatrice against the straps. They were starting to cut into her shoulders, making red lines.

"You take the line," Beatrice said. "You want him. You fish him."

"No, honey," Billy said. "You're going to bring him in."

"I cannot," Beatrice said. "I am much too tired."

"You're stronger than you think. I know. I've been on

the receiving end of your power. If you can fuck all night long, you can fish all night long."

I glanced at Ferdinand. He was red. He gunned the boat's motor.

"Hey, old man," Billy yelled up at him. "You're pulling the line too tight doing that."

"Sorry," Ferdinand said, and cut the engine back.

"I want this fish, Beatrice," Billy said. "You want to give me what I want. What I'm paying you gives me what I want, and then some. You fuck this up, you'll pay. You know that."

"Yes, Billy. Oh, God, Billy, please. My back feels like it is breaking."

"You're okay."

"My arms. I cannot hold them up."

"Sure you can."

"You want the goddamn fish," I said. "You take it. She's hurting."

"Nothing worth doing is easy," Billy said. "It's her fish, and she'll land it."

"Please, Billy," Beatrice said. "You can have it. It could be you caught it in the first place."

Then I really got it. He was mad Beatrice had caught the big fish instead of him, and he was punishing her with it.

I called to Ferdinand. "Cut it out. Let's take the boat in."

He looked at me, his mouth moved at one corner, but he said nothing.

Billy said, "I'm paying ten, no, twenty times . . . You hear me, old man, twenty times what you get for a charter. So you do it my way. Beatrice will do it my way."

"It is okay, Hap," Beatrice said. "I can land him. I can do it."

"You don't look like you could hold your leg up," I said, "let alone land that monster."

"I can," she said.

The boat stopped and the great fish sounded, dove way down into the deeps. The rod bent into a bow. Beatrice was beginning to shake. Her face was pale and her eyes looked as if they might roll up into her head. She was stretched forward in the straps so that her back was away from the fighting chair, exposed. I could see the cords of muscle there, knotted like the Gordian knot.

"She can't take much more of this," I said. "This is silly. I'll take the fish if you won't."

"You won't do any such thing," Billy said. "It's her fish and she'll land it. She caught it, she can bring it in."

"Billy," Beatrice said. "I feel faint."

He poured beer over her head. "Here, this'll freshen you up."

Beatrice shook the beer from her hair, began to cry silently.

Landis said, "Maybe it is enough, Billy."

"I say when it's enough," Billy said. "You just sit."

Landis shrugged. He might have a conscience, but it wasn't a strong one. Jason pulled a fresh beer from the cooler, popped it, looked off in the distance, possibly in search of Atlantis.

The rod began to bob up and down and the line on the reel was running out. The fish was still diving down.

Leonard said, "Lady, anytime you say it's finished, trust me, it's finished."

Billy sneered at Leonard.

Leonard looked at him and smiled. "And I might finish it before it's finished."

Ferdinand came out of the cabin. "I have killed the engine. The fish will sound. And will keep sounding. It is too much for her. My daughter cannot take much more. I must ask you to take the fish, señor."

"Me and Beatrice made a deal," Billy said. "She does what I say for a while, and you get a whole lot of reward out of it."

"I know," said Ferdinand. "But it is not enough. Not for such a thing as this."

My skin had begun to crawl. Not only because of what Billy was doing, but that her father was allowing, and worse yet, Leonard and I were allowing it. I couldn't imagine anything being worth this.

Billy slipped his hand beneath her bathing suit and began massaging a breast.

The shears Ferdinand had used on the barracuda lay on the deck behind the chair. I picked them up and cut the line. The rod snapped back like a whip. The line jumped over the side of the boat and the fish was gone.

Billy turned. But before I could hit him, Leonard was there. Leonard stuck the tips of his fingers in Billy's eyes. Billy's hands went to his face and Leonard kicked him hard in the balls. Billy went to his knees.

I looked at Landis and Jason. They were both on their feet. Jason dropped his beer onto the deck. It rolled up against the side of the boat and foamed.

I said, "I wouldn't."

"Naw," Leonard said. "Come ahead."

I was still holding the shears in my hand. Leonard had Billy by the hair, grinding his knuckles into the top of Billy's skull. He pulled Billy forward onto his face, dropped his knee across Billy's neck.

"Taste that boat," Leonard said. "Learn to like it. I plan on feeding it to you."

Beatrice was crying. "You do not know what you have done," she said.

"Maybe not," I said. "But enough is enough. Ferdinand,

take this boat back to port. And don't anyone give me any shit about it."

"Oh, no," Leonard said. "Please give me some shit. I'm already sweaty and worked up now. And I'm bleeding again. So I'm mad enough to need some shit. Come on, either of you pussies. I want some shit."

No one gave him any shit.

Ferdinand gunned us toward shore.

18

THAT NIGHT in our hotel, Leonard, wearing fresh bandages, propped himself up in bed with pillows. He said, "I enjoyed our fishing trip. Didn't you?"

I was sitting in a chair at the desk, drinking a diet cola. "So much," I said.

"Just a little rest. A vacation . . ."

"That's enough. I was trying to help the old man."

"You're always helping someone, Hap. Except yourself. And by the way, what do you think of the old man now?"

"I think he saved our lives, and he's a good old man, but . . . I don't know. That stuff with those dipshits. What's up with that?"

"She's a masochist, Hap. Where the fuck have you been all your life? Or maybe she has this big daddy thing goin' with Billy Boy. Boss me, and I'll be your slave shit."

"She seems intelligent."

"Probably is. She's just fucked up. Leave it at that."

"Or she's in some real deep shit and she and her old man are doing what they need to do to survive."

"Your idea was we were there to protect her today.

We did that. In spite of the fact I'm not so sure she wanted it. We haven't been invited back tomorrow."

"At least I won't have to put those nasty sardines on a hook."

"Do you know how long I had to shower to get that fish smell off?"

"You mean after we went fishing today, or before?"

"That's funny, Hap. Real funny. And I give up on the vacation."

"You talked me into staying."

"I know, and it was a mistake. We cannot take a vacation, Hap. It is not in the cards. Least not together. I miss John."

"Admit it. He might be your lover, but is he as much fun as me?"

"Trust me, Hap. You're not fun. And who knows, you might even call Brett and she might even like you calling."

"I must admit I think about her."

"She's all right, that one. You should try and stick with her."

"I have."

"No. When she gives you a little bit of coolness, you bail. Every woman you meet can't beat a drum all the time and blow a trumpet. They got to have their moments."

"Like you know anything about women, Leonard. You're a queer."

"But a smart queer. Brett, she's all right. We've known each other for a while now, Hap, old buddy, and I finally figured out why you don't stick with women."

"You mean besides the ones that double-cross and try to kill me?"

"Besides them."

"You mean like the one falls in love with a good friend and then goes off and gets killed."

"Well, besides her too."

"What's the answer, O Sage Queer?"

"What you got to do, my man, is give your relationships some breathing space. You're working so hard to have a relationship, you don't just let it happen. Hang with the moment, buddy."

"That's it? Hang with the moment? What kind of fuckin' advice is that? You haven't exactly had the best love life in the world either, if you'll recall."

"Got me there, but at least I figured out your problem. You meet a woman, you get that charge of being in love. That romantic, sexual rush, and then it gets everyday, and you don't know how, or don't have the character—"

"Watch it."

"Don't have the character to make it work when it gets into the everyday. I'm not one of those says a relationship should be a job. That's the case, get a part-time at the 7-Eleven. I am sayin', it ain't all about moony eyes and exchanging body fluids."

"This from the guy telling me that the size of John's hammer was what you were really impressed with."

"It is impressive. But . . . I been away from him awhile, and, you know, I'm beginning to rethink things. Not about the size of the hammer. I still like that part. But about love and life."

"Oh, shit. Love and Relationships by Leonard Pine. Save it. Write a column."

"Hey, listen to me, buddy. That's how I realized I'd turned a corner with John. I just let things be."

"You hung with the moment."

"Exactly: Bottom line. Don't try so hard. And this one.

Beatrice. Let it go. She's about two dogs short a sled team."

"I think I'll go to sleep now, Socrates."

"Fine. Just when you get in bed, try not to show so much skin. I don't like seeing you in your underdrawers."

"I thought queers liked men in their underwear."

"Not you."

"Well, you snore in your sleep."

"Yeah, and you fart. No wonder you can't keep a woman."

I slipped off my pants and shirt, turned off the light, climbed into my bed. I lay there silent for a while. I said, "Do I really fart in my sleep?"

Leonard snickered.

"Do I?"

Leonard snickered again.

"Do I?"

"Sometimes."

"What times?"

"When you fart. Now sleep tight, and don't let the bedbugs bite. And finally, my good man, shut the fuck up, will you?"

"Leonard?"

"Christ. What?"

"You may be right. It's tough loving someone and doing it right."

"Talk about tough, you ought to be a homo. You know me and John we can't even hold hands without people going bonkers. You, you can hold hands with a woman, no one thinks that's weird. I hold hands with John, people stand and stare."

"I've seen you hold hands with John. In public."

"I didn't say I didn't do it, but it isn't comfortable. Our love is ridiculed when folks can't just accept it. What the fuck harm does it do them?"

"None at all, Leonard. And if it's any consolation, I think John is a good catch. You done good. I don't know how. But you did."

"Good night, Hap."

"Good night, Leonard."

Next morning, early, there was a pounding on our door.

I sat up in bed. Leonard was already on his feet, stepping into his pants. "Who is it?" he said.

"Billy. From the boat."

"Yeah," Leonard said. "Just the man I don't want to see."

I pulled on my pants, was slipping on my shirt when Leonard opened the door.

Billy was standing there fuming, his fist clenched. His bright Hawaiian shirt was almost too much that time of morning.

"She here?"

"Who?" Leonard asked. "Helen of Troy?"

"You know who I mean."

"Beatrice?" I said.

"Yeah. Her. Where is she?"

"She's not here," Leonard said.

"Goddamn it," Billy said, reaching under his shirt, pulling out a small snub-nose revolver. "You're gonna tell me—"

It was quick, the way Leonard grabbed Billy by his shirtfront and started slapping him. I'm not exactly sure how many times he slapped Billy. It was too quick and economical to tell. It was over before it started. The slapping. And the disarming.

Leonard tossed the gun on the floor, stuck two fingers in Billy's nostrils, stepped behind him, jerked him to the floor.

Billy said, "Goddamn."

Leonard dislodged his fingers from Billy's nose, knelt behind him, wrapped his forearm around Billy's neck and squeezed. "Are you gonna be good, Billy," Leonard said, "or am I gonna have to open up an economy-size can of whup-ass?"

"I'm cool," Billy said.

"You ain't got enough time in your life to learn how to be cool," Leonard said. "What do you think, Hap?"

"We could kill him, cut him up, leave him under the bed."

"I like that."

"I was just looking for Beatrice," Billy said.

"I thought you were spending the night with her," I said.

"Can you please stop choking me?"

"You get up, play nice, and don't talk so loud," Leonard said, "you and me can tolerate one another."

Leonard stood up.

Billy stood up. Took a swing at Leonard. Leonard ducked it, grabbed the pistol off the floor, brought it around and caught Billy upside the head with it. Billy went down so fast it was like he'd stepped in an open manhole.

Leonard leaned over, tapped him again with the little gun, said, "You just think Rodney King took a beatin'. Wait'll I get through."

"Hold up, Leonard," I said. "That's enough. Save your strength. We may have to bury him later. And you don't want to open your wounds."

Leonard took a deep breath, tossed the pistol on the bed.

"Take a chair, my man," Leonard said.

Billy got his feet under him, went over and sat down at the little table. Blood was running from his nostrils, dripping onto his colorful shirt. His cheeks were bright and finger-marked.

I went in the bathroom, got some toilet paper, stuff you could use to sand your furniture, gave the wad to Billy.

He pressed it against his nose.

"You didn't have to do all that," he said.

"No," Leonard said. "I didn't have to. But I wanted to. Don't ever pull a gun on me, motherfucker. I'd been in a worse mood, you'd have to hire a winch truck to get that little shooter out of your ass."

"I thought she was here," Billy said. "I've spent more money on that bitch than the Republican party did their last election. I figure I got a right to know where she is. Me and her had a deal."

"You're spending money on her," I said. "You don't own her."

"That's a matter of opinion. I stayed with her last night. We had a fight. I wasn't happy with you guys. I didn't want you around, and she said fine, and then she really pissed me saying she fucked Hap here. That true, Hap?"

"I don't usually fuck and tell, but in your case, I'll make an exception. Yes. And I really, really enjoyed it."

"She told me she got herself in some kind of shit with a gangster or something. She needed money. Lots of it."

"So you took advantage of that?" I said.

"It was a deal she wanted to make," Billy said.

"Yeah," Leonard said, "and while you had her bent over a barrel, you thought you'd core her ass with your money. Am I right?"

"I came to her father about a fishing charter," Billy said. "He was recommended. Goddamn, I need more toilet paper."

This time Leonard came back with a wet towel. Billy took it, pressed it against his nose.

"Old man told me what he'd charge, and I agreed. Then I met Beatrice. She and I had a drink. We talked. She said she needed help. She needed money. She could make it a hell of a fishing trip, and in the meantime I could drop my line in her little water hole, if you know what I mean. Provided I came up with lots of money. She wanted too much money. Even for a good-looking ass like hers."

"So you had some ideas?" Leonard said.

"Yeah. I said, you do what I like. What I say for three days, and we fish too, I'll pay off the bill."

"How much is the bill?" I asked.

"Seventy-five or eighty thousand. It wasn't an exact figure."

I looked at Leonard. "You were actually going to pay her that much?"

"I figured I ought to fuck her old man too, for that price. Not that I wanted to, understand me."

"You have that kind of money?"

"Out the ass. That's no money to me."

"Are you going to pay her anything now?"

"I don't know. Probably not."

"So why are we hearing all this?" I asked.

"Because I can't find her and the deal's off. I'm giving the old man the money for the fishing trip. One day, but that's it. She threw me out last night, wouldn't answer her door this morning. I thought she was here."

"What would you care?" I said. "You were thinking about not paying the money. Right?"

"I don't like losing tail to someone else," Billy said. "Especially someone made me look like an asshole. And I've spent money on her, put her up in that hotel. She thinks I'm going to pay for today, her not letting me in like that, not answering the door, she can kiss my ass."

"No one had to work hard to make you look like an

asshole," Leonard said. "You were riding high there, my man. And understand you're getting this from the smartest nigger in the world."

"Smartest nigger in the world?" Billy said.

Leonard leaped off the bed, slapped Billy so hard it knocked him off the chair.

"I can say that," Leonard said. "You can't. How'd you vote last presidential election?"

"What?" Billy said, afraid to get off the floor.

"You heard me. You vote Republican or Democrat? And don't tell me what you think I want to hear."

"Republican."

"That saves you one whack," Leonard said.

"But it makes me want to hit you," I said. "Both of you."

"Look," Billy said. "I'm through with all this. I'll give her father the money, be on my way."

"I don't trust you to give anyone anything," I said. "And I think we should walk over to where Beatrice is, try that knock again."

We spent a little while cleaning Billy up. We even let him take off his shirt and rinse the blood out. We decided he could have his gun back. Without the ammunition.

Leonard said, "Don't let me see you pull that again, even if it's just to scratch your ass. You hear?"

"I hear," Billy said.

We walked over to the hotel where Beatrice was staying. It was a pretty good walk, took about thirty minutes.

We tried the phone in the lobby, but she didn't answer. The elevator was broken. We walked upstairs and Billy showed us the room. He knocked.

No answer.

I knocked and called her name.

No answer.

I beat on the door.

Still no answer.

Billy took a turn hammering on the door. "Wake up, you cunt," he said.

I touched his arm gently. "Don't say that."

"I was kind of expecting a guy to answer in his drawers," Leonard said. "I figured she got rid of both you bastards and got someone else."

"A guy in his drawers, huh?"

"Yep."

"Or, if your luck was in, without them."

"Don't tease me, Hap."

"Are you . . . ?" Billy said to Leonard.

"Careful," Leonard said.

"But you beat me up."

"And quite handily, I thought."

Billy dropped his head. It hadn't been his last two days. Lost his girl. Lost his fish. Got his ass beat by a queer. Several times.

I went downstairs, told the man in charge I couldn't wake the lady. He understood enough English to get the idea I wanted him to unlock her door, but he wouldn't do it. I offered him twenty-five dollars to check and see she was all right, but he wouldn't do that either. So much for Mexican corruption.

I went back upstairs and knocked again. I looked at Leonard. He said, "Enough of this using our brains and politeness. I suggest we resort to good old East Texas brawn and assholism. Stand back."

He jumped at the door.

He hit it solid and hard. So hard it knocked him backward on his ass. He got up, said, "Let's do it together."

"She could already be at the dock," I said.

"Good thought," Leonard said. "Glad you came up with

that. Maybe a minute or two earlier would have been better."

"You're supposed to go out again," I said. "Right, Billy Boy?"

"Well, yeah. But I told her I wasn't going out today. Not after last night. I told her that when she threw me out."

"Maybe she just left and went home," I said.

"Fuck it," Leonard said.

"What the hell," I said.

We hit the door with our shoulders, splintered it at the frame. We hit it two more times before it fell in. Even though it was morning, the curtains were drawn and it was dark in there. I switched on the light. There was a hallway, a bathroom on the left, and at the end of the hallway, on the left, was the bed.

Beatrice was on it. Her mouth was stuffed with something and her bikini top had been used to strap whatever was in her mouth firmly in place. Her throat was cut, wide and deep. Her head hung off the bed. Blood had dripped into her hair and some of it hung in ropy strings across the sheets where it had dried. Her face had been cut on. Someone had taken an axe or a machete to her as well. Her hands and feet were chopped off. The nubs of bone were clean, so the blade had been sharp and the blows had been swift.

There was a chair by the desk in the room, and there were four deep slashes in the seat of it; it had been used to prop up Beatrice's hands and feet for chopping. There were sprays of blood on the chair and on the wall near it. I didn't see her hands or feet lying around anywhere.

On the floor by the bed were a couple of knotted rubbers. They might have belonged to her tormentors or to Billy. Right then it didn't seem to matter.

"One goddamned thing," Billy said. "It wasn't suicide."

I turned to hit him, but Leonard was too quick. There was a sound like someone cracking a stick over their knee, and Billy flew back against the wall, hit his head against it hard enough to dent the sheetrock. His ragdoll body nodded to the left, collapsed to the floor.

"I was just made to hit that motherfucker," Leonard said.

I went quickly into the bathroom and splashed my face with water. I felt Leonard's arm on my shoulders.

"Easy, man," he said.

I raised up, moved away from the sink, then Leonard was splashing water on his face. "Goddamn," he said.

I looked where he was looking. The tub. In it were Beatrice's hands and feet.

The manager, having heard all the racket, arrived about then. He saw the shattered door, Billy on the floor, said something in Spanish. When he came forward, saw what was on the bed, he screamed and darted out of there.

Leonard and I got hold of Billy, dragged him into the hall. He didn't wake up. Or if he did he was smart enough to not let us know.

I reached back inside the room, cut off the light, waited for the policía.

19

THE COPS CAME and got us, thought we might have done it. It didn't help that Billy had a gun on him, even if it didn't have bullets. The police thought we were all buddies.

We were shoved into a Mexican jail with cockroaches big enough to work in an iron foundry, rats that reminded me of a roadside attraction. The guard, a tall, mustached man with a slight belly, looked like he'd nail our balls to a log and give us a knife to free ourselves.

Something about him, and the jail, didn't give me great confidence in the Mexican judicial system. I tried to tell them about Juan Miguel, and how I thought he might have done it or had it done. They listened to me, but said nothing. I might as well have been talking to those monoliths on Easter Island.

He did manage to ask in English where the knife was.

I realized then they were looking for the murder weapon. Obviously, we hadn't beat Beatrice to death with Billy's revolver, nor had we used it to cut her up.

Not finding the weapon seemed in our favor. We cer-

tainly hadn't flushed it down the commode or hid it in
our ass.

I reconciled myself with that. No murder weapon. What
didn't reconcile me was that jail and those goddamn rats.

Christ, they were big.

Once, many years ago, I stopped at a little trailer
parked beside the road that was painted up with exciting
pictures of behemoth rats, and above the painting was a
sign that read: SEE THE GIANT RATS OF SUMATRA. I couldn't
resist. I paid my money, went inside, found them to be
shaved possums. I said as much to the lady who owned
the exhibit. She said, "Yeah, you're right." No embarrass-
ment at all.

I said, "Everyone in East Texas knows a danged possum when they see it, shaved or not."

"I know," she said. And that was the end of that. She
didn't offer to give my money back. She didn't care I
knew they were shaved possums. It's like the world's
largest gopher I heard about. You pay and go in and it's
the world's largest all right, only it's a stone statue of a
gopher and they've already got your money.

The rats in the jail were near as big as those possums,
only they were very much card-carrying rats. They came
through a hole in the wall big enough to put your fist
through—up to your elbow. They came at night, scam-
pered and sniffed and nibbled about. I assumed they'd
bite. I kept both feet on my bunk, watched them in the
dark.

Rats. The dark. It brought me back to thinking about
Beatrice. I didn't want to think about her, but I did.
Thought about what human rats had done to her by lamp-
light. Slowly, methodically.

But why?

The money her father owed?

Wouldn't they let her pay it back after the fishing trip?

Why would anyone want money that bad?

Who in the hell had her father been in dutch with anyway?

Who was Juan Miguel?

What would be the point in killing her?

Break a finger maybe. I could see that.

But she's dead, how do they get their dough back? What's the advantage of dead over a living person you could hound for dollars?

Did it become a matter of pride over commerce?

She had to have let them in. The door was sound. But why would she? Did she think she could reason with them? Perhaps she had part of the money. Maybe she thought she'd have it all, that Billy would cool and she would talk him into doing what she wanted. She was probably used to that. Talking men into doing what she wanted.

No answers. Just questions.

So here we were, in a Mexican jail. Me, Leonard, and an asshole. It was a horrible place. Small and tight, all three of us in a damp cell with all those rats and one horribly stained shitter between us.

You had to sit right out there in the open and take a crap. Somehow I found that the most humiliating part of it. Me working out turds that, because of the food, came out like bricks, and Billy watching.

I don't know why he watched. Maybe he had nothing else to do. Maybe he liked to watch people shit. He certainly seemed to be watching me as I folded the thick toilet paper so I could do my duty.

After about midday of the second day, me shitting, Billy watching, I wiped my ass and rubbed the paper in Billy's face. He tried to fight back, but he was just big and strong and had no skills. I kneed him inside his thigh and dropped him. I got hold of his hair while he was on

his knees and gave him a couple of shots with a swinging elbow.

I regretted that. Got shit on my elbow. Had to wash
it in the sink with a pumice soap that nearly took the
skin off.

Billy lay down on the floor then, shit on his face,
whining. I felt like a bully, but not so much that an hour
later, when he was showing signs of recovery, I did it
again.

Hit him with an elbow I mean.

Had to use the soap again. Got it off his face and on
my elbow. That was starting to irritate me as well. It was
like washing up with lathered gravel.

Why couldn't he have washed his face?

That way, I hit him it would have been clean skin.

I know I wouldn't go around with doo-doo on my
face. No sir.

"Isn't he fun to hit?" Leonard said. "I'm thinking about
giving up sex just to save energy to hit him."

"In here you've given up sex," I said.

"So I can hit him lots."

I made a vow that I'd check my watch every hour,
and on the hour I was going to kick Billy's ass. But I'd
try and keep my elbow, hands, and feet off the shit on
his face. That crack he had made about Beatrice's death
not being suicide was still rubbing me raw. For that matter, I didn't know for a fact he didn't do it. I doubted he
had. Somehow it didn't strike me as his style. He was
abusive, but I doubted he was a murderer. He might kill
by accident he got mad enough, bitch-slap her to death,
but I doubted he'd plan anything like that. Torture. Am-
putation. Then bringing us over to see his handiwork.
Nope. Billy wasn't that calculating.

But he did deserve an hourly ass whipping.

However, the meanness went out of me. Billy even-

tually felt better, washed his face with the bad soap and
stayed in the corner away from us.

Leonard, who heard me make the vow to whip his
ass on the hour every hour, was a little disappointed in
my caving in. He thought it was the liberal in me. But
we decided, liberal or not, it was the best thing all around.

Later on, I felt a little ashamed of myself for doing
what I did.

Caving in like that.

After a couple days had gone by—because in Mexico
nobody gets in a hurry—they began to seriously suspect
we might not have done it. The authorities allowed me
to send word back to the States in the form of a phone
call. I got hold of Charlie. Told him to come see what
he could do, and to bring any kind of help he could
bring. The Army might be a good idea.

While we sat and waited, Leonard said, "I don't know
how you do it, Hap. You've just got the knack."

"What?"

"Trouble. You step in it the way kids step in mud pud-
dles. You just can't go around it, and when you try to
jump over it, you fall in it. It's a knack, brother."

"Poor Beatrice," I said.

"Yeah," Leonard said. "Poor Beatrice. And poor Ferdinand. I wonder about him."

We had warned the Mexican authorities that Ferdinand's life might be in danger as well, but again they
gave us the Easter Island treatment. It was the same when
we told them about Billy's friends. That was about as exciting to them as egg salad.

"If Ferdinand is alive," I said, "you don't think he thinks
we did it, do you?"

"Naw. Hey, Billy Boy."

Billy, who was sitting against the wall with his head
hung, looked up.

"Go over there and put your goddamn nose in the corner. I'm sick of looking at you "

Billy went, stood with his nose in the corner like a child.

"When I judge fifteen minutes, I'll let you out of the corner," Leonard said, "but don't you fuckin' look at me, you hear?"

"Yeah," Billy said.

"Change that to Yes sir, Mr. Pine, sir, or you ain't even imagined the beating you'll take, you piece of shit."

"Yes sir, Mr. Pine, sir."

"Now you're cookin' with gas."

We were sitting close together on Leonard's bunk, talking quietly. I said, "You don't think Billy did it, do you?"

"No. I think he got thrown out the night before, just like he said. He didn't get the lovin' he thought he was gonna get, and the next mornin' he was still mad, and when she didn't answer the door, he thought you were casting your harpoon, so he got the gun and came to scare you."

"But you scared him."

"I did. But, if you had answered the door, you would have scared him. Maybe not as good as me, but good enough."

Next afternoon Charlie arrived with Jim Bob Luke.

Charlie had gotten rid of the straw boater and had gone back to his porkpie. He was also wearing a Hawaiian shirt as usual.

Jim Bob is a private investigator and hog farmer out of Pasadena, Texas. A friend of Charlie's. He saved my life once.

He was wearing a blue western shirt with silver snaps, jeans that looked as if they had seen a lifetime of rodeos, and a white hat, creased, the brim turned up sharply on both sides. He had a little feather in the hatband and a toothpick in his mouth. The hatband was made out of rattlesnake hide and it still had the head on it, but he probably could have done without it.

He came and peeked at us through the bars.

"Damned, if this ain't the Ritz-Carlton, and you boys are uglier than I remember."

"And you're just as sweet as I remember," Leonard said.

"Gettin' lots of hog pussy, Jim Bob?" I said.

"Just if they get muddy," Jim Bob said. "That's the way I like it. They twist them little curly tails and it's all I can do not to cream my jeans."

"You're a sick sumbitch, Jim Bob," I said.

"I tell you," Jim Bob said, "you boys got a way of gettin' your dicks between the ground and a horse hoof, don't you?"

"Hap does. And I suffer because of it."

"Leonard, you're a fuckup that's got an excuse," Jim Bob said. "Without Hap, you'd fuck up on your own. It's just you boys' nature. I know. I'm the same way. Damn, it smells like a goddamn fart in here."

"They feed us a lot of beans," I said.

Charlie hadn't said a word. He took off his porkpie hat and slapped it on his thigh for some reason. His face wore the look of a very tired man or maybe just one who wished he had a better class of friends.

"I've got Veil in the other room talking," he said.

"No shit," I said.

"No shit," he said.

Veil had helped Leonard once after he burned down a crack house. His defense was basically Leonard thought he was exterminating rats by destroying it. It worked. Leonard got away with a warning. If there was anyone who could legally get us out of this thing, it was Veil.

Veil wasn't a big guy, average height, black hair gone gray, a slightly Mediterranean look, one good eye, the other covered with a black pirate patch. He had the demeanor of someone who could roll strikes in a bowling alley with his nuts.

"What's Jim Bob doing here?" Leonard asked. "I mean, I'm glad you might have brought him along to hold my dick while I pee, but what else is he good for?"

"My hogs speak highly of me," Jim Bob said. "Except for the ones I take to the packin' plant. I reckon their opinion of me lowers dramatically about then."

"We thought there might be trouble getting you out," Charlie said, "so I brought Jim Bob. He kind of likes trouble."

"Don't say that," Jim Bob said. "I don't like trouble. I just know how to deal with it . . . All right, I sort of like it."

"Well, I don't," I said. "Get us out of here."

"What about him?" Charlie said, pointing at Billy.

"He's on his own."

"Friends he had with him seem to have bailed," Leonard said.

"He guilty of anything?" Charlie asked.

"Birth," Leonard said.

Jim Bob, Charlie, and Veil took a room at the hotel, and Veil did his thing. Arguing with the law via translator. I thought with Veil on the case we'd be out that afternoon, but we weren't.

Billy, who was free to take his nose out of the wall, said, "You know, I didn't mean to start it off so bad with you guys."

"Sure you did," I said.

"All right, but I'm sorry now."

"I'm sorry I ever met you," Leonard said.

"Likewise," Billy said. "I'm sorry I ever came to Mexico."

Leonard said, "I'm sorry my best friend, my brother, talked me into a fucked-up cruise, got me left in Mexico, stabbed, and then into this shit. That's what I'm sorry of."

"Maybe if we'd taken another cruise line," I said.

"Look," Billy said. "I just want to get straight with you guys. I didn't do this to Beatrice. I wanted to fuck her, not kill her."

"You have such a way with words," I said.

"Yeah, well, maybe I'm not silver-tongued, but I got a few dollars. I'll get out of this."

"You're so rich, how come your lawyers aren't all over this?" I said. "I got my lawyer on it, and I'm not rich."

"Hey, you're a hero," Leonard said. "Remember? You got money in the bank."

"It's dwindling," I said.

"It's my father," Billy said. "He's making me suffer a little. He thinks I need to learn a lesson. I know him. I know that's what he's doing. I called him, had to leave a message. He could maybe be out of the country, though. So, would you please call him for me if you get out first?"

"Say you're a chickenshit cocksucker," Leonard said. "You hear me?"

"All right. I'm a chickenshit—"

"That's enough," Leonard said. "I just wanted to know you'd do it. Give me the number."

"Can we bury the hatchet?" Billy asked. "Well, maybe that's not what I should have said, considering Beatrice."

"Maybe not," Leonard said. "I get your drift. Unless it turns out you had something to do with this—like we'll ever know—consider it buried. At least as long as we're in this jail cell."

"Let me ask you something, Billy," I said. "If you're

without money now, waiting on your father, what were you going to pay Beatrice with?"

"Well, I would have had to get the money from my father."

"Would you really have done that?"

"Probably not," he said. "Will you still call my father?"

"Sure," I said. "We'll call once. He's not there, you're shit out of luck. I'm not going to make it a career."

"Thanks. I'll find a way to write out the phone number for you. You know, that guy in the cowboy hat is right. It does smell like a fart in here."

"Yeah," Leonard said, "and I smell it best when you open your mouth."

20

NEXT DAY we were out. I don't know what Veil did, but we were out. Basically, I think it was because they didn't have the evidence to hold us and Veil was one persuasive, smart sonofabitch. But I knew in Mexico, they can hold you anyway, so I figured some money had changed hands.

It didn't help Billy any. He was there when we left, looking like a friendly dog in the animal shelter, hoping someone would pick him before they came with the needle.

Although Veil and I had known each other for years, in an off and on sort of way, I couldn't quite figure Jim Bob being in Mexico. We weren't bosom buddies. Me and Leonard had only met him once before. But he'd apparently taken a liking to us, or maybe he was just bored with hogs, or owed Charlie a favor.

All I knew for certain was once, when the chips were down, and my balls were literally on ice, Jim Bob saved my life. It was a tense situation, punctuated with gunfire and death. But the way Jim Bob acted, you would have thought he had shown up to have a manicure and a massage.

I don't know I'd vouch for it being true, but Charlie once said Jim Bob was so cool and tough he made Leonard look like a sissy.

One thing for certain, those two ever went at it the sparks would fly so high and hot the moon would catch on fire.

We gathered at a table in the hotel where Jim Bob, Veil, and Charlie were staying. Charlie and Jim Bob were sharing a room. Veil had one of his own. That's the way Veil is. On his own. Even when he was with you he was on his own.

We bought some food at a café, had it wrapped, brought it up to the hotel. Tamales and fish stewed in some kind of sauce, tortillas and sodas.

We ate while we talked.

"So can we go home?" I said.

"Sooner the better," Veil said, eyeing me with his good eye. The tan Armani suit he was wearing looked as if it might have been previously worn by one of Jim Bob's hogs. "Mexican law officials have a way of changing their minds."

"Or they run out of the money you gave them," Charlie said.

"So money was paid," I said. "Jim Bob, was it you?"

"Why the fuck would I do that? I don't even know you."

"Oh."

"It was Charlie," Veil said.

"Sorry, Charlie," I said. "It's just you're so tight with money I wouldn't have guessed."

"Yeah," Charlie said. "It was my money, and I'm missing it already. I had plans for it. I was gonna do some work on my trailer. Maybe get me a blow-up fuck doll and a refrigerator with an ice maker."

"They're nice," Leonard said. "John's got one."

"A doll or a refrigerator with an ice maker?" Charlie asked.

"The refrigerator," Leonard said. "You got me, you don't need no blow-up doll . . . Besides, those male dolls, the dick doesn't hold air worth a damn. And the balls collapse right away."

"Don't suck so hard," Jim Bob said. "Besides, Charlie gets one, he'll want a ewe or a heifer. Right, Charlie?"

"Eat shit," Charlie said.

"Thanks again, Charlie," I said. "Seriously, we appreciate it."

"Jim Bob paid for the rooms," Charlie said. "I only go so far."

"Thanks," Leonard said.

"Shit," Jim Bob said, "I didn't have nothing to do. Divorce cases lately, and I'm sick of that. I had to sneak around last week and take photos of a fat husband cheating on his fat wife, and he wasn't even porkin' some kind of blond bimbo. Had him another porker. It was like I was back at my place, sittin' in the backyard watchin' the hogs fuck. Gettin' that on film, that was ugly. I think there ought to be some kind of law against it."

"I think there is," Veil said.

"What the hell were they doin'?" Leonard said. "Fuckin' out in the open?"

"They had them a picnic spot," Jim Bob said. "I'd tracked them to it before. It was night. They thought they were safe. But I have an infrared camera. I snuck up on 'em, first I thought two hot air balloons had come down in the park and were bouncing together. But nope, it was just two really fat, ugly people."

"Your friend, Veil, here," Charlie said, "you owe him some money too. He put up some of the air flights."

Veil grinned at me. It was the kind of smile barracudas are famous for. I knew he didn't want the money, but he sure wanted to make me think he did. It was his idea of a joke. Veil didn't travel in humor circles much so he kind of laughed at what amused wolves.

"So you all helped us," Leonard said.

"I brought everygoddamnbody," Charlie said. "I didn't have any idea what you two morons might be into. It's usually pretty deep shit. Actually, I think you got out easy this time. They could have held you until Mexico had a solid economy. In other words, for life."

"And I want you to know it's appreciated," Leonard said. "On the other hand, that appreciation is going to have to go a long goddamn ways. I haven't got any money to pay you back with. Hap does, though."

I sighed. "Yep. And it seems to be disappearing faster than sweat on an Eskimo's lip."

"I don't believe they call themselves Eskimos anymore," Charlie said. "They're Inuits. Eskimos is not an accepted term anymore."

"Yeah," Leonard said, "and the name of the black race isn't nigger anymore either, but I still hear it."

"Actually," Charlie said. "Black is passé. You are now an African-American."

"Charlie," Leonard said. "You can kiss my woolly black African-American ass."

We got transportation to Cancun up the way, flew out of there that afternoon, caught another flight in Mexico City, then headed to Houston Intercontinental. Veil didn't go with us. Next thing we knew he was gone. We neither saw nor heard him slip out. He was at the airport with us one moment, then he wasn't.

It didn't worry me. That's the way he operated. Showed up when you needed him, disappeared like the Lone Ranger. Or the Patched Ranger in this case.

Veil had his own agenda.

The flight from Cancun made me sick. It was a prop. It was all we could get. It bucked and weaved and threatened to strike the ground. Out of Mexico City it was a jet and a better flight.

Charlie and Leonard sat together, along with a red-faced man in a plaid jacket that liked to talk. I could hear him all the way in the back of the plane where I sat next to Jim Bob. Or almost next. The seat between us was empty. It was occupied by Jim Bob's hat.

I talked to Jim Bob about the events that led up to Beatrice's death. I figured I owed him as much of an explanation as possible, considering he'd left his hogs at home with a farmhand and had come all the way down to Mexico to help spring us.

I said, "They let us off easy as they did, I guess they feel certain we didn't do it? You talked to them. Do they have any idea who did it?"

"No. They sort of like your blond friend for it, but they don't sound real convinced. I speak damn good Spanish, amigo, and believe me I quizzed them. I'm always curious, even if it isn't any of my business. Especially if it isn't any of my business. They just think you guys are gringo assholes down there for Mexican poontang. They think Beatrice was whoring. Did you know she was a call girl?"

"What?"

"That's right. An expensive one. Or at least had been."

"Are you positive?"

"According to them. They say they knew her. But, keep in mind, those boys might lie to an old cowboy."

"Drugstore cowboy."

"Hogs may not be cattle, but they got to be tended to."

"I can't believe it."

"Really, hogs are a lot of work."

"I mean about Beatrice."

"Oh, well, as I said, that's what I was told. Said she usually worked pretty high-end, but in the last few years they hadn't heard from her. Then this. They think she tried to pull a trick, pick up a little extra, got the wrong man, someone who wanted more than a ride in the tunnel, and he did her in."

"Did they say why?"

"Because he wanted to. Bad hombre."

"So they don't really think Billy did it?"

"Being honest, I'm not sure what they think."

"Yeah, they were fairly inscrutable."

"I hate to perpetuate a stereotype, but those fellas were about as crooked as a dog's hind leg. Enough money and they'd think Walt Disney did it."

"He's dead."

"See what I mean."

"I guess it could have happened that way. But it would have been just what Beatrice feared. This Juan Miguel."

"Yeah. It could have been revenge against her father."

"What I'd like to know is where in hell was Ferdinand."

"The police would like to know too. That way they could pistol-whip him and have him explain a few things. I reckon you guys weren't Americans, you'd have gotten the bad end of a rubber hose. Irritating the American consulate, though, is not something they like. Pees in the tourist water."

"Ferdinand took off? That seems odd, considering what happened to his daughter."

"Maybe he could see the handwriting on the wall, Hap.

He knew this Juan Miguel would want him next, and him being killed wasn't going to bring his daughter back, so he took off in his boat."

I stewed over these revelations the rest of the way to Houston. At the airport, we caught a shuttle to airport parking. We rode back to LaBorde in Jim Bob's near-thirty-year-old, blood-red Cadillac, festooned with curb feelers. Inside, fuzzy dice and baby shoes dangled from the mirror, and on the windshield were silhouettes of dogs and people with slash marks through them.

"You fix this car up like this?" Leonard said. "Or is it some kind of punishment you got to bear?"

"This sonofabitch can outrun the Concorde," Jim Bob said.

"But does it stay on the ground?" Leonard asked.

"Sometimes," Jim Bob said.

"Jim Bob," Leonard said. "Thy middle name is class."

"Veil ride down with you guys?" I asked.

"Nope," Charlie said. "I called him, and he just sort of showed up at the jailhouse in Mexico. How long you known that guy?"

"Long enough," I said. "I don't see him that often, but trust me, he's aces with me."

"Seems it's the same with him," Charlie said. "I called him like you said, said you were in trouble, and he didn't even wait to find out what kind of trouble. He said, Yes, and where is he?"

"He's kind of an asshole, actually," Leonard said. "But he's an asshole worth having on your side."

"You're an asshole," Charlie said.

"I know," Leonard said.

"You too," Charlie said to me.

"I know."

"Don't even say it, Charlie," Jim Bob said.

21

W<small>E ARRIVED</small> in LaBorde just after dark, dropped Leonard off at John's house. When John opened the door he let out a yell. They embraced. With his arm around John's shoulders, Leonard turned and waved at us. John waved too. As they went inside a shape low to the ground came out of the dark, waddled into the light.

Bob the armadillo. The critter followed them inside while Leonard held the door open.

"Now that's weird," Jim Bob said.

"His name is Bob," I said. "He likes vanilla cookies, slow walks in the rain, and he doesn't carry leprosy like many armadillos."

Through the open door I could see warm yellow light and there was the sound of classical music playing.

Leonard closed the door.

I rolled up the window and we rode on.

My place was dark as a hit man's plans. Even in the dead of summer, it looked cold. When I got out of the car— the Red Bitch, Jim Bob called it—I could smell the stench of charred wood from the apartment below. Upstairs, where I lived, seemed like the place where a body ought to be laid out on a cooling board. My pickup was parked in the yard. No one had stolen it. No insurance money for me. No new transportation. Just this piece of shit.

"You guys don't stay up too late watching movies and spitting water," I said.

"Piss off," Charlie said, rolled up his window, and away they went.

He may have quit smoking, but late at night, or when he was tired, he grew kind of irritable.

I didn't have my key. I realized it when I was halfway up the stairs. No problem. I trooped downstairs, found the spare I keep in a metal box under a brick, went up, unlocked my door, and went inside.

The place smelled stale as an old maid's closet.

I turned on the light.

No dog jumped up to greet me.

Brett didn't come out of the back room in a negligee.

A small spider scrabbled across the floor, perhaps in greeting.

I stepped on it.

A few roaches were scuttling about in the kitchen. Making a sandwich perhaps.

I sat down at my kitchen table.

I got up and locked the door.

I sat down at the table again.

A roach darted out of the corner, stopped about three feet away. Perhaps he thought this was his home now and I was an intruder. He finally got tired of trying to stare me down, rushed away.

I noticed there were rat turds next to the refrigerator. I wondered if rats would use a sandbox like a cat. I wondered if I could train them. It was nice to know these were just average-sized rats. Not like the ones in the Mexican jail that could be saddled.

At least I hoped they were average size. Maybe the

Mexican rats had flown in with us, ridden in Jim Bob's trunk and had hustled into my house when I arrived.

Maybe I needed a lot of rest.

I got a diet cola out of the fridge. I didn't have an ice maker either.

I sat down at the table again.

I drank half the soda.

No roaches came back out to see me.

I didn't really want to think about rats anymore.

I was never going to have an ice maker.

It was tough having all these important things to think about.

I went to bed.

I was so tired, disappointed, and low on self-esteem, I couldn't even manage enough energy to abuse myself.

Next morning I lay in bed for a while and thought about that poor girl in the hospital, wounded by some nut for no reason. I thought about Beatrice, and I felt weak and lonely, like a pine straw being buffeted by the ocean. Lately I was having a lot of those thoughts, feeling my mortality. Realizing more strongly than ever before that I had lived more life than I had left, and I wasn't liking that revelation at all.

I often told myself I didn't mind aging, but now I found myself constantly wishing I was young and that I could do it all over again, and differently.

Wished my hip didn't hurt so bad, that all those places where my ribs were broken had not been broken. When I was young my fight injuries, received while defending myself, or just because I shot my mouth off when I shouldn't, were a badge of honor. Now the badges hurt. The pins that held them to me were buried in my hide too deep and time was causing them to go deeper. The badges were feeling heavy as anvils; they were tugging at the pins; they weren't worth wearing.

I got up slowly, twisting gingerly to make cracking noises come from my back, hip, knees, and ankles. I felt like something made of Tinkertoys, but screwed down way too tight and somehow rotten at the center, fearing that if I turned just a little too far in one direction the whole of me might come undone.

While I was brewing coffee, I noticed the light blinking on my answering machine. I looked at it, saw it registered five messages.

I listened to them. A couple were phone sales. But three of them were from Brett. Two supported the first. The first I played over three times so I could hear her voice.

"Hap. This is Brett. You know what, life sucks if you let it. I've been letting it. No more feeling sorry for myself. My daughter is going to turn tricks if I want her to or not. I'm thinking about getting a new puppy and a wax job. One or the other. Or maybe I'll get a puppy and give that little scooter a wax job. Give me a call. Better yet, come by and see me. Bring your dick."

Pure Brett. I was at a stage in my life where I really hoped it was more me she wanted to see than the dick. Though, like all males, I could tolerate that part if I had to. No arm twisting necessary.

While my coffee brewed I looked for something to eat, but there was only spoiled milk and moldy bread. I put the bag of bread and the plastic milk carton in the trash.

I showered, dressed, poured up a cup of coffee, went down to my car and out of there.

I went by a little café and bought some biscuits and bacon, drank their coffee. I drove to the hospital then, went up to where Sarah Bond still had a room.

I didn't know if I was allowed or not, but I opened the door and slipped in. She was asleep. She didn't have as many tubes and wires in her this time, but she looked only marginally better. Her face was pale as Lazarus before Jesus raised him. She was still patched and taped up. Only a little of her face showed. I reached over, patted her hand, and went out.

As I walked down the hall to the elevator, I thought about what Leonard had told me once. About how things didn't happen for a reason, they just happened. And he was right. But Sarah being attacked, me trying to help her, had set a series of events in motion.

I wondered if things would have been different for Beatrice had I not come along. Maybe I shouldn't have cut that fishing line, put her and Billy at odds with one another. I could have let her do what she wanted to do, as distasteful as it might be to me. She might have gotten her money if I had. Might have paid her bills and spared her life.

I wondered if Brett was on duty. We had met in this hospital. It was a very romantic memory. She had stuck a needle in my ass.

I went down to the desk and asked. She wasn't on duty, still worked the night shift. Of course, I knew that. I was just hoping against hope. I drove over to her place.

The yard was ripe with sunburned brown grass, and a lawn chair had been gathered up and near turned over by the foliage. It was as if the lawn had grassy hands and it was using them to tip the chair.

I went up and knocked on the door. Gently at first.

No answer.

Less gently.

I heard someone moving behind the door.

I hoped it wouldn't be some man.

That would certainly be a disappointment.

Brett opened the door. She was wearing an oversized T-shirt and slippers made like bears. Her red hair was wadded around her face. She smiled slightly, said, "Well, if it isn't Hap Collins. Come on in."

"I've missed you," I said.

"You sure you haven't just missed what's between my legs."

Brett was like that, vulgar, to the point. Being Gilmer High School Sweet Tater Queen some many years ago hadn't gone to her head.

"I missed that too," I said. "I was thinking maybe that's all you missed about me."

"Well, I missed what was between your legs, Hap, but there's plenty of that around."

"Oh, good. Now I feel better."

"I finally think I've got my head on straight. Killing people can kind of dig itself in deep, like a tick. I think I pulled off the body but the head's still in me."

"That's one way of putting it."

"You don't have some other floozy you're porkin' do you?"

"No. But God how I've tried."

"There hasn't been anyone else, Hap. Not for me."

"Well, there has been someone else, but . . . that's over."

"Wasn't the same as with you and me, was it?"

"Nothing is. Also, she's dead."

"That'll kill a relationship, all right. Sorry I said that. Are you still sad about it?"

"Darlin', I'm always sad about something."

"Sit down, sweetie, tell me all about it. I haven't had breakfast. Want some? Breakfast, I mean."

"Just ate. But I'll drink coffee with you."

Brett clanged some stuff around, came back with a piece of toast for herself, poured us coffee. We sat down at the table. She put one hand on my leg.

"I really have missed you," she said.

"Same."

"I know about how you saved that girl. You saved my girl too, Hap. You saved me. You're always trying to save somebody. Everybody but yourself. You ever think about that?"

"Sometimes."

"I don't want you to think I didn't appreciate what you did for me and my daughter."

"I admit, I wondered. I shouldn't. That isn't the way you're supposed to be. You do something with the best of intentions, it's supposed to be with the best of intentions and nothing else. But I did wonder. Leonard chastised me for it."

"Leonard's a mutant."

"That must be it."

"The rest of us wonder about those kinds of things. Hap, it isn't that I'm ungrateful. Or that I don't love you. I adore you. It's just that I've been a little lost. Tillie went right back to takin' strokes for money."

"Yeah. You told me."

"Can you believe that?"

"Leonard said she would."

"Again, Mr. Know-It-All."

"I get to thinking he's so smart, what in hell is he doin' hangin' around with me?"

Brett laughed. I loved that laugh. It was rich and smoky.

"Tillie may not have changed like I hoped," she said, "but I like to think she's safer. As safe as anyone can be in that business."

"I hope so, Brett."

"You know I went to the Gilmer Yamboree this year. I told you I rode a float there once. When I was a teenager."

"Yep. You were Sweet Tater Queen. I've seen the photographs. The float is a giant sweet potato. As I recall, you told me you thought it looked like a giant turd."

"That's right. And you know what, they didn't even have a goddamn sweet tater over there this year. Not even as a float."

"Modernization, what you gonna do? Everybody's eatin' McDonald's french fries. There's people don't even know you don't make french fries out of sweet taters."

"Actually, you can," Brett said, "but they don't taste right. But, shit, you'd think they could find a sweet potato somewhere . . . Hap, this woman. The one who's dead. Did you love her?"

"No. I didn't love her."

"Do you want to tell me about her?"

"Maybe not just now."

"You want to leave this shitty coffee and go sweat up the sheets?"

"Boy, do I."

I guess it was about a week later. Me and Brett had taken to living with one another, and it was working out fine. She had gotten neither puppy nor wax job nor waxed puppy. She did let me shave her pubic hair, however, and I liked that.

We had her daughter, the whore, visit from Tyler. She had dinner with us. Tillie decided she was going to spend the rest of her time taking the basic courses at Tyler Community College, turning tricks less and less. Perhaps a career as a brain surgeon was in her future.

Or maybe she just wanted to learn how to count up her trick money better at the end of the day; run her own whorehouse.

Brett's son, Jimmy, had finally gotten rid of his Christian Scientist girlfriend. Or rather fate had gotten rid of her for him. She died. Should have had that kidney checked when it first acted up. But she believed in the power of prayer. Her God, however, had other plans. So Jimmy was free. And doing better. Had gone on a bender to Mexico, Brett said. Came home with a box of Chiclets, a sombrero, and a dose of the clap. Nothing penicillin couldn't clean up. He was no longer teaching Aikido; having gotten beaten up in Mexico he decided he needed more lessons.

Anyway, Brett and I were together again. She had only one new rule for me, having doled it out after I had told a friend she was nursing. I was told to say she was a nurse and never say she was nursing. Brett thought it sounded like she was wet-nursing a baby.

"Could I just say you're nursing me?" I asked.

"No, you cannot."

Me and Leonard were back to work at the chicken plant. We were happy as people can be protecting chickens. I learned to never make friends with incoming chickens. Under the circumstances, even a chicken knew it was insincere. You could see it in their eyes, way they held their heads.

One afternoon before Brett and I went to work, we went over to my apartment to start cleaning it out. I had decided at the end of the month to let it go. I had pretty much moved in with Brett anyway. We were talking about marriage and a different house that we might rent, or even buy. Some place big enough to hold all our things and anything else that might come to us. I was seriously thinking about trying to start a real career. As always I was stalled on knowing exactly what. I thought about President of the United States for a couple hours, but I didn't really want to move out of East Texas. Astronaut was an idea, but considering I disliked flying any more than I had to, I had to rule that out. Plantation owner was another thought. But I didn't have any land or money and

Leonard wasn't the butler type, so I had to dismiss that. I thought about what was most likely. I kept coming up with chicken plant guard.

It was depressing.

I was thinking more and more about Charlie and Hanson, their offer to work for them.

At my place me and Brett cleaned out the refrigerator, tossing stuff in the trash, packing up the good stuff to take over to her place. There was a lot more trash than good stuff.

While we were at it, Charlie came by.

The door to my place was open. I had quit running the air conditioner, trying to save money. It was a time of the year when it was starting to cool down a little. Nothing to get excited about. No igloos were about to go up. We were merely having a mild streak.

Charlie came in and took off his hat. He smiled. I knew it wasn't for me. It was for Brett. She was wearing white shorts and her pale lightly freckled legs were a wonderful thing to see. Her bright red hair was cut so that it fell around her face like a feathered helmet. She had on a loose top and no bra. She was one of the few older women I knew who could get away with that, though it was her claim her days as a swinging tit were almost over.

"Hey, Charlie," she said.

"Hey, Brett. Good God, woman. What do you see in this man?"

"I don't know," she said.

Charlie and I shook hands. Charlie said, "I've come by a few times, but haven't caught you."

"I'm mostly at Brett's," I said.

"I'm glad to see you two back together. How's Leonard?"

"He's good. We only see each other at work these days. He's got John and I've got Brett."

"Good for both of you. Me, not so good. I got Hanson. We're putting together our agency, you know?"

"That's right," I said. "Got clients yet?"

"Not really. We're not quite ready. I've been enjoying my retirement till the money runs out. I been lookin' for you because I wanted to thank you for payin' the money back from the Mexico thing."

"You're welcome. I owed it. You saved my bacon. You're lucky I had some money and could pay it back in one chunk."

"I'd have liked to let it go, but . . ."

"Don't be ridiculous."

"I can make some coffee, Charlie," Brett said. "We were thinking about having some."

"That would be nice."

Charlie sat on the couch, put his porkpie hat on the armrest. "You're moving out?"

"I am."

"Well, that kind of log-jams the other reason I came by."

"And that is?" I asked.

"I wanted to see I could stay here one night soon. So I could have my trailer painted. And boy, does it need it. I bought it off a couple had a bunch of kids. They must have wiped shit on the walls, way that place stank. I got some cheap new furniture in storage. Been sleeping on a pallet. It's killing my back. I was gonna do the painting myself, but I'm a shitty painter. Fact is, I'm bringing in painters to repaint what I fucked up. I started trying to do it, but a brain-damaged chimpanzee could have done a better job. Thing is, the smell. Not just from the kids, but the new paint. Man, I can't take it. I thought about staying with Hanson, but his wife doesn't like me. I thought I'd ask you. That doesn't work out, I can ask John and Leonard. I thought it just being you it would be easier, but I see it isn't just you anymore. And you're moving out."

"Well, Hanson's wife just doesn't know your charm," Brett said.

"Yeah, charming, that's my goddamned middle name."

"I hear you, honey," Brett said. "When they were passing out ass, I thought they said class, and I asked for a lot of it. And I got it."

"It looks all right to me," Charlie said.

"I'm not complaining," Brett said. "It sure beats being bony when you fall on it."

I said, "I've got another week or two on this place, Charlie. You can stay here. I'm stayin' at Brett's, so you'd have it to yourself. I can leave the coffee, any of this food you want. Though the rotten stuff might not be too appetizing."

"No. That's all right. Well, just the coffee."

"Not a problem."

I gave him my spare key.

"I can start tonight?"

"Sure," I said. "I've spent my last night here."

22

As I GROW OLDER, my belief in a higher power has not only disintegrated, it's become negative. As my lawyer friend Veil once said, "If there's a God, let him explain babies with AIDS."

I think about the silliness of it. This whole God thing. Two teams praying before a football game. Not to get injured is all right, but they're also praying to win. As if the Wildcats are more in God's favor to win a fuckin' football game than the Beavers.

How does God judge that? Best-looking cheerleaders? Quarterback with the best hairdo? Linebacker with the biggest dick? What's the criteria on that?

In other words, what the hell was God's plan for doing what he did to me and mine?

So, here's what happened. I'm trucking along happy-like. Living with Brett. Playing house. Eating good. Going to work at the chicken plant. Not exactly the life of a high roller, but like the GED, the Good Enough Diploma that's almost a high school diploma, I had a Good Enough Life, which was almost like a real one.

One morning after I got off work, I drove over to my

place to tell Charlie if he needed a few days more, he had them. Until the end of the month actually. On that date, the landlord, a real shithead of a guy, was going to level the apartment and put the property up for sale.

I drove over there. Charlie's car was in the yard. I parked next to it, started up the stairs. When I reached the top I saw the door was splintered at the frame. The door itself hung slightly open.

I felt a cold chill get hold of the short hairs on my neck and shake them. I felt a tightening in my stomach, a shrinking of my testicles.

I still had on my guard outfit, including gun, so I pulled the revolver, a .38, and went on up, thinking, Good God, don't let that motherfucker I fought at the chicken plant be up here. Anything but that.

I don't know exactly why that came to mind, but that was my first thought. He had escaped, was looking for me, had gnawed a hole through the jail bars with his god-damn teeth, and now he was waiting to leap on my head, bite my skull, and suck out my brain.

I eased up to the door frame, listened. Off in the distance I heard a kid yell and a dog bark. I gingerly pushed the door completely open.

Inside the apartment the only sound was a drip from the sink.

I slipped inside. It was a little dark. The blinds were drawn, but it wasn't a place a person could hide, unless he was a leprechaun or the Invisible Man. I pointed the revolver around just for the hell of it. I called Charlie's name.

He didn't answer.

I was reminded of something else.

The hotel room in Mexico. The bed with Beatrice on it.

All of a sudden the apartment seemed like a place I'd never been and didn't want to be. The ceiling was too low, the walls too close. I thought the floor might tilt up and drop me off the edge of the world.

I called Charlie's name again, this time real loud. Just for good luck I cocked back the hammer on the .38.

As I moved inside my feet bogged in something wet on the carpet. I lifted them. They were sticky. The carpet was like the carpet of an old theater gummy with spilled soft drinks and smashed candies.

The carpet only partially covered the living room. The rest was wooden floor, and parts of it were coated in something congealed. It had seeped out from behind the couch. My nostrils quivered with the stench of it; sort of road kill meets dried copper baking slowly in a smutty oven.

I put one knee on the couch and leaned over and looked down.

There was a burst of blackness that struck me in the face, sent me stumbling back, swatting.

Flies.

I took a breath, put a knee on the couch, and looked over again. Now I knew why Charlie hadn't answered. You can't yell loud enough for someone in that state to hear.

Charlie lay behind the couch. He wore only jockey shorts. His throat had been cut. But before that he had been worked on. He was missing some teeth. His nose and cheeks had been cut on, as if whittled. He wore an expression that seemed to say, "Oh, shit." His hands were tied behind his back with strips of one of my sheets or maybe a pillowcase.

The flies were settling on him again.

I couldn't help myself. I let out a little bark of pain and fear and bounced off the couch.

I wiped my feet on a dry part of the carpet. I was

trembling so bad I thought I was literally going to shake my gun belt off.

I started to back out of the doorway, but I gathered up my courage. It was like trying to gather up ten pounds of yarn and poke it in a two-pound basket. But I did it. I went to the bedroom. Opened the door and yelled. I don't know why I yelled. To scare whoever might be in there. To encourage myself. Hard to say.

The bed was blood-drenched. The stench in there was strong enough to grow legs and dance up the wall. There was a bloody handprint on the wall. As if someone had leaned there, tired from his work. Or maybe Charlie broke free, pushed his attacker back, forcing him to put out a hand to keep from falling.

But whoever it had been was fast enough to catch up with a wounded man. And he had. And he had cut Charlie's throat.

As for the handprint, it was huge.

A little suitcase sat on its side by my chair. On the chair were Charlie's clothes, a Hawaiian shirt draped over the back of it. The shirt pictured a bursting sunset against a blue-green sea, bordered by palm trees and a strip of beach. On the seat of the chair, on top of his gray slacks, was his porkpie hat. Beside the chair, his Dr. Scholl's shoes with black and red clocked socks sticking out of them like tired tongues.

I eased the rest of the way into the room and looked around. I even bent down and looked under the bed. Lots of cobwebs. I opened the closet door.

Empty, except for a dead beetle.

I took a deep breath. I checked out the bathroom.

I pulled back the shower curtain.

Nothing.

I holstered my gun, went to the front room, picked up the phone, called Leonard first. I don't know why, but things go wrong, I call him. It's a wonder I don't call him when I have a hangnail. When I explained, he said, "Goddamn. Godalmightydamn. Charlie? You're sure?"

"I'm sure."

"You're absolutely sure."

"He's behind the goddamn couch, Leonard. He's cut up. It's him. I'd let you talk to him, but he's dead. Dead, goddamn it."

"Easy. I'm coming over . . . You all right, Hap?"

"Peachy."

I dialed 911 next, told the police who I was, gave them the address and details.

I went outside, took off my gun belt, put it on the front seat of my car. I didn't want any gun-happy cops popping me.

I sat down on the bottom step of the apartment and took in long, slow breaths. I was away from the stench of blood, but I could still smell it. I felt as if it had soaked into my skin. In the distance I could hear a siren. More than one.

Then I really began to think about who was upstairs. My good buddy, Charlie. I thought about what had occurred, how horrible it had been, and that it must have been meant for me.

As I've pointed out, I'm not exactly a lucky man. But I did get a bit of luck. The head honcho on the case knew me. His name was Jake. I had met him several times but I could never remember his last name. He had been a patrol cop when I first met him. He was a detective now. Part of that was due to Charlie leaving, opening up a position. He and Charlie had been friends.

He was a big dark-haired guy with a belly made pregnant by too many beers and not enough exercise. He had a naturally sad face, and today it was sadder. He wore a

very nice suit and very nice shoes. I found myself looking at his shoes a lot. I didn't like the fact I was all teary-
eyed. Even under such circumstances one tries to be
macho. It's expected.

We were leaning on my car, talking. I was giving him
the poop I knew. Which, of course, was limited. I didn't
mention the Mexico thing. I knew I should have. I even
knew they were connected, but right then I didn't mention it.

Leonard drove up. The cops didn't want to let him see
me, but Jake signaled him through.

"You okay, brother?" Leonard said.

"I suppose," I said. "I'm not exactly up for Pancho's
Mexican buffet, but I guess I'll make it."

One of the blue suits came over, said, "There's a handprint in blood on the bathroom wall. It's big. If the rest
of that motherfucker goes with the hand he'll be just a
little smaller than a Tyrannosaurus rex."

"You getting prints?"

"I'm just a blue suit, like you used to be, Jake, but I
thought of that. We do that when we do police work. We
take photographs and try not to step in stuff."

"All right, all right," Jake said. "I get you."

"Did I say this motherfucker is big?" the blue suit said.
"I mean big."

"You said he was big," Jake said.

"He's so big he hurts my feelings. I wear like a size
eight shoe. Everyone's bigger than me, but this motherfucker, he's bigger than everyone else."

"We get the point," Jake said. "Go supervise. Get a
doughnut. Something. You're gettin' on my nerves."

"Now that you're a detective I get on your nerves."

"Ned, you always got on my nerves."

Ned went away. Jake said, "You have no idea why
this happened?"

"I think whoever it was was looking for me," I said. "Charlie was in the wrong place at the wrong time. It could have been robbery. They wanted something I didn't have. I had moved most of my stuff out. Disappointed, they took it out on Charlie. It could have been like that."

"Could be that way," Jake said. "But before you said robbery, you said they were looking for you. You kind of tacked that on, like maybe you wished you hadn't said the first part. Why would *they* be looking for you?"

"I live here. Charlie isn't normally here. Maybe someone had a grudge and came to settle it."

"What I know about you guys, lots of people could have grudges. You got any names of these grudge holders?"

"You'll need a computer," Leonard said.

"Yeah, but I can't think of anyone who would do this," I said.

"So no one comes to mind?" Jake said.

I shook my head. "No. Not really."

"What about you, Leonard? You know Hap well. Anyone you can think of would want him dead."

Leonard put his arm around my shoulder. "No."

"And Charlie was here why?"

"He was going to stay a couple nights while his trailer was painted."

"You wouldn't hold back anything, would you, Hap?"

"I don't think I am."

"That's not quite an answer either way."

"No, it isn't, Jake. I'm a little rattled right now. You'll have to forgive me. I just found a good friend with his throat cut. Tends to make a man tense and a little confused."

"Hey, he was my friend too," Jake said.

"I know."

"You called Leonard, obviously. I don't suppose you

called and told Hanson. They were like brothers, you know."

"I do know," I said. "No. I didn't call Hanson."

"I'll take care of that. You got some place to go?"

"I'm staying with my girlfriend. Brett Sawyer."

"He'll be with me for a while," Leonard said. "You know my address."

"Who in law enforcement doesn't?" Jake said.

"I can give you my boyfriend's address too."

"Oh. Well . . ."

"Forgot I was queer, didn't you?"

"Bingo. You just don't . . . I don't know . . ."

"Act queer?"

"Well, yeah."

"Guess what? Some of us don't wear feather boas. But just so you don't feel all confused, me and John, sometimes we hold hands and kiss and I did give him a little promise ring."

"Man, I don't want to hear that," Jake said. "Your boyfriend's address isn't necessary. Give me Brett's address, Hap, and go. I need to ask any more questions, I'll look you up."

I gave him the address, started to get in my car.

Jake said, "I assume the gun on the seat goes with the guard uniform?"

"Goddamn, you are a detective," I said. I was trying to come across as cool and calm and still ripe with humor, but the words came out flat and a little desperate. It's funny the way men try to be men.

"Follow me to my place," Leonard said. "We can talk."

When we got to John's, and Leonard explained what happened, John immediately put a pot of water on the stove. Leonard once told me when things get tense, first thing John did was heat water and make tea.

"Motherfucker thinks he's from England," Leonard said.

"Tea is soothing," John said. "I've got some cookies. Vanilla, of course."

"You put ice in tea," Leonard said. "Anything else is un-American. Besides, I like milk with vanilla cookies. We got the wafers or the ones with the creme in the middle?"

"Like it matters to you," John said. "Vanilla cookies with shit in the center would be all right for you. Long as they're vanilla."

We sat at the table while the water heated. Leonard said, "You didn't mention Mexico to Jake."

"No, I didn't. And you didn't either."

"You thought Jake didn't need to know, I couldn't see any reason to mention it. But it's too much like Mexico to be coincidence."

John poured hot water into cups with tea bags in them. He said, "May I ask why you didn't tell the police? You want the killer caught, of course."

"I want his ass. I want it personally. Beatrice was a fool, but she was all right at the center. She didn't deserve to die and then have it all swept under the rug. I left that to the Mexican police. Obviously, it didn't work out. I don't think it'll ever work out. I been thinking about that. Me just going off to let it work out in whatever manner it worked out. It's in my craw."

"Frankly," Leonard said, "it's in my craw too. She and her old man did help us when we needed it."

"Damn right. And Charlie, he was a good friend. He was staying at my place and was killed because whoever did this thought it was me. I want to get even."

"Doesn't that violate your kinder and gentler nature you're trying to preserve?"

"It does. And I want to find out why anyone would

want to kill me. What the hell could I know or have that would interest them?"

"I think it's more like what they think you know or have," Leonard said.

"Another thing," John said. "Wouldn't it be best to tell the cops? Just for one simple reason."

"Which is?"

"They might actually catch him. I mean, come on, from what Leonard's told me about you two guys, about the only thing you can catch is a cold."

"Hey," Leonard said. "We stumble around long enough, we get what we want."

"Think about this," John said. "Guy's out there running around right now. You think he came all this way just to break down a door, kill Charlie, catch a plane back to Mexico?"

"Well, no," I said.

"He could have thought you were Charlie," Leonard said. "He somehow knew a Hap Collins was involved with Beatrice, and for whatever reason he killed her, he connects you to it, comes to kill you, gets poor Charlie, thinks his job is done, and goes home."

"Bless Charlie," John said. "Could be just that. But don't you think at some point in the torture, Charlie would have been inclined to tell this big man who he was, and maybe where you were?"

"He'd done to me what he did to Charlie," I said, "I'd have told him anything he wanted to know. I'd have sucked his goddamn dick and given him a shoeshine. I don't see how Charlie could have kept from it."

"Brett," Leonard said.

"Shit," I said.

"You stay here," Leonard said to John.

"And why is that?"

"Because you're the bitch in this relationship."

We were on our way out the door when John said, "Piss on you, Leonard. You male chauvinist pig."

"But you're male too," Leonard said. "So how can that be male chauvinistic? Oh, shit, they could be looking for me as well. I mean, it could be that way, right?"

"They know about me, they may know about you," I said.

"That means they might come after me, and John's here."

"You are not leaving my sweet ass behind then," John said.

Leonard rushed to his closet, took out his shotgun, plucked a few shells from an overhead shelf. We hustled over to Brett's in John's car, and before I got in I got my gun out of my pickup.

That morning, when I had left to go over to Charlie's, it was my plan to drop in on him and take him to coffee. Take some coffee and doughnuts back to Brett. She had pulled a hard shift the night before and was sleeping late. I thought it would be a nice surprise. But my plans might actually have put Brett in the line of destruction.

When we pulled up in Brett's yard, the lawn chair was still wrapped in grass and the front door was intact.

Of course, our man could have come through the back door.

I got out with my revolver in my hand, Leonard behind me with the shotgun held against his leg. John kept close to Leonard. He was carrying a fistful of shotgun shells, just in case our enemies came in waves.

John said, "That lawn chair. That's one of ours."

"That's nice," Leonard said.

"Circa nineteen ninety-five. We don't make them like that anymore."

"It's a fuckin' antique," Leonard said. "Now shut up."

I used my key and went in.

Everything looked like it always did.

I hurried to the bedroom, my stomach sour with fear.

Brett was in bed with the covers under her chin. She was snoring in a very unladylike fashion. I sighed, glanced up at a whirling shadow. It was her panties hanging from the slowly rotating overhead fan. That was my signal to wake her. Waking her was always worthwhile.

I gently patted her and went out, closed the door, sat down on the living room couch. Leonard sat down beside me, the shotgun draped across his knees.

"I feel drained," I said.

"Understandable," John said. "I'll find a pot and boil some water. Uh . . . Brett does have tea, doesn't she?"

Leonard looked at me, said, "See?"

About twenty minutes later, Brett came out of her bedroom. We were sitting on the couch sipping tea. We turned to look at her. She was wearing a half T-shirt that covered the tops of her breasts. She wasn't wearing panties.

She looked at us. We looked at her.

"Well," she said, "ain't this a fine howdy-do? You on the couch, and me dressed like Huckleberry Hound. I hope you'll excuse me."

She turned, showing us her ass, and disappeared back into the bedroom. She came out a moment later with shorts on. As she came into the room, she said, "You know, it's hard to act cool when you've just shown three men your beaver and found your underwear dangling from an overhead fan."

"Sorry," I said.

"If it helps any," Leonard said, "me and John go for dicks."

"And I've seen it before," I said.

"Well now . . . Is there still some tea?"

"There is," John said. "I'll fix you up."

"A gal shows off her canoe, even if it's by accident, you'd hope someone thought it was worth riding in."

"I didn't say I wasn't interested," I said. "I'm very interested."

"It looked very nice," Leonard said. "I guess. I mean, I don't really know what all of that's about, you know."

"You mean you're still queer? Sight of me didn't jerk you into a heterosexual frame of mind?"

" 'Fraid not," Leonard said.

"But if anyone could," John said, "I'm sure it would be you."

"Thank you, John. I'll cherish that. May I ask what I owe the joy of this gathering to? I'm kind of surprised you didn't fix me breakfast, Hap. I figured a fuckin' like I gave you last night ought to at least warrant toast and coffee. Good God, all three of you have the longest goddamn faces."

"Actually, I went out for doughnuts, but I got detoured."

"Have I faded from your thoughts that quickly."

"There's been something come up. Charlie."

"Is he in the bathroom? Now he's a hetero. He would have respected my entrance. I can tell by the way he looks at me with my clothes on, he would have loved a view of the canyon. Last I heard, he wasn't gettin' any, so that might make me look even better."

"If he were in the bathroom, he'd be horrified at what he missed," I said. "But he's not. And that's why we're glum. Hon, Charlie's dead."

"What?"

I told her the story. I told her the background.

"I'll be damned. I can't believe it. Charlie's dead."

"Yeah. It's hard to believe."

"We just saw him yesterday."

"I put you in danger, Brett. I didn't even know I did it. Somehow, sorry doesn't seem like enough to say. I don't know what would be enough."

"You didn't know this was going to happen. No way you could have. It doesn't matter. You didn't do it on purpose."

"On purpose or not, this monster might have shown up here. I don't like to think about that. Seems you and me get together there's always trouble."

"You and anybody get together it's trouble," Leonard said.

"Jesus, poor Charlie," Brett said. "He was such a nice guy."

"That's right," I said, "he was."

"And you didn't tell the cops about what happened in Mexico?" Brett asked.

"I didn't."

"That means you plan to settle it, doesn't it?"

"I plan to try."

"Which means, of course, that Leonard will try with you."

"I've dragged Leonard into enough shit."

"Oh, shut the fuck up," Leonard said.

"You're the one complains," I said.

"Yeah, I complain. But you know well as I do, they're doin' it to you, they're doin' it to me, brother."

"But they're not doing it to me," John said. "I don't like the idea of you doing this, Leonard. You said you were backing off doing things with Hap."

"I tried," Leonard said. "I can't help myself. It's like we're Siamese twins or something."

"I don't want you to do it," John said.

"I love you," Leonard said. "But Hap's family."

"What the hell am I?"

"Family. But Hap and I had a relationship first. Do I chunk that out now just because I love you? What's that say about me? About my feelings toward Hap?"

"I don't know, Leonard," John said. "What does it say?"

"It says I've got to take care of my brother. That's what it says."

"But he isn't your brother. If you haven't noticed, he's not as dark as you are."

"I don't tan well," I said.

"Look, John," Leonard said. "It hasn't got a damn thing to do with genetics. It's got to do with spirit."

"Spirit. That's rich."

"I'm closer to Hap than I am my own kin. He's done more for me than any relative. He's been there when I needed him. He's stood by me through thick and thin. I can't just throw that out."

"I appreciate it," I said. "But you know what? Things do have to change. You've talked about it more than once. We're not getting any younger. It's time we settled down. It's time you settled down right now. Maybe," and I looked at Brett, "when this is all over, I can do the same."

"I understand," Brett said. "You do what you got to do, Hap."

"I don't see how you can say that, Brett," John said.

"Hap's done for me what no one would. I wanted something from him that was dangerous, and he did it without question . . . I fear for him, John: But I stand by him. I want to help too."

John sighed loudly. He got up and went to the bathroom.

I said, "Leonard. I know you'll do what it takes, my friend. But John, you don't want to lose him. I've never seen you happier. And I'm a goddamn jinx."

"Yes you are," Leonard said. "Shit, man. What a fucked-up thing. Charlie, he was all right."

John came out of the bathroom. He went over and sat on the couch. He said, "Leonard. I love you. I don't want you to do this. I'm afraid you'll be hurt. But . . . I love you no matter what. You do this thing, I'll be waiting when you get back. But I can't do it with you. I'm not like Brett. I can't help. I can't break the law. I can't do anything like that. It just isn't in me."

"I understand that," Leonard said. "Never expected you to. I don't like it either. But it's got to happen."

"No it doesn't. You could still tell the police."

"And we might," I said. "I just want to look into it a little first. Find out what I can. It looks to be something I think the police can solve, or will solve, then I'll tell them what I know."

"Why wouldn't they solve it?" John said. "I don't get it."

"First off, it's personal," I said. "I like to take care of my own problems. Especially when it involves some asshole trying to kill me. Second, Mexico didn't solve their case. In the future, they may, or may not, figure out and punish whoever killed Beatrice. But I wouldn't count on it. Mexico is known for its corruption. It's become a lifestyle in Mexican government, especially the police force. How do I know whoever murdered Beatrice didn't pay someone off? How do I know it wasn't someone involved with the police to begin with? Hell, police officers tried to rob me and Leonard, and they cut Leonard. Hadn't been for Beatrice's old man, they would have killed us both.

"And if this monster came here to kill me, thinks he has, has gone home, and I tell our cops, can they get him out of Mexico? It might require a lot more than they can manage. Extradition can be a bitch."

"Christ," John said. "For the first time in my life I got a real relationship. I don't want to lose that."

"You won't," Leonard said. "I'm indestructible."

"Yeah," John said. "What about that knife wound?"

"I had an off day. Hey, even monkeys fall out of trees."

"Leonard. Please don't fall. Promise me."

"I promise," Leonard said. "Hap will be my support line."

"Shit," Brett said. "Let's find the sonofabitch killed Charlie, cut his nuts off, and feed them to a German shepherd. Or better yet, one of those little bitty dogs without hair."

23

Two days later we had Charlie's funeral. It was a simple one. No church or preacher was involved. He wouldn't have liked that. His body was cremated and services were held at a community center. It was packed. Friends. Relatives and cops. Mostly cops. Jake was among them. He said to me, "I got a feeling more and more that I don't know all I know about this thing. Get me?"

"I haven't a clue what you mean."

"Hap, don't get caught. Whatever you're doin', don't get caught. Whoever did this to Charlie, if you're after the sonofabitch, I hope you succeed. But you break a law and I know about it, you know what I got to do."

"I do. But I don't intend to break any laws. I haven't a clue what you're talking about."

"Yeah, right," Jake said.

One at a time, people got up and told things about Charlie. Stories. Incidents. Or just expressed their feelings. I was included. I said: "Charlie was a good friend. He died badly, but I know he died as bravely as is humanly possible. His killer will be found."

I didn't go as far as to say how he would be found.

That was still a card to play, and only Leonard, Brett, and John had seen it.

Jim Bob Luke showed for the funeral. He got up and said a few words. Then Leonard.

Hanson was last, and the best. He had known Charlie the longest, had worked with him closely when they were both on the police department.

Hanson was in his motorized wheelchair. He rode it to a place beside the podium where everyone else had stood and talked. Charlie's porkpie hat was in his lap. Hanson's wife, Rachel, a striking black woman in a purple dress, took the microphone off the podium and gave it to him.

Hanson held the microphone for a while, as if he might not actually speak. Then he said, "Charlie Blank was the friend everyone wanted, and if he was your friend, you were proud of it. He made you proud of yourself. Figured a guy like Charlie liked you, you had to be all right. He was a simple guy. Loved his friends. Was a wonderful cop. He loved the smell of a woman's hair. Told me that many times. He liked dogs and hated cats. In many ways, he saved my life. He made me know it was worth living after my accident. He's helped me with my physical therapy, and he listened to me whine about how life wasn't worth living, and he convinced me it was worth living. I thank him for that. Right now, even with what happened to Charlie, I'm very convinced it's worth living again.

"He loved Wal-Mart. He was a nut for Wal-mart. And before Wal-Mart, Kmart. He was shattered when the Kmart folded. He was depressed for days, had a hard time shifting his loyalty to Wal-Mart, but when he did, he did it wholeheartedly.

"He liked porkpie hats. In fact, I have his here. I'm going to start wearing it. I always wanted to anyway. I thought Charlie looked cool in it. I was too embarrassed to let him know. Instead, I made fun of him. From now on, I'll wear his hat. He liked Hawaiian shirts. The gaudier the better. He liked tennis shoes and Dr. Scholl's shoes, which he bought at Wal-Mart, and he wore a pair of one or the other every day of his life. He did jogging, played basketball, he had on those tennis shoes or Dr. Scholl's. He went to a wedding or a funeral, he had them on. Me, Hap Collins, Leonard Pine, and God bless her, Brett Sawyer, all wore black, tie-up Dr. Scholl's today in his honor. We love you, Charlie. We'll never forget you."

Hanson put the porkpie on and Rachel wheeled him away.

We had a small get-together at John's house. Me and Brett. Leonard and John, of course. Hanson and Jim Bob. John fixed hot tea for all of us.

Hanson said, "Well, what are we going to do about this?"

"You too?" I said.

"Been thinking about things," Hanson said.

"I have plans," I said. "Sort of."

"Then that means Leonard has plans too," Hanson said.

"That's right," Leonard said.

"They won't be very smart plans," Jim Bob said. "No offense, but from my time with you guys, I'd say you're as dogged as pit bulls, but about as smart as two slices of bologna rubbing together on dry bread."

"Thanks," Leonard said. "Nothing like a good compliment. You're lucky you got slack with me for saving Hap's ass that time. Otherwise, a remark like that I'd have to see if you bounced."

Jim Bob grinned. "What you'd find is that I not only bounce. I bounce back."

"Ooooeeeeee," Leonard said. "Now my nuts are suckin' up. You are so scary."

"What I'm sayin' is it's what I do," Jim Bob said. "Detecting. And making things happen. What you and Hap do is fuck things up."

"There's a certain truth to that," I said.

"Motherfucker did this, is about as mean as a rattlesnake with a stick up its ass," Jim Bob said. "And he's big enough to pull a building down on us. What you need is someone like me knows how to sniff this shit out. You want him found, I'm your man."

"That's true," Hanson said. "Me and Charlie were going to pick Jim Bob's brain to start our investigations business. He's the best."

I thought he probably was, and so did Leonard. But there was some kind of macho shit between them, and Leonard wasn't eager to give Jim Bob credit for much. Not and like it. I think it had something to do with Jim Bob saving me that time. Leonard may have thought that was his job and he slacked on me. Then again, maybe he was just disappointed he didn't have it to hold over my head.

"Hot tea, anyone?" John said.

"Christ, enough with the tea, already," Leonard said. "I'm floatin' in the stuff."

"I'm nervous," John said.

"Plan I got is this," Jim Bob said. "You folks set tight. I'll make a little trip to Mexico. Do some investigating. I have a friend or two down there. They're in the detecting business too. Mexican. Both of them. They know where all the bodies are buried. Maybe me and them can dig up the ones we need. In the meantime, might I suggest you folks stay close and stay ready. We don't know for sure this behemoth has gone home. He may be waiting for another chance. He may know he didn't get the right person. If we're lucky, he went back to Mexico thinking he did what he needed to do. Or he may have just gone back anyway and plans to come back and finish the job. We'll have to find out."

"Who says Mexico is his home?" Hanson said.

"Wouldn't it be?" Brett asked.

"Hanson's right," Jim Bob said. "Assume nothing. That's the first rule of good detecting. And always wear clean underwear in case you have a wreck. Mother told me that. I've tried to live by it."

"Have a bad enough wreck," Brett said, "you can bet even clean underwear will fill up."

Jim Bob wrinkled his brows. "You know, I hadn't even considered that."

24

WE STAYED HOME and Jim Bob went to Mexico. During that time, we played it careful. Leonard decided to pack up his shotgun, vanilla cookies, John's tea, and move John and Bob the armadillo back to his place for a while. It was out in the country and a little harder to find, and small, easier to protect. There was no certainty that he, or any of us, was in danger, of course, but it was a case of better safe than sorry.

Brett and I hunkered down at her place. I escorted her to work and picked her up, still wearing my chicken plant uniform, my chicken plant revolver on my hip.

Brett wore a little automatic hidden under her nurse uniform. It was in a holster fastened to her thigh. Certainly against hospital rules, but what they didn't know wouldn't hurt them.

When she changed at night it was a ritual. She'd lift the hem of her dress and show me the little revolver in its white holster, which matched her white nurse uniform and white hose. Then she slid the dress up high enough to show me her panties. Off came the dress, the revolver, the hose, the panties. Finally she was wearing nothing but a smile and a thin fringe of red pubic hair growing back into place.

Now and then, while wearing my chicken plant guard uniform, I'd insist I was the law and thought she ought to be strip-searched, and she'd let me. It was foolish and fun.

We made love a lot during the two weeks Jim Bob was gone. Deep down maybe we figured things could go wrong. Thought we'd try to make up for all the love-making we might miss if one or both of us got killed. Something silly like that.

Whatever, that part of the waiting wasn't so bad. And I realized that I didn't just love Brett, I was crazy in love with her. I had never met a woman who made me feel this way.

I thought my first wife, Trudy, was the only one that would ever give me those feelings, but Brett, she was the best yet. She made me truly realize just how childish and puppylike my love for Trudy had been.

At work Leonard and I found ourselves telling Charlie stories. Hadn't been for Charlie, there were a few times when I wouldn't have gone home at night, and now, in an odd way, it was my fault he was dead.

I began to gather up guilt. Had I been where I was supposed to be it would have been me. It was supposed to be me.

And then I'd feel something else.

Shame. Shame because I was glad I hadn't been home, that it hadn't been me. It was a mix of noxious feelings that didn't set well on the stomach.

I told Leonard how I felt. He said what he's said to me before. "Things don't happen for a reason, Hap. They just happen. It's got nothing to do with either you or Charlie deserving to die. The guy did this wanted you, you weren't there. That's good for you. Charlie was there.

That's bad for Charlie. It's simplistic, but that's all there is to it. Some idiot might say things happen for the best. And for you that would be true. But what about Charlie? Was that for his best? Of course not. Neither of you deserved that, but he got it. No rhyme. No reason. Just the way it came together. Once you start realizing it's got nothing to do with deserving it, you'll deal with it better."

"Would you have felt guilty had it been you?"

Leonard was silent for a moment. "Yeah. Yeah I would have. But not like you, brother. I'd have brooded on it for a day, told myself just what I told you, and I'd have moved on. I might have a bump in the night from time to time thinking about it, some wiggle in the back of my brain. But I'd put it in its place, and day by day it would grow smaller, and then it would just be what happened. I'd still love and miss Charlie, but I'd know it wasn't my fault."

"Are you saying that just to make me feel better?"

"A little. But I also mean what I say. You can't carry everyone's problems, every bad thing that happens to someone you know around on your back like a boulder. That boulder is going to get heavier and heavier, and finally, you won't be able to bear it. You'll go down before your time. My advice is feel guilty only about the things that happen to me because of our association and jettison the rest."

25

AFTER TWO WEEKS or so, in the middle of the night, on a weekend, mine and Brett's nights off, the phone rang. Brett was so deep in sleep she didn't hear it. I had become so accustomed to sleeping part of the day, I found it difficult to sleep at night on the weekends. Brett, on the other hand, would have shamed a hibernating bear.

I rolled out of bed and went around on Brett's side where the phone sat on a nightstand. I sat down on the bed and answered it, expecting it to be one of Brett's worthless children with their tit in the wringer, their dick in a crack.

It was Jim Bob.

"Qué pasa," he said.

"Where are you?"

"I'm at a phone booth in the center of town. I called John's place, but no answer. I called Hanson and he's coming in. We thought we'd gather up at John's place or Brett's. That okay?"

I thought about it a minute. I said, "Come over here. But don't knock the house down, Brett's asleep."

"Can you get in touch with Leonard?"

"I can. I'll have him meet us."

"Be there in a moment. And I got a little surprise for you."

"I didn't know you knew my size. Is it revealing?"

"Just in all the right places."

"Well, come on then."

I called Leonard's place and he answered. I could hear country music in the background.

"You having a hoedown?"

"Me and John was dancing. He dances like someone sawed off about half his foot."

I told him what Jim Bob had said.

"We're on our way."

"Well, don't let Bob drive."

"He's grounded. Sonofabitch rooted around one of the blocks holds up the porch, made it collapse. No movies, dates, or giving him the car for a week."

Jim Bob arrived first. He knocked gently on the door and opened it. He said, "I really didn't know your size, so I got you something else."

"And what's that?"

Jim Bob stepped aside and I saw Ferdinand standing there, wearing a simple white shirt and blue jeans. There was a scabbed scar on the right side of his face. He was leaning on a cane.

"Well, I'll be goddamned. Come on in."

Ferdinand came in, suddenly grabbed me and hugged me. He started to cry. "You must think me an awful man," he said.

I peeled him off of me and guided him to the couch. "I don't think anything," I said. Which was a partial lie. I had my opinions about Ferdinand. Some of them good, some not so good.

"How did you find him?" I said.

"Let's wait until the others are here. I'd rather not tell it twice."

About fifteen minutes later Hanson arrived. He was wearing Charlie's porkpie. I was surprised to see him using a walker.

"You're out of your chair?" I said as I let him in.

"Your skills of observation are as sharp as ever," Hanson said, his black face beaming. "Feeling is back in my legs. Been using this for about a week now. Doctor thinks I keep up the physical therapy, martial arts training, the feeling will come back completely."

I sat him on the couch, introduced Ferdinand.

About thirty minutes later John and Leonard arrived. When Ferdinand saw Leonard, he got up and extended his hand. Leonard took it. Ferdinand began to weep.

"Just sit down," Leonard said.

"I'll make tea," John said.

"Of course you will," Leonard said.

I decided to slip back in the bedroom for a moment. When I got in there, Brett was stirring. I said, "Baby, if you don't want to repeat your Gypsy Rose Lee act, I'd advise you to dress before you come in the living room."

"What's going on?"

I told her.

"I'll be out in a moment."

John was pouring tea into cups and putting the cups on a tray when Brett came out. Her hair was beautifully tousled around her face. She was wearing a white T-shirt and white shorts. I introduced her to Ferdinand. She sat on the arm of the couch.

Jim Bob was sitting in a chair near the coffee table. He sipped his tea and set it on the table. He said, "I've got an interesting story for you people. I'll try and give you the *Reader's Digest* version.

"To sort of capsulize the theme, let me say, Hap, that you inadvertently stepped into a nest of vipers."

"Hell, I know that."

"No. You don't know. This thing has some twisties and some turnies."

"Twisties and turnies?" Leonard said. "Is that some kind of exotic underwear?"

"Sophisticated private eye talk," Jim Bob said. "Don't you fret none now, Leonard. It's over your head and it isn't your fault."

Jim Bob turned his chair backward and sat so that his arms lay on the back rest. He said, "I'm gonna nutshell for you what this is all about. Ferdinand filled me in on some of it, and me and him sort of guessed out the rest, but I figure it's pretty accurate.

"Beatrice's father borrowed money from someone known for loaning money and not being nice about it. High interest. Strongarm tactics. It was the only way he could get the money he needed to send Beatrice to the States to go to the university. Deal was, she'd graduate in four years, and then pay back what was borrowed with money from her new job, whatever it was. In the meantime, Ferdinand had to pay something back every week. And this amount didn't count toward the amount borrowed. It didn't even count as interest. The man who loaned the money, Juan Miguel, saw it as collateral on the major loan. Best I can describe it."

"If you don't mind me saying, seems like a pretty dumb kind of loan," Leonard said.

"Yes," Ferdinand said. "But I wanted for her what I could not give her. She was to pay it back."

"Let me finish this," Jim Bob said. "Beatrice goes to the University of Texas, and bails. That's the bottom line. She gave up on it and came back to Mexico without the debt paid. That meant Ferdinand had to pay every week

and she had to help. In the long run, this being a lifetime deal until they could pay back the loan in full, this
might not have been a bad way for Juan Miguel to go.
Just have them keep paying until they're both in the grave.
This might surpass the loan. And say somehow they make
back the loan, pay it all off, well, okay. He gets his money
back with interest, plus all the money they've been paying weekly to keep him from breaking something.

"Then there's a new wrinkle. Through old contacts at
the university, Beatrice finds out that some Mayan facades—"

"What?" John asked.

"Mayan facades are painted stucco on the fronts of
temples. These had been found by looters in the jungle,
and they had contacted university scouts to let them know
they had them available for a good price."

"Is this kind of thing legal?" Brett said.

"Nope. The scouts aren't sanctioned. They're just people who work for the university and occasionally field information of a dubious and illegal nature. Lot of things
you see in museums came through university contacts that
weren't on the up-and-up. It's a coup for the university
as well as the museum. Though it's harder to pull that
kind of thing off these days. Used to, there wasn't much
to stop that kind of commerce. That leads us to the rest
of the story, as old Paul Harvey is fond of saying.

"Well, the university offers a whole shitload of money
for this thing, and the looters say yippie. We'll bring it as
far as Playa del Carmen. You come get it. Secretly, of
course.

"Here's the corker. The looters load this stuff on trucks
and arrive at the pickup point, just outside Playa del Carmen, and the university people don't show. They've gotten cold feet. New attitudes are in place, and what was
once smart archaeology is now considered looting. Not

only by the obvious looters, but by the university and museum folks as well. That's always been the attitude, openly, but underneath, this kind of thing was okay as long as no one got their tail in too tight a crack.

"University decided it was putting the tail of its reputation in just such as crack, and they backed out. So guess what? The looters decided to hide the stuff away and sell it to another bidder. They decide to hire a boat. Ferdinand's boat. They moved the stucco facades by boat to an island Ferdinand knew. He occasionally took people there to fish, and the looters were paying pretty good money, and he thought he could put this money away and add to it later to pay off what he owed Juan Miguel.

"How am I doing, Ferdinand? Am I telling it right?"

Ferdinand nodded.

"So, Ferdinand, with the help of his daughter, transfers the facades to this little island, hides 'em away, then on the return trip the looters decide—or have already decided—they don't really want Ferdinand and Beatrice to go back with them. In fact, they don't want them to go back at all, and they don't plan on leaving them on the island to Robinson Crusoe it. They decide to use machetes and chop the old man up."

"Well, seeing that he's here, and having seen him in action," I said, "we know how that turned out."

"Exactly. There were two of them. He took the machete away from one of them and killed them both. Dumped them in the ocean. Is that right, Ferdinand?"

Ferdinand nodded.

"You are one bad dude," Leonard said.

"They did not expect one so old to be so willing," Ferdinand said. "And they did not know that I grew up training with the machete."

"Not something you'd expect," Brett said. "Machete training. I thought you just chopped with it."

"Whatever," Jim Bob said. "He and Beatrice survived. So now Ferdinand and Beatrice have an ace in the hole. Or so they think. Beatrice goes to Juan Miguel and tells him she knows the whereabouts of these facades. She believes that the University of Mexico will be interested in them, and that they will pay heavily. She offers to trade the facades to Miguel to sell to the university for the cancellation of her debt.

"Juan Miguel is a nut not only for money and meanness, but dig this—if you'll pardon the pun. He loves archaeology. He likes to think he's adding to the world's knowledge in this area. You know, loan shark a little, kill a little, and do a little archaeology. Or rather buy a little archaeology. He sees himself as a Renaissance man of sorts. So, he agrees to go with Beatrice. He contacts the Mexican university, and sure enough, they will pay for these facades. And considering they don't have to be sold out of the country, it's a legal deal.

"But in the meantime, Beatrice decides she's screwed the pooch. She should have offered to sell them herself, cut out the middleman. This way, she thought, she could pay off Miguel, and come out with enough money to take her and her father to the States.

"Now we have Juan Miguel having negotiated with the university through his contacts, and suddenly, when he's ready for the information to reveal the location of the facades, Beatrice isn't talking."

"I did not know she had done this thing," Ferdinand said. "I would not have let her. Sell them to Miguel for our debt, yes. But to double-cross him . . . no."

"Juan Miguel was," Jim Bob said, "to put it in casual terms, about ready to piss vinegar and turn it to wine. He was embarrassed. He's like a kind of mafia don in Mexico, and all the underworld knew he was brokerin' this deal, and now some woman, a former prostitute . . . No offense, Ferdinand . . ."

"It is the truth," Ferdinand said. "But when she goes to the university, she leaves this life behind. Until this man Billy . . . Please, continue, Señor Jim Bob."

"Well, he doesn't like it that she backs out on him and throws shit in his face. He is not a happy little criminal. He's as embarrassed as a priest caught jacking off during a confession. He goes to Beatrice and says, Hey, we had a deal, and she lies and says, I have another deal in place, and I'll have all the money I owe you, promise. You won't get the facades to give to the University of Mexico, I'll do that, but you will get your money *in toto*. Juan Miguel doesn't like this, but he accepts. But, to make sure Beatrice understands he's tired of dickin' around, he has his man cut off the tip of her little finger."

"She told me it was a fishing accident," I said.

"She lied," Ferdinand said. "I would have killed this man had I been there."

"Maybe not this guy," Jim Bob said. "Maybe not any of us this guy. But I'll come back to him. So he cuts off Beatrice's finger, tells her he'll kill her and her father if she fucks this up.

"Beatrice isn't through, however. She meets you and Leonard. And you get involved, and then she meets this Billy. Billy's a blowhard and as full of shit as Beatrice. No offense, old man. But it seems your daughter had enough bullshit to fertilize about half the globe."

I saw Ferdinand's eyes glow, but only for a moment. He hung his head.

"She wants what she wants so bad she will deal with the devil," Ferdinand said.

"And she did," Jim Bob said. "And besides the devil, she dealt with Billy. Billy says he'll pay her a lot more than three days of fishing are worth if she throws herself in and agrees to do whatever he wants her to do.

"As I said, before she went to the university Beatrice was a call girl in Mexico City. She's not afraid of this deal. She's seen some things, done some things. It turns out Billy, who is Billy Sullivan, is full of it and doesn't really have any money. He's a blowhard but Beatrice falls for it. He gave a little down payment, but the rest of it he didn't have and wasn't about to ask his father, who, though not rich, is fairly well off."

"Know what," I said. "I never did call his old man. I forgot all about it."

"Doesn't matter," Jim Bob said. "He finally got in touch with him and his father came down with lawyers and money and got him out of jail and took him home. I traced him down when I got back from Mexico. And, guess what? He's dead. Someone went all the way to Indiana, which is where he's from, and cut him up. Same way as Charlie."

"Poor old Billy," I said.

"Fuck Billy," Leonard said. "I wouldn't have shit a hot meal in his hand if he was dying of hunger."

"Way I figure it," Jim Bob said, "Beatrice gave names or had addresses on her, something. Somehow she led them to you, Hap, or rather Charlie. I don't think they knew the difference. Then they went to Indiana and got Billy. For all I know, they got all your addresses from the police and Beatrice didn't give them shit. Enough money, information tends to change hands. And not just in Mexico."

"But why would he want us?" I said.

Jim Bob shrugged, said, "Juan Miguel wanted vengeance and he thought you and Billy were in on the scam. Maybe Beatrice, to prolong her life, told them that. How's that for a guess? I think it's that simple. Juan Miguel, he doesn't like taking a fuckin', and if he does take one, then he makes sure whoever gave it to him takes it up the ass as well. A sort of permanent fuckin'. 'Course, could be he thought you or Billy, or both of you, knew about the facades and maybe he thought he'd find that out. He'd still want them, I think."

"What about Leonard?" I asked.

"I don't know," Jim Bob said. "No one tried to kill him, so maybe she didn't give his name, died before she could. I don't know. No way of knowing."

"I gave my address," Leonard said. "Not where I was staying, with John. The ironic part is after Charlie was killed I moved John and me out to my house for a while, because I thought it was safer."

"By then it was," Jim Bob said. "The killers had gone home. Maybe they decided they had the main two, and after torturing Charlie and Billy and getting nothing, they decided neither of you knew dick about the facades."

"That seems like a pretty good guess," I said.

"And Ferdinand?" Leonard said.

"He was going to kill Ferdinand too, but Juan Miguel made the mistake of not sending the Jolly Green Giant. They sent some everyday fucker, and guess what? They sent him to do it with a machete. It's kind of their trademark, death by machete.

"Guy comes to get Ferdinand on his boat. Ferdinand disarms him, beats him like a circus monkey, makes him tell why he's come. That's how Ferdinand finds out about Beatrice.

"Then, Ferdinand ties up his attacker, takes him out to sea, and dumps him in the ocean."

"Tied up?" John asked.

"Yes," Ferdinand said. "That way he cannot swim."

"Yeah," Leonard said, "tied up cramps a fella's breast stroke all right."

I thought, Damn. This is one mean old man.

"How the hell did you find all this out?" Brett asked.

"Hey, I'm a detective, lovely lady. And I had some help. Guy down there, a Mexican, runs a little private eye agency. I've worked with him I don't know how many times. I heard this name, Juan Miguel, I thought it rang a bell. My acquaintance down there, César, he had a partner who met a nasty end not long ago, and the whole thing's connected with Juan Miguel. That's where I had heard the name, year and a half ago. It didn't mean much to me then. Just something they had got themselves into.

"I didn't know the details, just that some gangster named Juan Miguel was responsible for César's partner's death. The partner I had met, but hadn't dealt with much. Not directly. I always dealt with César. Fact is, César helped me find Ferdinand."

"How did you find him?" Leonard asked.

"Me and César found him by finding the boy you told me about. José. The one helped him fish. He didn't know Ferdinand was in trouble, just that he was gone, and César simply asked him did Ferdinand have a place he went that few people knew about, and how about three hundred dollars if he told us. He was loyal to Ferdinand for about five minutes, then he was loyal to three hundred dollars. For him, that's like a thousand, at least.

"The boy told me about a little island. Said that was where Ferdinand sometimes went to fish for himself and to be alone. Said he had gone with him a couple times. No one else had asked José that. No one else had offered him three hundred dollars either. No one thought or knew to ask him the question. We told José he should say nothing else about it to anyone. César rented a boat and we went out there, found Ferdinand. And the facades. That's the island where they're stored."

"What about what really counts to us?" Hanson said. "Justice for Charlie."

"There's the rub," Jim Bob said. "We might could put together some pretty good information for the Mexican police. But in that little town of Playa del Carmen, Juan Miguel's pretty much the man. He's pretty much the man throughout Mexico when it comes to crime and payoffs in cocaine, money, and poontang."

"So," Leonard said, "might we assume you're saying that would be a worthless approach to taking care of Charlie's killer?"

"Right."

"I say we go to Mexico and get the sonofabitch," Hanson said. "Him and this giant. Or whoever gets in the way."

"First off, you're not going anywhere," Jim Bob said. "No offense, but in your state you'd just fuck up the mission."

"All right then," Hanson said. "What are you and the others going to do? And how can I help?"

"I like Hanson's idea," Leonard said. "We kill the sonofabitch."

"It's an idea," Jim Bob said, "but not an easy one to pull off."

"I been in on a designed killing once, and I didn't like it," I said. "I'm still dealing with it. I just don't like the idea of a guy pisses you off, you kill him."

"Pisses you off," Jim Bob said. "He killed Charlie, man. I'm more than pissed off."

"You want justice for your friend, Charlie," Ferdinand said. "I want justice for my daughter. We all have a price to pay. Vengeance is a price, but it must be paid."

"Not me," John said. "You know how I stand. I'm an observer. And not a happy one."

"Killing him seems awful heavy to me," I said.

"You're fuckin' me," Leonard said. "What do you suggest, we humiliate him? Shame him? Bad dog. Smack him with a rolled-up newspaper? I think you ain't got no peas for your pea shooter, Hap. Why don't we just call him a bad name or knock his hat off?"

"Or write he sucks dicks on some bathroom wall," Jim Bob said. "Hey, meant nothing by that, Leonard. John. Anyone else in here suck dicks?"

Brett raised her hand.

Jim Bob burst out laughing.

"Listen," I said. "I was thinking we get some photos of these facades. We say to Juan Miguel we got these facades and we'll sell them to you for such and such, and then we spring the police on him. You know, have them in waiting, so they got to arrest him when he shows up to buy them."

"They'll arrest us for setting up the scam," Jim Bob said. "It implies we stole the facades in the first place, even if we didn't. And if it did work, you keep forgetting, he's got the Mexican law's dicks in his pockets. It's a stupid idea, Hap."

"So we have to kill him?" I said.

No one said anything for a time. Finally Jim Bob said, "Before we start passing out the ammunition and a sack lunch, might be a good idea I tell you a little about this guy Juan Miguel, and his main henchman."

"Henchman?" Leonard said. "Shit, I just love that term. I think I used to read that in the Fu Manchu books. Henchmen."

"César helped me find out a lot of stuff on this dude. Juan Miguel is rich because he's run more drugs than Johnson and Johnson. He started out a petty thief, worked himself up to a higher level, killed off the right guys in the Mexican mafia, and eventually, he's head dick. Got him some class along the way. Money buys class, you know. And very expensive suits, in all shades. When he wears a suit. He's a practicing nudist much of the time."

"A nudist?" Brett said.

"Yep. A classy nudist. At least in his own eyes. In reality he's about as classy as a ball peen hammer to the back of the head. Which is something he's done. Used a ball peen on his enemies' skulls. But he's too cool for that now. He's got hired hands that do that."

"The henchmen," Leonard said.

"That's right."

"Is he hard to get to?" Hanson asked.

"He's got a little fortress of a house in the hills surrounding Playa del Carmen. Nice pad. You can drive a car right up to it, but there's guys with guns to greet you. One of the guys, according to César, is about six eight, weighs about three eighty-five, and only the bits between his fingers and toes is fatty."

"Sounds like hyperbole," John said.

"Could be," Jim Bob said. "They call him Hammerhead."

"An old family name," Leonard said. "Surely he's a junior."

"Point is," Jim Bob said, "what we got here isn't a cakewalk. This guy is dangerous. The people who protect him are dangerous. We can't drive up to his house, knock on his door, ask if he can come out to play and shoot him in the head."

"Any weaknesses?" I asked.

"Maybe at bridge," Jim Bob said, "not much else. Well, there is one thing. A mistress. A real stunner. She lives in a fine house with some pretty nice guards herself. Provided by Juan Miguel, of course. She likes to travel to Mexico City and shop in expensive shops. We followed her three times in one week to the airport. And we even got on the flight once. The guards were with her. She shopped Mexico City to death. Only thing she didn't do was buy the coats off the bears at the Mexico City zoo. She had the two plugs with her carrying all this shit. Clothes. Shoes. Whatever the crap is women buy, and I bet me and César sat outside those stores in a rented airport car most of the day. We didn't even eat lunch."

"She's the key," Leonard said.

"Yep," Jim Bob said. "I suppose so."

26

THAT NIGHT THE RAIN blew hard against the house, rattled the windows like teeth chattering in a cold face. Only it was warm, sticky warm, even in the house with the central air and a fan blowing at the foot of the bed.

Brett, who I thought was asleep, rolled over and laid her arm across my chest.

"You aren't sleeping?"

"I know. And neither are you. Surely you don't want sex again? I think I'm pooped out."

"We didn't have sex tonight."

"I'm still pooped out . . . You sure we didn't?"

"I'm sure. Man, is that rain gonna wash us away?"

"We'll float on the bed. We'll be okay."

"Will there be room for all the animals, Noah?"

"We're the only animals that matter."

"Hap. Can we do this?"

"You don't need to do anything. Me and Leonard, Jim Bob and Ferdinand, we can do it."

"The plan sounds kind of lame to me."

"He's actually using part of my idea."

"Like I said, the plan sounds lame."

"Jim Bob said it was a better plan than he expected the bunch of us to come up with."

"Finding an extra pecan in your pecan sundae is better than you expected, but it isn't exactly a whole pie. Jim Bob's so smart, why doesn't he come up with a better plan."

"You're knocking the plan?"

"I'm just saying Jim Bob saying it's a better plan than he expected doesn't make it the best plan devised."

"It's better than me or Leonard running the show."

"It's still not a plan that makes me feel confident."

"Would any plan make you feel confident?"

"Probably not."

"It's what we've got. Or what we've got without you. You don't need to go at all. You have a job to worry about."

"You're not doing anything without me. I got a little money put back. I can probably get off for a couple weeks. How long does it take to hunt down and kill a guy anyway?"

"Christ, don't say that, Brett. I still wake up with the other on my mind."

"Me too. I even wake up screaming about it sometimes. But I'd do it again. I'd do what we're about to do twice. Charlie was a good guy, Hap. He didn't deserve this."

"No, he didn't."

"You did a thing for me once that I can't imagine anyone else doing."

"Leonard did it too."

"You always say that, and he did, but he did it for you . . . Okay. I can't imagine anyone but you two doing it for me, and now here's my chance to pay you back."

"I don't want that. You're not paying me back. This

has got nothing to do with you paying me back. It's got to do with me paying back that cocksucker in Mexico."

Brett got up, went to the bathroom, came back, and snuggled in with me again. I said, "Frankly, I hate to admit it, but I been thinking about walkin'."

"No you haven't."

"I haven't?"

"Oh, you might consider it. It's in your head. But you know what you'll do, and so do I."

"Am I that predictable?"

"Except that part where you bent one of my legs sideways and came at me from that weird angle. I didn't expect that. But, other than sex, yes, you're predictable."

"Hey, we're together long enough, I'll be predictable there too. Then you'll have to get rid of me."

"I don't think you're altogether joking."

"I haven't had the best luck with love, my dear."

"Hap. I don't care you're not young, you're not rich or overly handsome, or even well hung—"

"Hold it now, goddamn it, you're stepping across the line."

"I thought that would wake you up. I'm saying I don't care. I don't care about any of those things, but I care about you, and I can't just kiss you bye and send you to Mexico not knowing what's going to happen. And when it's over, when we come back here, I want to make this deal permanent. I'm not saying you have to marry me, though that would be nice, but I want us to be together. And that means being together when you go to Mexico. I don't want to be sitting here waiting on my man to do what a man's got to do like some cheap-ass Western movie."

"That's kind of what it boils down to, though, isn't it?"

"It boils down to you and me. From now on, I want it you and me. Except when I'm doing some serious business in the bathroom. I don't mind you come in I'm doing a number one, but a number two, no way. Unless maybe it's to hand me the toilet paper if I forgot to put it on the roll, but other than that, not a number two. You stay out then."

"You're fucking nuts, Brett."

"I know."

"Brett, I don't know I can go through with it. I think about it I clench up inside."

"Whatever you do. Whatever you decide. I want to be there with you. Except that bathroom part that I've already explained. And that goes if you're doing number two as well. I don't want to see that."

"Brett, thy middle name is class."

"I keep telling you that."

Next day they fired Brett when she wanted time off. She'd already used all her time off dealing with her worthless daughter.

I was with her at the nurses' station when the head nurse told her it was all over and that they'd been thinking about firing her for some time because of her mouth.

"My mouth," Brett said. "My fuckin' mouth. You old dried-up cunt. You'd be so lucky as to have my cunt for your mouth. Turn it sideways, and it'd go better with your mustache than the mouth you got, you fuckin' Wicked Witch of the West. I ought—"

I got her by the arm and pulled her out of there. On the way out she yelled back what they could do with their thermometers.

Later that day, Leonard and I went to our boss. It was tough. I knew Bond felt he owed me something, and I didn't want to put him in a position of feeling he had to let me have more juice than I deserved, but there was nothing else to do.

His office was in town, away from the chicken plant. There were, however, pictures of chickens on the wall, and charts with chickens. There was also a big wooden desk, a black leather chair, and a black and gray striped couch.

Bond actually hadn't been in the office, but I had called and he had called back and said he'd meet me there. He ended up meeting us out in the parking lot, riding up with us in the elevator.

"I don't come here much," he said. "I'm really too rich and too far removed from what's going on anymore to have opinions. I just like to collect checks and leave the work and the organization to people I've handpicked."

"It's a nice life if you can get it," Leonard said.

"Yes it is," Bond said.

Leonard and I sat on the couch, shuffled our feet for a moment. Finally I came out with it. Told Bond something had come up. That we had to go away for a while. But we'd come back. And we'd like our jobs back, if that was possible, and not to think we were trying to take advantage of him. To my ears, I sounded like a kid making up some bullshit excuse for not doing his homework.

Bond looked at us, said, "You do whatever you want. I won't even cut your pay."

"You don't owe me that," I said. "You sure don't owe Leonard that."

"Thanks," Leonard said.

"No," Bond said. "I do owe you that. Go with my blessing."

"I want you to know I'm not trying to take advantage of you," I said. "Something really did come up."

"I believe you. Go with my blessing. And the assurance your jobs are waiting."

"How is Sarah?"

"She's much better. She has been moved to a less critical wing of the hospital."

"I'm glad to hear it."

"She's talking now. Some of her old spirit is back. She speaks highly of you, Hap."

"That's kind of her," I said.

Bond was starting to look teary. We got up to leave. Bond said, "Hap. Leonard. I got an idea you two aren't just going on a hunting trip."

"Actually," Leonard said, "that's exactly what we're doing."

"Be safe."

We thanked him and left.

Jim Bob booked me, Brett, Leonard, Ferdinand, and himself on a flight to Cancun for the next afternoon. I took Brett to a nice store in Tyler and bought her an expensive outfit or two. Still, we packed light.

That night we slept hardly at all, got up early, muddled about. Hanson came by to wish us off. Told us to keep him posted. Early afternoon, we headed for Houston Intercontinental in Jim Bob's car, the Red Bitch.

"What about guns?" Leonard asked.

"César," Jim Bob said, switching lanes to the sound of a car horn blaring. "He'll provide what we need. He has his own grudge he'd like to take care of. He's been nursing it for years, and now he's ready. You brought some of that money you got, didn't you, Hap?"

"I did."

"I sold some hogs cheap, fired all my help, so now I got some extra bread too."

"I brought some," Brett said. "But I didn't have much. I plan to suck off Hap when we get home."

"That sounds enticing," I said.

"You know what I mean," Brett said.

"I didn't bring any money," Leonard said. "I don't even know what color a dollar bill is anymore."

Jim Bob changed lanes so close had the car behind us had another coat of paint, it would have been in the back seat of the Red Bitch.

"You are one scary driver," Brett said.

"I'm just getting you folks primed for the really scary stuff."

27

We arrived in Cancun, rented a car, headed off toward Playa del Carmen. As we neared the town, a slice of sunset the color of a fresh-sliced salmon fillet stained the horizon. As we watched, darkness corrupted it, then it all sank away as if into a tar pit.

It was a night full of clouds and no visible moon. Darkness dripped over the car like ink poured from a jar, but as we neared the city pinpricks of colored lights jumped into view. We cruised past a McDonald's and a T-shirt shop and on into town.

We ended up staying at a nice hotel near the sea. Brett and I took a room, Jim Bob, Leonard, and Ferdinand took one together. Leonard ended up on a rollaway.

In our room we opened a window, pulled back the curtains, let the sea air in. There was a palm tree near our window. The limbs and leaves scraped the wall like a cat scratching. There were lights on poles along the edge of the beach and they made the sand and water and the pedestrian walk, Fifth Avenue, look like one of those paintings you do by numbers.

Seabirds were coasting low over the water, dropping birdshit like napalm, hoping for a late fish snack before hanging it up for the day.

People walked along Fifth Avenue, talking and laughing.

"Since this is gonna cost us anyway," Brett said, "what say we order room service, enjoy that, then fuck like two rabbits in a lab experiment?"

"That's my kind of night," I said.

We ordered room service, but what we ended up doing was not fucking like rabbits in a lab experiment, but lying in one another's arms watching a late movie, *The Man With the Golden Arm,* starring Frank Sinatra. It was in English. Something cabled in for the tourists, I guess.

Next morning we got up early, had room service, then went with Jim Bob in the rental to meet César. Leonard was walking a little funny. I thought maybe his bad hip was acting up.

"You all right?" I asked.

"It's not my hip, if that's what you're thinking. It's that damn roll-away. I fought that motherfucker all night. It finally threw me. I ended up sleeping with a blanket and a pillow on the floor. Now I know how those poor racked sonofabitches felt during the Inquisition."

We piled into the car. As we drove near the beach, I saw Ferdinand look out at the sea. I said, "Where's your boat?"

"I sold the boat," he said. "Some rich American who wanted his own fishing boat."

"I'm sorry."

"I needed the money . . . I know what you must think of me, señor. All of you. But I did what I could do. I tried to help my daughter. I did not make her a whore. She chose that for herself. When I thought she could get the money needed to keep her from dying, I let her do what she had to do. It was never for me. You must understand I was only letting her do what I thought she must do. It is all nothing now. She is dead. I am dead."

"Time heals things," I said.

"No, señor. It only heals some things. An open wound heals. This, this does not heal. But I can put salve on it. I can help kill this man who had my daughter killed."

"If it's any consolation," Leonard said. "Knowing now what you were up against, I understand why you did what you did."

"It is something, señor. It is something."

César's place was very nice. Nothing like what I expected. It was nestled amongst palms and foliage, one long story made of wood and stone, not far from the beach. The garage contained a Jaguar and an older-looking dirt-brown Plymouth.

"Looking through people's windows, prowling through their underwear drawers, seems to pay pretty good," Leonard said.

Jim Bob looked at Leonard and smiled. Leonard may have forgotten that Jim Bob and César were in the same business, but I doubted it.

We walked up a little crunched seashell path, and before we could knock, the door opened and a little fat man in a red shirt opened the door. He looked to be in his late thirties or forties, had very little hair, and what hair he had was black and gooey with oil. He had a face that would have looked at home on the Buddha, providing the Buddha had one cauliflowered ear. He shook our hands and hugged Jim Bob and Brett.

"Would you come in," he said. "It is so good to meet you, señores, and it is even better to see this delightful señorita. Or is it señora?"

"Señorita," she said.

"Surely, you are but an angel visiting from heaven."

"That goes without question," Brett said.

Inside the house it was also very nice, with colorful Mexican rugs hung on the wall, fine furniture, and nearby a young Mexican lady with blond hair and black roots. She stood near a stone fireplace, almost at attention. She wore a white pants suit with a long, near-waist-length strand of black beads that had gotten slung sideways, so that against her white suit it looked as if she were a cracked porcelain doll. She was pretty, but the look on her face was like that of someone who had just discovered her asshole has been sewn shut.

"This is my wife," César said. "Her name is Hermonie."

"Is Hermonie a Spanish name?" Brett asked.

"I have no idea," César said. "She is very shy . . . Ah, Jim Bob."

He and Jim Bob embraced. "Didn't we just do this?" Jim Bob said.

"What?" César said. "It is not as good the second time? Come, I have had a late breakfast prepared." He spoke pleasantly to Hermonie in Spanish.

She led us out the back way, as if leading us to our execution. Leonard leaned toward me, said, "I don't think these two are a love match."

We ended up at a table under a canopy. The table was covered with fruit, fried meats, and eggs. There were tortillas and coffee. There were also a few flies, but César brushed at these with his hand as if they were but part of the ambience.

"Please," César said. "Sit. Eat. Drink. Talk."

We sat. Jim Bob said, "Actually, César, we would like to get right to things. We're on a limited budget and we've got time restraints."

"Ah, you Americans. You do not understand time. Time

is time. It has no movement. Revenge is revenge, now or later."

"Drive-through burgers, drive-through pharmacies, and drive-through revenge," Jim Bob said. "That's us."

César grinned. "Of course. Try the cantaloupe. All the fruit is fresh."

Hermonie went away, then showed up with a small pitcher of cream, sweeteners for the coffee, then she disappeared again.

"Will Hermonie be joining us?" Brett asked.

"Actually," César said, looking sadly, "she is shy, and she hates Americans. For that matter, she is not too fond of me. She married me because she thought I had money. And I do, but not the sort of money she is looking for. She wants big money for big cars and big things. I make money that allows the middle-sized things. She made a mistake.

"But that is all right. I tolerate her and she tolerates me. She is as lovely a woman as an ugly fat man like myself will get, and I am most likely as rich as she will find. And I love Americans. My good friend, Jim Bob, I love him."

"I'm a Texan," Jim Bob said.

"Texas was stolen from Mexico," César said. "It should not be part of the United States."

"Mexicans helped steal it," Jim Bob said.

"Would it be okay if you two didn't fight the Alamo all over again?" I said.

"Ah," César said. "I love this guy. He loves me."

"Well, before you and I mate, César," Jim Bob said, "maybe we should get right to it. We have a plan, and being no friend of Juan Miguel, we thought you might help us tweak this plan."

"I am certainly no friend of this man, Juan Miguel. I have been waiting until my time is right to do what I need to do. Waiting, and praying to God to help me have my revenge."

"He helps in those matters?" Brett asked.

"If he does not, then we will do it without him," César said.

Jim Bob briefly outlined our plan.

César said, "Oh, you got some big stones, my friends. Big stones. Pardon me, lady."

"Forget it," Brett said.

"Let me tell you. We can do this. We must plan more carefully, but we can do this. By myself, I could not get even with this man. But with your help. Yes. I can. We can all eat a fine dish of revenge.

"Let me tell you about Juan Miguel, amigos. Many years ago a rich lady, a Mexican lady, she hires me to follow after her daughter who she thinks is being naughty with a man in Mexico City. Did I say she was a rich lady?"

"You did," I said.

"She offered me very much to watch this girl. My partner, Toño, was to help me. We, how is it you say it . . . double-teamed her, you see. It is easier that way. One can rest while the other watches. After a day or two we determine that, yes, she is in fact being naughty. She is with another man. They are spending many hours together in his hotel room and they did not have cards or dice with them. They are certainly playing that other game we all like to play. Toño takes photographs of her and this man going in and out of the hotel. We think this is good enough to show the lady. Show her that her pretty daughter is in fact running with this man. And we find out who this man is. He is Juan Miguel's son, Carmelo.

"We report all of this to the lady, and she sends her daughter away to the U.S. to study in the university, away from this man. So what happens? The girl, she pines for

Carmelo and she decides to climb to the top of the University of Texas tower and jump."

"Jesus," Brett said. "I wanted a man that bad, I'd just hop a plane."

"Who is to understand the thinking of the young?" César said. "And there is another thing. When her mother sends her away, this Carmelo, he finds a new woman. It is not true love to him. It is true lust.

"But that is not all. The mother. She is distraught. She hires us to show her where this Carmelo is. And we find him again for her, and he is in a beach house near Cozumel, and we go away. And this woman, she comes back there another time, and you know what she does. She shoots and kills this boy.

"Then, she is not happy yet. A week after the boy is dead, she sends word to Juan Miguel she knows how his boy died, and he agrees to see her, and she has the photographs we took of Carmelo and her daughter, and when she explains the connection, so he understands, you see, she tries to kill him with a knife she has concealed, but they take it away from her. And then he tortures her. He wants to know how she killed his boy, how she found him. She tells them about us. She tells them Toño took the photographs. She mentions me, but she tells him Toño took the photographs. She remembers Toño because he wanted her. He wanted her badly. He tried to lie with her in his bed. It didn't work, but I believe when it came time to call names, she called his because she knew him better. She said he took the photographs and that I worked for him.

"He cuts off her nose and sets her free. She does not go to the doctor. She goes home, she takes pills, and she is dead. She could not face having no daughter and no nose. Juan Miguel, he sends his men to see Toño. I do not know what happened to him. Not really. They come to see me and tell me they have killed Toño. They say I was Toño's boss. I was not the one who took the photos, but in case I should ever want to bother in their business, they would leave me a reminder. This big one. Hammerhead. Or Oso as I called him. He beat me. He cut off the tip of my finger."

César held his right hand up. The tip of the little finger was missing, same as Beatrice.

"And he gives me this ear. Here. He hit me so hard with a slap he did that. I do not hear as well in that ear anymore. They let me live. That was a mistake."

"Did you try the police?" Brett asked.

César shook his head. "No. I know this place too well. Many of the policemen, they are good. They would do the law. But Juan Miguel, he owns those at the top. They run things as they see them, and they see them with money."

"We're sorry about your friend," Brett said.

"Sorry is not important. Toño worked for me. He was not a friend. I did not like him much. He was good at what he did, but he was no brother. What I am mad about is my little finger and my ear. Juan Miguel, he will pay. But, unlike the woman, I do not go off half-cocked. I have waited my time. And now, with this tragedy of the woman . . ."

César reached out and patted Ferdinand on the arm, ". . . and the tragedy of your friend, the time is correct. He shall now pay. Tell me more of your plan."

"We thought we'd kidnap his mistress," Jim Bob said, "but we need you for that. We need to corner her somewhere. As for the bodyguards, you got me, Hap, and Leonard to take care of them."

"No offense, gentlemen," César said, "but are you capable?"

"I'd bet my life on them," Jim Bob said.

"Oh, you will," César said.

28

It WAS A TIGHT FIT in the rental, but thankfully, the trip was brief. César drove the car to a spot on the beach and parked us next to a high wide pile of large white stone slabs.

"There was to be a house here," César said as we got out of the car. "But it fell through. These stones. They were cut to be part of the foundation. The man having it built, he must have lost money. Or lost his wife. Or maybe he builds it for his mistress and she leaves him. I cannot say. Something went wrong. Perhaps he is still the owner of this land. There, where the grass grows up to the beach, that was where he was to build. This was the beginning, these stones. And they were the end."

The huge stones were cut in even rectangles four inches thick and maybe four feet long, and three feet across. It was obvious they had once been stacked neatly, but weather, or perhaps people climbing on them, had caused them to shift in places. Some of the stones had fallen and broken against others. At the peak of the pile was a colorful bird. I had never seen that kind of bird before. As

I watched, it took to the sky. It looked like a bouquet of flowers exploding.

César had placed a telescope in the trunk, and now he got it and the stand out, climbed to the top of the slab pile with it, moving his little round body as sure-footed as a mountain goat. He fastened the scope to its tripod, positioned it on a flat piece of rock, focused, looked through, called down, "Come see."

I went up first, realizing that going up was not as easy for me as César had made it look. I felt slabs shift under my feet. I yelled down for the others to watch out, went carefully, finally found the top.

A moment later the others worked their way up. We clutched together at the top around the telescope.

"This is a good telescope," César said. "I use it in my work. After what happened to me and Toño, I began to find out more about this Juan Miguel. I come here . . . and to another spot higher up, among the trees there, and observe from time to time. Juan Miguel spends much time at home. He likes the middle of the day to eat his lunch and answer his phone. Come look for yourself."

I looked. The sun was bright on the house and there was a blinding reflection off a great satellite dish that looked like a flying saucer that had landed on its edge. There were palms and shrubs and flowering plants to the left of the house that grew so thick they completely concealed anything that might be behind them.

It was a huge house, mostly glass and stone, surrounded by a fence of rock and mortar positioned at the peak and around a great rise of land covered in greenery and scrubby trees. The way the rise sloped toward us, you could see the close-clipped backyard and the swimming pool and patio. Their view from up there would be terrific. You would see the road below, the greater highway, and beyond that the sandy white beach and the deep blue sea.

There was a man sitting at a table under a patio roof, shirtless, shoeless, wearing a pair of khaki shorts. He was talking on the phone. He was middle-aged, brown, a little heavy.

Closer to the fence was the pool. Someone was swimming in the pool. I watched. It was a woman. She climbed out. She was tall and lean and dark with shoulder-length black hair. She looked middle-aged, and she looked to have worn well. I could tell that even from a distance. She was topless and proud of it. Walked with her back straight, shoulders back, her breasts forward like copper headlamps. The bikini she wore was a dark color and covered her in the front but did little to hide anything else.

"Damn," I said.

"Ah, that would be his wife you are seeing," César said. "Is she nude?"

"Damn near it."

"She likes to go without the top. Sometimes she wears nothing at all. Juan Miguel. He often goes nude. They are very much into the nudity. They travel to nudist camps worldwide I am told. They think the life is healthy. And then there is Hammerhead. Do you see him?"

"Nope," I said. "Damn. She's a beauty . . . And he's screwing around with another woman?"

"Alas, it happens. And she too is magnificent, this other woman. And younger."

"They always are," Brett said.

"If the guy takes off his pants," Leonard said, "let me know. Then I'll want a look."

"I would like to see," Ferdinand said.

"Look," I said.

He looked through the telescope. "I want him to see my face before he dies. I want him to know why."

"We all do," Brett said. She stood with her arm around my waist.

"I'd just settle for him being dead," I said. "A good rifle, and bam, he's out of here."

In fact, I knew it was a shot I could make if I had the right instrument. I had learned to shoot a rifle on my daddy's knee, and though my close vision wasn't what it used to be, I could still see far away and well.

"No," César said. "I agree with Ferdinand. He must know."

"After he knows, he's got a long time not knowing," I said. "What's the difference? We got to do this thing, why not just do it?"

Because I will think of it forever," César said. "And I will cherish it forever. The look on his face when I explain."

"You have to have time to explain."

César grinned at me.

"I don't think you're going to find this type of revenge all that satisfying," I said.

"Oh, I will," César said. "Are you losing your stomach for this?"

"I'm beginning to think I never had the stomach for it."

Brett took hold of the telescope, said, "Let me take a look."

She said, "Oh, my God. That must be Hammerhead. Jesus Christ. You put a sock and shoe on his dick, stroked it a couple times, he could use it as a third leg."

I took over the scope.

"My Lord."

The man was monstrous and naked. He had come into the yard carrying a barbell decked with weights. I saw now there were other weights in the yard, and there was a weight rack. Hammerhead was completely nude. Miguel's wife had stretched out on a towel and was rubbing her long legs with lotion. She had put on sunglasses. Her head was turned in Hammerhead's direction, head tilted slightly like a dog that had spotted a salami, and in way, she had.

Hammerhead's body coiled and the weights rose, he uncoiled and they lowered. He repeated the process. Muscles crawled and knotted under his flesh like angry pigs struggling in a sack. He was the biggest man I had ever seen. Not the tallest, or the heaviest. Just the biggest. His shoulders were broad enough to maybe just hold up the sky. His chest was like the Hoover Dam. His arms were big enough to be used to beat the World Wrestling Federation to death all at the same time. His penis hung long and limp and seemed as big around as my wrist.

"He is one big motherfucker," I said.

"Is he as big as Big Man Mountain?" Leonard asked, referring to a wrestler we had crossed paths with once.

"He could hide Big Man Mountain under his nut sack," Jim Bob said, glancing through the scope. "I told you he was big, didn't I, Hap?"

"Let me look at this," Leonard said. He took a look. He said, "Good God, his goober and balls look like grapefruits hanging off a fence post. He got that thing up someone's asshole they'd have to get it out with crowbars, maybe dynamite it free. He is one creepy motherfucker. Maybe a rifle shot for the both of them isn't such a bad idea. Or in his case, maybe a couple land mines."

"No," César said. "I will not do it that way."

"Nor will we," Jim Bob said. "Now we need to get started."

29

WE HAD TO WAIT a few days and watch the mistress. Actually, I didn't watch anything. César, Ferdinand, and Jim Bob did the watching. They took turns near the mistress's house, parking nearby and observing, sometimes from a distance with the scope.

Me, Brett, and Leonard got the cushy part of the deal, which probably meant Jim Bob was afraid me and Leonard would fuck things up.

Brett and I stayed at the hotel, in bed a lot. Leonard spent time in the swimming pool. Each day the three of us met for lunch, and in the afternoons, Ferdinand and Jim Bob, or Ferdinand and César, or some combination of the three would meet us back at the hotel for dinner while the other watched. Ferdinand was very uncomfortable when he was one of the two who joined us for dinner. He was not used to restaurants.

It was one of the few times in my life I had lived like I had money, and I was enjoying it.

I did have money. But it was seeping away daily, like a sand angel washed by the waves.

About four days after we arrived in Playa del Carmen,

Jim Bob met us for dinner without Ferdinand or César. We were sitting at a poolside table, and Brett had ordered margaritas for herself and Leonard, and they were going at it when he walked up.

"Just you today?" I said.

"That's right. César and Ferdinand are on their way to Mexico City."

"The mistress went shopping?" I said.

"Looks that way. She went to the airport. César gave me a cell phone, left me sitting under a palm tree, followed her in the car, then called me back. They were at the airport. He said she was getting a ticket to Mexico City."

"How does he know?" Brett asked. "She might have been getting a ticket to Juárez."

"He knows," Jim Bob said. He smiled at her. "He's a detective. Remember?"

"Ah," Brett said.

"César and Ferdinand were about to get tickets to follow. Guess they did. He said for us to meet him in Mexico City at the Presidente Intercontinental Hotel. After I got all that, I walked a couple miles, hitched a ride, and here I am."

"When do we leave?" Leonard asked.

"Not before dinner," Jim Bob said. "I can assure you of that."

The summer days were long, so it was still full light by the time we finished dinner and took a taxi to the airport in Cancun. We bought tickets, waited about an hour, and flew out. The plane was poorly air-conditioned, so it was a stuffy, hot flight.

Brett and I were sitting together with a spare seat between us. We were holding hands like teenagers, but it was too humid, and by mutual unspoken agreement, we let go.

I opened my shirt collar, adjusted the air-conditioning vent, but no help there.

"I got sweat beads in my crack," Brett said. "Both cracks."

"Overshare," I said.

There were no clouds and the sun was beginning to dip as we flew into Mexico City's airspace. We circled for a while. Through the window I could see mountains and snow-capped volcanoes bathed in the red of the dying sun.

Finally we flew in closer to the city. A haze of pollution thick enough to wear overalls hung over everything. Mixed with the sunlight the air achieved the color of a dried wound. Buildings jumped up at us and the streets below were as confused as a ball of twine.

Soon we were landing, hustling our luggage, trying to move through a sweaty crowd of people toward the street and a taxi. Jim Bob spoke to a driver and got us a ride. The car was once blue, but was now spotted like a pinto horse with gray filler. The tires were so worn-looking the rubber seemed attached to them by no more than a prayer.

We packed our luggage in the trunk, which smelled as if fish had recently been stored there, and no sooner had we closed the doors of the taxi than the driver gave it gas and leaped us out in front of traffic like a sacrifice.

Horns blared. We cruised at top speed through lights that once they turned red were shaded by at least three or four cars before anyone actually took heed of their color. We bounced the curb a couple of times, as if our driver might get points for pedestrians, and he may actually have clipped the ass of a slow-moving woman carrying a shopping bag. It was hard to tell if she was knocked or she jumped. She just went leaping away, her long blue dress fluttering, one shoe flying, the bag swinging on her arm by its rope handle.

I turned to look out the back window to see if she got up, but we turned so fast everything behind us became a blur and we edged in on another taxi as if to initiate a duel.

I glanced out the left-hand window of the back seat, saw we were close enough for me to put gas in the other taxi's tank, but that wasn't close enough. Not for our man. He edged in tighter, so close that if the elderly lady in the back seat had rolled down her window, we could have French kissed.

The lady looked to be on the verge of a stroke, or at least a very heavy-duty bowel movement. She glanced at me, swallowed. I smiled as our taxi driver cut down on his horn hard enough and loud enough to alert any ship channel within a thousand miles, then we shot away from the car beside us as if we had just vaulted to warp speed, changed lanes tighter than a suppository in a fat man's ass, went weaving, honking, and being honked at all the way to the Presidente Intercontinental.

As our driver pulled into the driveway at the hotel and I stepped out on solid ground, I felt like a ripped-up teddy bear that had just had its legs sewn back on, but without all the stuffing.

Our driver lugged our luggage out of the trunk with the care of a murderer disposing of a body in a tar pit, and a fellow who looked as if he could bench-press the taxi came out, threw our bags on a rolling rack, and showed us he had all his teeth and every one of them yellow. Jim Bob paid the taxi driver, and we followed our toothy man with the rack to the front desk.

"I haven't had that much fun since my last yeast infection," Brett said.

"I just kept my eyes closed," Leonard said.

Jim Bob talked in Spanish to a pretty woman at the desk with too much eye makeup. They smiled at each other a lot. Jim Bob borrowed the desk phone.

The phone conversation was short. Jim Bob talked to the lady at the desk again. She gave him some keys.

Jim Bob said, "César already has our rooms. You and me, Leonard, we're roomies."

"Oh boy," Leonard said. "Up late spitting water and reading fashion magazines."

"Hot damn," Jim Bob said.

We rode the elevator up with the man with the luggage carriage, got our stuff loaded in our rooms, paid the guy off, then took a walk down the corridor where Jim Bob knocked on a door.

César opened up and let us in. "Qué pasa," he said.

He was dressed in a navy blue shirt that fit him tight as a grapeskin. His pants were tight as well, and too short. He looked like someone who had tucked his belongings into his crotch and was trying to wade high water.

Ferdinand appeared, wearing what must have been one of César's shirts; it was black as the grave and the collars were flared as if they were wings. He was silent as usual, sat at the table near the window, looking down at the streets and the hot sunshine. He was drinking a Mexican beer. Another was on the table, opened.

"Would you like drinks?" César asked. He opened up the little bar with his key. Brett and Leonard took a beer, I took a Diet Coke. We sat on one of the beds, César took a chair at the table. He said, "Our little mistress is quite the busy one already."

"Aren't we supposed to go out and spring on her or something?" Leonard said.

"In due time," César said. "I have followed her before, remember. Jim Bob and I followed her. But I have watched her before that."

"Why?" Brett said.

"I have watched her because I have watched everything there is to know about this Juan Miguel. I am very
patient, you see. But I must confess, this idea of kidnap-
ping her, it had not occurred to me. It is a good idea for
what you have in mind. I should have thought of it some
time ago."

"We are masters of crime," I said.

"She is in this hotel," César said. "It is where she always stays. She will go to the Museum of Anthropology.
She will shop, and she will come to the restaurant here
to have her dinner. This is her schedule in the past."

"What if she changes it?" I said.

"It is possible, but I will chance that she does not."

"You're chancing our money, César," I said. "I only
have so much. I can't run around all over Mexico."

"Trust me," César said. "Tell them, Jim Bob."

"Trust him," Jim Bob said.

"I feel better," Brett said.

"What's up with the Museum of Anthropology?" Leonard
asked.

"That is for Juan Miguel, or so I believe," César said.
"I think she is trying to sell certain pieces that Juan Miguel
has to the museum. She goes there each time she comes
here. Juan Miguel, as I'm sure my friend Jim Bob has explained to you, is known to have an extensive collection,
known to traffic in antiquities. So it is possible."

"And maybe," Brett said, "the reason she's his mistress
is she shares Juan Miguel's interests. Maybe she isn't just
a poke piece, but someone who is smart, sophisticated,
and loves anthropology and archaeology, and maybe his
wife doesn't."

"And she's a poke piece," Jim Bob said.

"That too," Brett said. "But Hap and I are attracted to
each other because we share interests."

"Like what?" Jim Bob said.

"Chickens. He protects them, and I deep-fry them."

"I was once asked to masturbate a rooster," I said.

"I don't even want to know about that," Jim Bob said.

"I think that I would, señor," said César.

Even Ferdinand looked interested.

I told them about being offered a job to garner rooster sperm. César laughed as if I had told him the best joke he had ever heard.

Brett said, "That's my man."

"Yeah," I said. "Hard to believe I turned them down."

"About this thing we're doing?" Leonard asked. "You know, the thing that's not as exciting as jerking a chicken's nub, but this thing with the woman . . . She has her body-guards with her, of course?"

"Of course," César said.

"Are they big?"

"Big enough, señor."

"As in big and mean?"

"I would say so. Yes, señor, big and mean."

"Shit."

"Armed of course?" I asked.

"Unless those big bumps under their arms are breasts that have slid sideways, I believe so, señor."

"Maybe we could talk them into just arm wrestling us for her?" Leonard said.

"Will you two just shut up," Jim Bob said.

I looked at Leonard and grinned. He wrinkled his mouth into a near smile. Brett reached over, patted me on the leg. She either loved my humor or was kind enough to make me think so.

"The best time to grab the woman would be when they come up from dinner to their room," César said. "They have a very nice room at the top of the hotel."

"You know they're in this room because they always are?" I asked.

"Yes. Juan Miguel pays for this, so he sees she has the best. Tomorrow, that will be the day when she does the serious shopping. It is too late today, and I am too tired. I say we have a good dinner, rest, and tomorrow, I will tail them. Is that how you say it, Jim Bob, tail them?"

"Yeah," Jim Bob said.

"I will tail them, and then when she has her dinner, you will be prepared when she comes up, and you will take care of the guards—"

"Hey, I don't want to kill these guys," I said. "That's not part of the deal. We want Juan Miguel and the walking haystack, but these other guys, I don't want to kill them."

"Then do not," César said. "But take care of them. Make your choice. Take the woman. Make her quiet."

"Then what?" Leonard said. "Do we knock her unconscious, beat her up in the hall?"

"Do not worry," César said. "I have brought the chloroform. You put it on a rag, give her a whiff, and she will fall to the ground. You can do it with the guards too, but they may not fall so fast. They are big and strong and most certainly willful. I leave that to you."

"You know," I said to Jim Bob, "I think your additions to my basic plan aren't all that better than the basic plan. My plan sucks, and this is better?"

"Believe me," Jim Bob said. "It's better. And there's more to it. Most of it will be passed on to you on a need-to-know basis."

"Boss," Leonard said. "Dat a good idea. We don't wants lots of stuffs in our haids might be confusin'."

"You got that right," Jim Bob said.

"I suppose Jim Bob has told you that you are all listed under false names?" César said.

"He failed to mention that," I said.

"I was going to," Jim Bob said. He told us our false names.

César said, "Meet here at four P.M. tomorrow, local time. If you have watches, make sure they are set correctly. Come to this room and wait until you get a phone call."

"From who?" I asked.

"From me. I will be watching her. Ferdinand will let you in so you can wait. I will call when they are near."

"What about guns?" Leonard said.

"I will take care of that, my friend," César said.

Jim Bob said, "I'm going to my room now, going to watch a little Mexican TV, then get a good night's sleep. What about you, Leonard?"

"I got a key," Leonard said. "I'll come along shortly."

"Suit yourself," Jim Bob said, and left the room.

Leonard went with me and Brett to our room, had another drink. I said, "This thing is starting to involve more people than the U.S. Army. And it seems like there's more people to hurt all the time. All I want to do is nab the woman, set her up as an insurance policy for us so we can do what we have to do."

"It'll be okay, Hap," Leonard said. He stood up. "Good night, brother. Good night, Brett."

30

Next morning after breakfast I couldn't bring myself to sit in the hotel room, because all I did then was brood on our plans. The old saw about revenge is a dish best served cold is bullshit. Revenge is only sweet in the heat of the moment.

Brett was willing, so we went walking. The streets were crowded and the air was blistering to the eyes. Within fifteen minutes the pollution had done a job on my throat. It felt as if a little man with a bad temper had moved into my mouth and sandpapered my tonsils.

We walked over to the Anthropology Museum and looked around. I loved it. Deep inside me I felt old longings. As a child I had often thought of teaching, perhaps archaeology or history. Here I was, in my forties, a night guard in a chicken plant. I didn't even have a college education, just a piece of one. There wasn't much point thinking about what might have been, but as we walked about and looked at things, I thought about it anyway.

"I wish we had time to go out and see the pyramids," Brett said. "The Temple of the Sun and the Moon aren't far from here. A day's excursion."

I looked at my watch. "How about lunch instead?"

"Lunch is good."

We left the museum and walked until we came to an interesting restaurant. It wasn't fancy, but it wasn't exactly a hole in the wall either. No one spoke English there, so we pointed at the menu a lot, not sure of what we were getting.

It turned out to be something the waiter called mole de quajalote, and it was good. It tasted like some kind of bird, maybe turkey, in a very sweet sauce. We also had a dish called cochinita pibil, which I could tell was made from pork.

When we finished with the meal, they brought out a sweet bread and a kind of pudding made of milk, fruit, sugar, and stuff I couldn't identify. It was too sweet for me.

Feeling like funnel-fed geese, we decided to walk off the meal. Outside the air was rawer than before. It had a stench, like gasoline mixed with sewage, tortillas, and frying meat. The last two smells came from the large number of vendors who cooked you meals on the spot. Chances were, you ate the stuff in the square, you could get a case of the squirts that would make a mud slide seem tame.

We looked at huge and beautiful churches, took a short walking tour that was guided by a man that almost spoke English, though it was certainly better than my Spanish, and finally we ended up at the Mexico City zoo. It was a huge zoo, well tended, but as always, like circuses, it made me sad. Polar bears housed in southern regions do not consider themselves on a tropical vacation. They just look lost.

About three in the afternoon we caught a taxi, found out our first experience had not been a fluke. This taxi ride was just as scary, and by the time we arrived back at the hotel, the sweet sauce I had eaten was nestled in the back of my throat.

We went up to our room, brushed our teeth, looked at our watches. We were about fifteen minutes early. We checked to make sure both our watches said the same thing. They did. Finally, we said fuck it, walked over to César's room, knocked on the door.

Ferdinand let us in. About five minutes later, Leonard showed up.

"You sightsee?" I said.

"Just the back of my eyelids," Leonard said. "I slept in. Jim Bob snores like a goddamn bear. I didn't sleep good last night. I'm sort of pissed off, actually. I don't like it when I don't sleep well."

"Where's Jim Bob?" Brett said.

"He was gone when I got up. I grabbed some lunch, read a Western Jim Bob had brought with him, went to the bathroom a lot, blew my nose, looked out the window, and here I am."

"Quite a prosperous day," I said.

There was a knock on the door. I looked through the peephole. Jim Bob was shooting me the finger.

I opened the door, said, "What an adolescent."

"I drop these pants, boy, you'll think adolescent. Calling me a child is like calling—"

"Oh, just come in and shut up," Brett said.

There were two suitcases setting on either side of Jim Bob. He picked them up, carried them into the room. He put them on the bed.

"What you got there?" Brett asked. "Sex toys?"

"You wish," Jim Bob said. "César's contacts. They're bad boys."

Inside one suitcase was something wrapped in a white towel. Jim Bob removed that, laid it carefully on the bed. It was a bottle of chloroform.

He removed a folded duffel bag from the suitcase and unfolded it. It was about six feet in length. Beneath it were a couple of blackjacks, a slapjack, and four nine-millimeter automatics. The other case contained ammo clips and several pieces that went together to make a rifle and a sawed-off double-barrel shotgun. The rifle had a scope and a silencer. There was ammunition for both guns.

"I still think shooting him from a distance is the way to go," I said.

"He must know who it is that kills him," Ferdinand said.

"Yep," Jim Bob said. "It's a grace note. Five seconds of knowing you're about to die, for whatever reason, is a long goddamn time. Shooting him from a distance is just doing the motherfucker a favor."

"All right," I said. "Outline it."

"For what we're doing here," Jim Bob said, "the guns are out. We take the blackjacks, or the slapjack, our hands, whatever. We use the chloroform. We get these two guys down quick, we nab the woman, put her out of commission, and we're out of here."

"How are we out of here?" Brett asked.

"We stick the woman in the duffel bag, we check out, we get in the black van out front that César will have waiting, we go to the airport, and he drives the woman back to his place. We meet there."

"Why don't we just put her in our pocket and walk out?" Leonard said. "A duffel bag? That's it? A fuckin' duffel bag?"

"It'll work," Jim Bob said. "Trust me."

"So we're supposed to meet them as they come up the elevator," I said. "What if someone rides up the elevator with them?"

"They won't," Jim Bob said. "César says they never

ride up or down with anyone. They wait until they have it to themselves. Safety precautions."

"Don't these guys know what what César looks like?" Brett said. "I mean, hell, they cut the tip of his finger off and slapped his ear silly."

"These men may or may not," Jim Bob said. "But they won't see him if he doesn't want to be seen. César's good. Almost as good as me."

"Why so much protection?" Brett said. "Is she made of gold?"

"She's protected because of people like us," Jim Bob said. "Juan Miguel protects his property, and to him, she's property."

"So the elevator opens on this floor," Leonard said. "What's to prevent someone else being in the hallway, seeing us go at these guys?"

"Nothing," Jim Bob said. "We deal with that if it happens."

Just before six the phone rang. Jim Bob answered, listened, hung up. He turned to us.

"Yippie ki 'eah."

I put the slapjack in my back pocket, Leonard took a blackjack, and Jim Bob brought only himself. Ferdinand said, "And me?"

"You're going to have to wait in the room," Jim Bob said. "When we knock, you be right by the door and let us in. Got me?"

Ferdinand nodded.

Brett opened the door for us and tagged along behind carrying a towel. She had poured it full of chloroform, and the stench of it was strong in the hall.

"This is so fucked," she said.

"I'm about to swoon here," Leonard said. "Brett, you think maybe you got enough of that crap on the towel?"

"Too much and you'll kill her," Jim Bob said. "Hit her with it quick, then get it off her face."

No one was in the hallway. We stopped at the elevator. The numbers on the elevator light were racing toward our floor. Then the other elevator started moving up.

"Which elevator are they in?" I asked.

"I don't know," Jim Bob said.

"Oh, shit. That's good."

We tried to stand casual, just a wad of folks waiting to get on the elevator. The door opened. A short, stocky woman just shy of three thousand years old with sparse hair dyed shoe polish black and at least twenty-five whisker hairs to match, also dyed, stepped out of the elevator carrying a white poodle with a leash.

Brett leaned close to my ear, spoke softly. "Maybe we should sap her once for not getting rid of that mustache."

"Twice," I said. "She also has a poodle."

The woman moved slowly, putting the dog down, leading it on its leash. She had just turned the corner away from the elevator, out of sight, when the other elevator's light hit our floor and the door opened, and there was one of the most astoundingly beautiful women I have ever seen.

She was probably five seven, a little over a hundred pounds, well built, face like an angel, large black eyes and soft black hair that flowed to the middle of her back. She wore a short blue dress and matching high heels. Her legs were fashioned from a dream. She looked very elegant.

The guys on either side of her were well dressed, but not so elegant. They would have looked the same in thousand-dollar suits or tablecloths. They looked about as casual as meat gravy stains on a white shirt.

As they stepped out of the elevator, Jim Bob said something pleasant in Spanish, stepped aside. As they passed, the guard on the left eyed Jim Bob. Brett took hold of her skirt, pulled it up and scratched her leg, causing the skirt to ride almost to her hip.

The guy looked.

Jim Bob sapped him. It was a good lick. The guy stumbled, Jim Bob leaped on him, started beating him like a hamburger steak.

The other guy was on the move now, his hand going inside his coat. Leonard grabbed that hand with his left, poked the man in the eyes with his right. The big bastard grunted, his hand came out of his coat, he tried to reach for his face, but Leonard had that hand. Leonard twisted slightly, and the dude flipped, hit the floor hard, banging the side of his head. I kicked the poor bastard hard as I could. He didn't go out, but he didn't act as if he was in any hurry to get up.

Leonard bent down over him and went to work with the sap. It sounded like a carpenter driving a pesky nail. Even after I thought the guy was out, I heard the sap ring a half dozen more times.

Brett had wrestled the woman to the floor and was trying to push the chloroform-filled towel over her face, but no luck. The woman started to scream.

Jim Bob pulled Brett off the mistress, brought his palm down swift, but not too hard on the woman's forehead, just above the eyebrow at the left corner.

She went out.

I was standing, panting. The place stank of chloroform. I had moved away from the elevator wall, and now I could see down the hall. The woman with the poodle had stopped, listening to those screams.

Brett stepped into the hallway. "A bug. A spider. It frightened me."

The woman looked puzzled.

Jim Bob stepped into view, he spoke Spanish. The

woman grinned, said something in Spanish. She and her dog went on down the hallway.

"What did you say?" Brett asked.

"Just what you did. I told her you saw a spider."

"What did she say?"

"What a sissy. Words to that effect."

"I'm not sure I like that."

When the old woman was out of sight, Leonard removed the guns from the bodyguards, got one of the guys by the leg and started dragging him down the corridor toward Jim Bob's room. Jim Bob got the other guard by the leg, and I picked up the woman. She was as small as a child.

I looked down at her. A small purple bruise was forming at the corner of her eye. She was so gorgeous I felt as if her beauty were sucking out my soul. I could see why Juan Miguel would leave his wife. It's a hard thing to admit beauty alone can make you crazy, but a woman like this, good God, she *could* make you crazy.

"When we get her to the room," Brett said, "maybe you could tuck her in, give her a bottle."

I made a snorting sound. "I hope you're not jealous of someone we just tried to chloroform and hit on the head."

"I'm jealous of someone who looks like a magazine cover, that's what I'm jealous of," Brett said.

Jim Bob knocked, Ferdinand opened the door. Jim Bob and Leonard dragged the guards inside. I carried the woman and put her on the bed. She had begun to stir. She opened her eyes. Brett, smiling, leaned forward and pushed the chloroform-filled towel over her nose. The woman struggled briefly, went out.

Brett pulled the towel away.

"Tie up and gag these mooses," Jim Bob said. "And quick before they wake up. Tie her up too, and pull her dress down. I don't need to see that. I like it, but I don't need to see it. I better not see it. Damn, those panties are sheer . . ."

"We get the picture," Brett said.

31

W<small>E BOUND THEM</small> and gagged them with strips of sheets. We poured the chloroform down the sink, put the towel in the tub. The air was still fairly stout with it. We opened a window. We turned on the TV set, sat the bodyguards on the floor with their backs against the bed.

We found a Spanish game show. Jim Bob patted them on the head and we left out of there, the woman in the duffel bag, slung over Leonard's shoulder.

We rode the elevator down. As Jim Bob and Brett stopped at the desk with our keys, prepared to check us out, Leonard and I walked outside to the curb. There was a black van there. César got out of it, nodded at us. He opened the side of the van. Leonard put the duffel bag on the seat, closed the door.

"We will see you in Playa del Carmen in a while," César said. "We must drive the whole way. Where is Jim Bob?"

"Coming," Leonard said.

Jim Bob and Brett came out. Jim Bob got in the van. Before he closed the door I looked at the duffel bag on the seat. "She's moving," I said.

Jim Bob reached inside his coat, pulled out the black-jack. With a motion a ballet dancer would have appreci-ated, he shifted in his seat and smacked the bag where the head was. The bag quit moving.

"Goddamn, Jim Bob," I said. "It's not her we want to hurt."

"You want I should take her to a bullfight?" Jim Bob said. "A bump on her head is better than us in a Mexi-can jail. You should know."

I closed the door, César drove them away.

We had a slightly better ride to the airport than from it. I was able to get out of the taxi without feeling faint. Our life had only been in danger maybe half a dozen times.

We caught our flight out without incident, arrived that night in Cancun, took our rental back to Playa del Car-men. We didn't have reservations, but we got our same hotel without trouble. Leonard got a room. Brett and I shared a room.

That night, when she finished brushing her teeth, Brett said, "Do you think that woman is beautiful?"

I was stepping out of the shower. "Ravishing," I said.

"She was very pretty."

"Ravishing."

"Don't overdo it if you want Mr. Happy to actually be happy tonight."

"But with that knot on her head from the blackjack, not so beautiful. And you know what? Jim Bob may have hit her again. Maybe a lot of times. She could be real ugly by now."

"That's better. And dry under your balls. I hate it when they're sticky on my ass."

"You say the most exciting things," I said.

"Do you know what they're planning to do?"

"About as much as you do. They'll drive her to César's, taking their time. Maybe stop along the way a couple of nights. Tomorrow, a couple of us go to see the man, tell him we have her, and then we lay the trap."

Brett had slipped out of her clothes, and I was enjoying watching her pull on a nightie with no underwear. No underwear was always a good sign.

32

THREE NIGHTS LATER, about three A.M., we got a call.

"Come over." It was Jim Bob.

"On our way."

I woke Brett up. Called Leonard's room, fifteen minutes later we were in the rental, wheeling our way to César's house.

César let us in. He was colorful as usual, a purple shirt with red and green parrots on it, white slacks and slip-on white shoes without socks.

Jim Bob looked his usual self, but for the moment, he was without his hat. I was surprised to discover he had hair.

Ferdinand was sitting quietly in a chair, hands rested in his lap. He looked calm, as if he were waiting to drop the lever on a guillotine. He smiled thinly at us, nodded his head.

Hermonie sat on one end of the couch, looking pretty and inscrutable in a pale yellow pants suit. When we came in, she didn't speak, didn't change her expression. There was nothing about her to acknowledge we had entered the room except a lifting of her eyes.

On the other end of the couch, her hands cuffed in front of her, a chain fastened to the center of the cuffs on her ankles, was the mistress. She looked like a goddess, except for a faint blue bruise above her right eye. I assumed, under that luxurious mane of black hair, would be at least one blackjack knot. She was smoldering. I half expected the couch to burst into flames.

On the coffee table in front of the mistress was a plate of food, untouched from the looks of it.

"More bastards!" she said. "You are all bastards!"

"Actually," Brett said, "technically, I'm a bitch."

"Bastards! All bastards!"

"Her English," Jim Bob said, "is quite good, especially when it comes to cuss words. We took our time getting here, and we've had her here awhile, doing a bit of interrogation."

"Juan Miguel will kill you," she said. "He will have you skinned. He will nail your skins to walls and he will piss on them."

"Do you want to be gagged?" Jim Bob said. "I'll use my dirty underwear again."

The mistress went silent, but the looks she gave Jim Bob were almost enough to skin him without Juan Miguel's help.

"Her name is Ileana," Jim Bob said.

"Fuck you, you pig," Ileana said. "Fuck you. Fuck you."

"Dirty underwear, dear," Jim Bob said. "Ones with the Hershey stains in the seat."

"Jesus," Brett said. "You're not even threatening to gag me and I'm scared."

Ileana went silent again, but she wasn't happy about it.

"What's next?" I said.

"We have already contacted Juan Miguel," Jim Bob said. "Told him we had his woman. He really wants her back," Jim Bob said. "I don't know he cares for her so much—"

"He loves me," Ileana said. "He loves me much. He will hate you much."

Jim Bob put a finger to his lips. "You be quiet now. As I was saying, I don't know how much he cares for her, but he wants her back, talks like he's lost a wallet or something and wants it back. He doesn't talk like she's a person."

"Neither do you," Brett said.

"No, I don't, lady. It makes things easier not to. He wants her back, so I arranged a meeting. You and me, Hap. We'll do it."

"Will it be safe?" Brett said.

"Safe as we can make it," Jim Bob said. "We got something Juan Miguel wants."

Jim Bob stopped at a phone booth on the way into Playa del Carmen. He didn't want to chance César's home phone or cell phone number. If the number could be traced, Juan Miguel might have the contacts to trace it.

César had somehow gotten Juan Miguel's number, either through research or from Ileana. I hoped he had not done anything bad to her to get it.

Jim Bob called and talked while I stood outside the old rickety phone booth. As he talked, three young Mexican men wandered over in our direction.

I knew their intent. I had seen it many times. Thugs come in all colors and sizes, but they all walk just alike. I figured a phone booth that worked, located in a dark place, this time of night, was a great spot for them to pull off a mugging.

By the time Jim Bob finished talking and came out of the booth, they were about ten feet away. He reached in his coat and pulled out one of the nine millimeters, said something in Spanish while he waved it around.

The three thugs bolted away into the darkness.

"You have such a way with words," I said.

"Ain't that the goddamn truth," Jim Bob said.

"How'd it go?"

"They're expecting us."

"Jim Bob."

"Yeah."

"Ileana. You didn't really hurt her, did you?"

"I think that sap shot hurt pretty good."

"I mean beyond that."

"No . . . You planning on dating her?"

"I merely meant I don't want to see her hurt. I feel scummy. She's an innocent bystander."

"In a manner, but in another, she knows who Juan Miguel is. She knows what kinds of things he does. She profits from this, Hap. Don't get too fuckin' sentimental just because she's a looker. She got in bed with this mangy, flea-bitten dog, and she's got his fleas on her now. That's the long and the short of it."

We drove along the beach toward the great house that belonged to Juan Miguel. It was full of light up on the rise, stood there like a gem growing out of the ground.

We came around on its back side, stopped at a wide metal gate. There was a box you talked into, and Jim Bob did that. The gate opened. Jim Bob took the nine millimeter out from under his coat and pushed it under the car seat.

"They're gonna search us anyway, take it away," he said. "You got anything?"

"A wallet."

"Put it under the seat. That's what I'm doing."

I did that. He said, "Anything else?"

"Nothing that isn't attached."

"Let's hope they let us keep that stuff," Jim Bob said.

We drove through the gate, down the drive, up to the house. Juan Miguel's home was even more awesome close up, like something I thought the movies made up. Three stories high, lots of glass, the rest of it pink stone with a red tile roof and a front porch big enough to build a tennis court on. The porch was made of stone too, but snow white, as if it were bleached daily and polished. The house and porch gleamed fairy-tale-like in the soft glow of the night lights that poked out of the shrubs and palm trees, but the tall tinted windows deadened the light like cataracts.

Surrounded by low-cut shrubbery was a well-lit pool. It was to the right of the house, the color of a sapphire, the shape of a kidney. A diving board perched above it like an extended tongue. It was a big pool, and I knew from my telescopic eavesdropping it was smaller than the one at the rear of the house, which had through the looking glass appeared big enough and deep enough to provide Shamu the Killer Whale with a vacation home.

"Damn sure beats a double-wide, don't it?" Jim Bob said.

"I once knew a fella fastened two double-wides together," I said. "That was pretty nice."

Jim Bob chuckled.

The door opened and two guys in tan suits came out on the stone porch. From where we sat, they looked like two fleas standing on canvas, about to go through their act. They were the two guys we had beat and tied up at the hotel in Mexico City.

As we got out of the car, Jim Bob said, "At least there are two people here who know us."

"They are sweet," I said, "but my guess is neither of them will be bringing pot luck lunches to Mensa's next Christmas party."

The air was stuffed with the smell of fresh-mowed grass and recently manicured shrubs. There was a touch of chlorine from the pool. If it had been daylight I'm sure a butterfly and bluebird would have lit on my shoulder.

The two came down the great steps carefully, as if they were afraid their pants might rip. It seemed to take them forever to cross the green, clipped lawn, make their way over to meet us. First thing they did was clobber the both of us. I took an uppercut in the belly and went down. I wanted to fight back, but didn't. I took another clip to the side of the head, was yanked up and kicked in the ass. I made a note to remember that kick in the ass. Not to mention the fact I had a headache about the size of Alaska.

A moment later we were searched and four pesos I had in my front pocket were taken and Jim Bob lost a pocketknife out of the deal. We should have put those under the seat.

Next Jim Bob and I were hustled in front of them, toward the pool. Jim Bob had lost his hat in the beating, and it had been stepped on before he recovered it. As he walked along he was at work straightening it.

"They took it personal," he said.

"Looks like."

"I didn't take the beating personal myself," Jim Bob said. "But stepping on my hat was just mean, and I won't forget it."

"You're like Leonard about his hats," I said.

"I've never seen him in a hat."

"They get stepped on."

We went through a gap in the wall of shrubbery, between palm trees with lights on them, out to the side pool, which was bordered by copper-colored tile and on the far side there were plenty of bushes and trees and a fountain in the shape of an angel with wings spread wide.

There was plenty of light on the sapphire pool and someone was in it, swimming. We were taken to a glass table,
pushed down into white plastic chairs, spoken to in Spanish.

"They want us to stay," Jim Bob said.

"I figured that much. Goddamn, my gut hurts. That
fucker has quite a punch."

"My guy hit like a sissy," Jim Bob said.

"You're lucky," I said. "He hit any harder than he did,
you'd look like E.T. on that side of your face."

The person in the pool was obviously Juan Miguel. He
swam a couple more laps just for show, then climbed out.
He was butt-naked. One of the buffaloes gave him a long
white towel and he went to drying himself.

He came over, flipping his dick and balls with the end
of the towel. I didn't know if he were merely drying himself, or if it was some kind of greeting.

Up close I could see Juan Miguel was older than he
had appeared through the telescope. He was in good
shape, with a slightly protruding belly, but solid muscle
tone. He had all his own hair and certainly dyed it. He
was probably about five ten, one ninety and proud of
himself.

"Qué pasa," Juan Miguel said, and he smiled so big
the light bouncing off his teeth nearly put my eyes out.

"How's it hanging?" Jim Bob said.

Juan Miguel thought about that, then slowly he laughed.
"How is it hanging. That is good. How is it hanging. As
you can see, my man, it hangs quite well."

"Yeah. It almost looks like a real dick."

Juan Miguel said something in Spanish. One of the
buffaloes stepped forward, slapped Jim Bob so hard he
was knocked out of the chair and the chair went spin-
ning. He lost his hat again. It rolled backward all the way
to the shrubbery.

Juan Miguel looked at me. "Do you have a comment, sir?"

"I'm cool," I said.

Jim Bob got up, straightened his chair, recovered his hat, sat back down. "Where do you get these guys? A girls school?"

Juan Miguel made a movement with his mouth that wasn't quite a frown or a smile, but was certainly unpleasant. I thought Jim Bob was due for another slapping, or worse, but Juan Miguel took a breath, looked down at his package and continued drying it as if he were polishing a precious stone.

"Do you find nudity unpleasant?" Juan Miguel asked us.

"Yours, yes," Jim Bob said. "But your woman, hey, I think she looks pretty good."

Juan Miguel snapped something in Spanish, and this time both buffaloes jumped on Jim Bob. I wanted to help him, but I knew that wasn't our game. Jim Bob took a short but rapid beating from their fists, then lay on his side and was kicked for a while.

I said, "You do that much longer, I can assure you, you'll never see your mistress again, unless it's in a ditch with a zucchini stuffed up her snatch."

"Alto," Juan Miguel said.

Jim Bob lay awhile longer this time, but finally he got up, brushed himself off, righted his chair, recovered his hat, which was the shape of a paper wad, and sat down. "The two of them together, working hard, are almost a man," he said.

"You are crazy," Juan Miguel said. "You want to die. And you will."

Jim Bob spat blood on the stones. "Not unless you want that mistress to end up like my partner said. Only I'll make sure she gets a zucchini in every hole. Maybe even a melon. No more beatings. No more bullshit. You listen to us. We don't come back soon, call in, your girl-friend, she's gonna end up in a bad way. You hear me, you cheap-ass Mexican Godfather wannabe. We're just hired help, and it don't mean a thing to us one way or another, except we want to come out of this alive and happy, and if things work out, you get your bitch back alive and happy, and we come out of it with some money. And let me tell you, I'm gonna talk to you, you get some drawers on, or wrap that towel around that limp piece of spaghetti, sit down and listen."

"You are on my turf, you American turd. Nudity is healthy. I am sixty years old, and I know I do not look it. It is the nudity. The fresh air, the sun. I swim nude every night in this pool, and it has done wonders for me. Man was meant to have fresh air, sunlight, and exercise."

"It's dark," I said.

"Yes, but there is the night air," Juan Miguel said.

"We're on your turf," Jim Bob said, straightening his hat, "but we've got your muff. Let me tell you about nu-dity for health, Zorro. Tried it when I was twelve. Stripped off and played Tarzan. Climbed up in a tree and got a sunburn, damn near fried my pecker off, turned my ass the color of a Washington apple. I didn't find it so healthy. You get a good sunburn on your general and it starts to peel, let me tell you, it's highly uncomfortable."

"You idiot," Juan Miguel said.

"You gonna sit and deal, or you gonna bore me with your lifestyle choices?"

"You fool," Juan Miguel said. "You think I am losing true love here? My wife, she is my true love. Ileana, she is a dalliance. A hobby. A pastime. She is one of many."

I felt my stomach go sour. What if Ileana didn't mat-ter to him? What if he had women all over Mexico?

Then I thought: Like Ileana? Not likely. Who the hell was he fooling?

"I think we're wasting time," I said. "You want her, we best get to talking, and talking now."

Juan Miguel studied us, as if to be certain we weren't mirages, some stupid dream. He wrapped the towel around his waist, pulled out a chair and sat down. No sooner had he done that, as if on cue, out of the darkness near the pool, on the far side, something moved.

At first I thought one of the palm trees had come loose of its roots and was about to topple, but the base was much larger than the palms, and as it stepped into the light, I saw it was tall, but shorter than a tree. It looked like someone had stacked some brown tires in a pile, put sumo wrestler legs and arms on it, fastened a vague facsimile of a human head to the top, and tied an anaconda between its legs. It was, of course, our living Michelin Man, in the nude.

Juan Miguel saw our gaze had shifted from him to somewhere over his shoulder. He grinned. "Hammerhead, we call him."

Hammerhead leaped into the pool with a splash that almost started a tidal wave. He swam across the pool with a couple of strokes, climbed out dripping on our side. He ambled toward us. Moby-Dick gone bipedal.

"What do you think?" Juan Miguel said, as proud as if he was showing us a pet, and I suppose he was. "Is he not something?"

Jim Bob, naturally endearing, said, "An ambulatory shit pile. But I wouldn't want him to fall on me."

As Hammerhead grew closer, he became even more frightening. Through the telescope I had not been able to see how strange his head was. The front of it protruded, then sunk toward the nose, which lay flat against his face like a splattered man who had jumped from a great height. He had more scars than a Gurkha division and there were little pale scars like road map lines against the darkness of his body. It was hard to tell his nationality. He was dark, but his features were almost blank. He had Asian eyes and a little mouth that held tiny white childlike teeth. When he moved, water trapped beneath the rolls of his flesh squished out. He came to stand next to Juan Miguel's chair.

"You're a cute couple," Jim Bob said.

I thought, that's it. Jim Bob's gonna be dead so fast Juan Miguel will forget why we're here. But nothing happened. He just stared at Jim Bob for a while. Then at me. He said, "You listen to me. You hurt Ileana, Hammerhead here, he will beat you to death."

"He could probably do that with that sausage between his legs," Jim Bob said. "Considering that peanut you carry, I'm surprised you keep this guy around. Seems like it would remind you of your shortcomings."

Juan Miguel leaped to his feet, his fist crashed down on the table and the glass split and splattered into thousands of fragments that caught the light and ricocheted images of trees and shrubs at us.

When the glass fallout was over, Jim Bob, in a bored voice, said, "You broke your table."

"Enough!" Juan Miguel said. "It is enough!"

"I guess he's had enough," Jim Bob said to me.

"Reckon so," I said.

Juan Miguel was panting. "What is . . . How do you say it? The deal? What is it? Tell me now, or I have you killed."

Juan Miguel's hand was bleeding. He pressed it to the towel at his waist.

"The deal is this," Jim Bob said. "We want half a million dollars for your little doll, and we want to tell you why we want the money."

"I know why you want the money," Juan Miguel said. "I know why anyone wants the money."

"No," I said. "No, you don't. We want the money because of Beatrice and Charlie."

"Who?"

"We want the money because you wanted to kill me and the old man. I even want it for Billy, and I didn't even like that sonofabitch."

"What is it that you are talking about?" Juan Miguel said, his words becoming more accented and purposeful. "What is the fuck you want?"

"That's what the fuck," Jim Bob said. "That's the way you say it. No slight there, just thought you might like to know that for future reference."

"You do have half a million?" I said. "We'd hate to think you don't. 'Cause you don't, we got to take less, well, you get her back, but without a little finger or a thumb. You know what I'm saying?"

"Let me tell you a little thing you have not thought of," Juan Miguel said. "I get her back with any part missing, her hair cut, a scar on her thigh, I do not want her back. She must come back as she is supposed to be. She does not, she is of no use to me, understand?"

Definitely not true love, I thought. And, unlike us, he wasn't bluffing.

"Very well," I said. "She comes back pretty quick if you act pretty quick."

"How dare you threaten me."

I knew we were beginning to play it pretty close. Maybe Juan Miguel was thinking now he could let Ileana go, shop for another. Then again, she was special. Unique. And she was his, and he liked to own things, and once owned, he didn't like giving them up.

I said, "Here are our demands. And we want you to know our reasons. So just listen. And tell Gorgo here to go play somewhere. He makes me nervous."

Juan Miguel spoke something in Spanish. Hammerhead's face stayed just the same. Not a flick of an eye-lash. He went to the pool, dove in, began to swim.

"Because of his size, the way he looks," Juan Miguel said, "you might think he is a fool. He is not. He is very strong. And very loyal. He would do anything I ask. I want you to keep that in mind as you deal with me. You must prove to me that Ileana is alive. That she is okay. That she is unharmed merchandise."

"We can do that," Jim Bob said. "That's how we'll begin the down payment, with proof she's okay?"

"What kind of proof?"

"A phone call. She can speak to you to let you know she's all right. We come back here, you give us half the money."

"How much is this half?"

"This half is two hundred and fifty thousand dollars. The other half, well, obviously we're talking half a million here. But you try to be smart. You try to get by not paying the money, I'll send her head home to you in a box. Comprende?"

Juan Miguel said, "Very well. But what has this to do with the people you named?"

"You're making me mad," I said.

"That bothers me so greatly," Juan Miguel said.

Jim Bob looked at his watch. "We're not back in half an hour, they kill the girl. So you had best listen and cut with the shit. Tell him, Hap."

I gave him a brief outline of the events I thought he needed to know, and when I was finished, Juan Miguel said: "That was a personal matter. She had it coming. She lied to me. She did not do as she said. That I cannot allow. I will not allow it with you. Do you understand?"

"What about Charlie, the man you killed because you thought it was me?"

"I thought you had helped her to try and con me. I

did not like that. The same with this Billy. Mistakes. I can see that now. I was angry. I like to make a clean sweep, as you Americans say. I have her killed. She gives your name. They find this other man's name on a card. I send Hammerhead to the States. He does the job. He comes home."

"That's it?"

"That is it, señor. Nothing mysterious. That is all."

I wondered how a giant like Hammerhead had wandered around LaBorde without the cops hearing about him from some source. Juan Miguel must not have been kidding about him being smart.

I suppose I had wanted there to be more, some semi-valid reason for all the deaths, but there was none. It was as Jim Bob had figured. Juan Miguel cleaning up after himself, not wanting any messes left over from his dealings with Beatrice.

"So, this is your plan," Juan Miguel said. "I could hold you, of course. I could make sure you do not leave."

"We been over that," Jim Bob said. "Fuck with us, the woman's dead. For whatever reason, even if the reason belongs to someone else, you fuck up, she's toast."

"Toast?"

Jim Bob slapped the back of his hand into his palm. "Burned. Done. Wiped out."

"Very well," Juan Miguel said. "But do not make a mistake. Take care of Ileana. Very good care. And when I get her back. When you have your money. Please run. Run very far. For I will be at your back, my friends."

"We'll remember that," Jim Bob said.

"There's just one more thing," I said.

"There always is," Juan Miguel said.

"The archaeological items you wanted from Beatrice. They are real and they are available. They are for sale."

"You must be out of your mind," Juan Miguel said. "I would not buy them from you."

"Well, you see," I said, "they sort of go with the deal."

"Then we are not talking half a million of your dollars, are we?"

"I suppose not. I will reveal the location of the facades when I see the money."

"I no longer want them."

"That doesn't matter. You'll pay for them anyway. And then I won't give them to you. I'll donate them to the Anthropology Museum in Mexico City."

"How much?"

"That'll be another half million."

"A million American dollars. That is outrageous. No woman is worth that."

"Well, considering you can buy pussy for about two dollars in some places, I reckon you're right," Jim Bob said. "But if this woman is someone you like specifically, and can't be replaced easy—and let me tell you, she looks to me hard to replace under any circumstances—well, then, at least to you, she's worth a million dollars. It was me, and I was in your position, I'd buy her back. Oh boy, would I. And you want her, good buddy, you better let us leave in less than five minutes so we can stop and make a phone call along the way, say the deal's on so she doesn't get snuffed. And don't follow. I wouldn't like it."

"My men could work on you until I knew what I wanted to know," Juan Miguel said. "They are very good at that sort of thing."

"That's nice, but we made a pact with our group. We don't know anyone's real names. That way, you can torture us all you want, and we can't even tell you where each other lives, except the two of us. We know each other. But you got us. So how would that help? And it don't matter we did know, we told you where she is. By the time you get through doing what you got to do, it'll be way too late. I can hold out that long, I promise you."

Juan Miguel looked at his men, then he looked at us. I tried to remain cool and calm. I glanced at Jim Bob. He looked like he was waiting on a waiter to bring him a beer.

"Go," Juan Miguel said. "Go. I will be waiting for her call. And she must answer me. It cannot be thought to be a recording. I must ask a question and she must answer so that I know she is alive and unharmed."

"Fine," Jim Bob said. "Remember, we'll be listening. And I better not see your men, or your giant, anytime during the dealings. And when it comes time to trade, you'll do it our way. Just you. And dress up, would you? And by the way, before we leave I want my pocketknife, and he wants his four pesos back."

We went out to the car. Jim Bob drove us out of there. When we were away from the house, he checked the rearview.

"Well?" I asked.

"No one's following."

"Good," I said, letting it out like a sigh.

Jim Bob held out his hand. It was shaking violently. He said, "Will you look at that?"

I held up my own shaking hand.

"Twins," I said.

33

THAT NIGHT, in the hotel, Brett and I sat by our window in chairs pulled close together. I had wrapped some ice in a towel, and was holding it to the back of my head, trying to bring the swelling down on a knot one of Juan Miguel's Golems had given me.

We sat there with the shades wide, looked at the pedestrian walk and the sea beyond. The water looked oily and there were a number of dead fish washed up close to shore and they too were covered with something dark and slick.

The moon was a nasty slice of limburger, spotted by clouds that looked like soggy boles of field-spoiled cotton.

Jim Bob had dropped me off and driven out to César's.

"You really think Juan Miguel will come through with the money?" Brett asked.

"Truthfully, I don't know. And it doesn't matter. We don't want the money."

"But he might come through with it."

"You want the money, right?"

"Of course not. It's blood money. I don't want that. But what if he did come through with the money?"

"We meet him, he has the money, we kill him. We leave the money."

"It would be a shame to leave all that money. A quarter million first time, right? I mean, that's a lot of money to just leave lying around."

"Brett, I don't steal from the dead."

"I know. But listen. What if you took the money and gave it to Ferdinand? He could buy a new boat. He could go on with his life. If anyone deserves the money, it's him. His daughter was killed by that animal. Charlie, he doesn't have anyone he'd want to have the money. Certainly not his ex-wife."

"You got a point. It works out that way, okay. Ferdinand gets the money. Maybe César will have other ideas. I don't know. But it's okay with me."

"You're going to have him deliver half, right?"

"It's all he'll ever deliver," I said. "We're going to kill him, remember? Then let the girl go."

"You want to do this right, want to get him good, have him pay all the money, and on the last delivery kill him."

"You're cold, Brett."

"We're going to kill him anyway, right?"

"Right."

"He's a piece of shit, right?"

"Right."

"So we kill him, and we take him for a million. Ferdinand would never have to worry. And with that kind of money, neither would we."

I turned in my chair and looked at her.

"Brett, I'm not sure I believe my ears. Didn't you just say you didn't want the money?"

"It's a lot of money."

"It's not like we're finding it in a pig track. It's blood money."

"I was just thinking out loud," she said. "Jesus. Will you listen to me? Money does corrupt. I feel like Humphrey Bogart in *Treasure of the Sierra Madre.*"

"Well, one thing you got going for you, you don't look like Bogart. And if it's any consolation, I've thought of the money too. You can't help but think about it. But we start getting greedy, even if we get greedy for someone else, we're gonna end up messing up."

"Don't you want the Anthropology Museum to have those facades?"

"Brett, we don't need money for them to have the facades. We just give them a tip-off on where they're hidden. They'll do the rest."

"Oh yeah, I forgot. But you know what?"

"What?"

"You could quit working at the chicken plant. You could do what you want. So could I."

"For a while. Even if we took the money, it would be split between everyone, our share would be small for a lifetime. We could live on it for a while, but then what?"

"We invest it."

"And maybe we lose it."

"True. I don't know anything about the stock market. We could live off of it while you figured out what you really wanted to do. Maybe you could go to college. You got some hours, right?"

"Right."

"You could get a degree, maybe teach or something."

It sounded good. But it sounded wrong. Still, I sat and considered.

Brett said, "When does Jim Bob let Ileana talk to Juan Miguel?"

"I don't know. He's playing it loose, making sure Juan

Miguel is tense. He's also giving him time to get the money together. Mostly though, it's just Jim Bob playing a waiting game."

"You think he knows what he's doing?"

"Much as anyone knows. You should have seen him at Juan Miguel's. He was as cool as an ice tray. He had Juan Miguel eating out of his hand. Juan Miguel tried to act like he was in charge, but I tell you, Jim Bob, he was running the show. We left, his hand was shaking bad as mine, but he didn't show it, not with Juan Miguel."

"Did you?"

"I don't know. Jim Bob says I didn't. I hope I didn't."

"You wouldn't want to be outmachoed by Jim Bob, would you?"

"I wouldn't," I said, "but I got to tell you, that sonofabitch is more macho than my brother, Leonard. I'm surprised he doesn't go around with a wheelbarrow in front of him so he can carry his balls."

"Remember," Brett said, "Leonard's macho and queer as a duck in a tuxedo. He's starting one square lower on the tough guy scale. So, you got to sort of give him special points."

"I wouldn't let him hear you say that."

"Hap, we come out all right on this, you and me, we're gonna stay together. Right?"

"We're gonna get married," I said. "If you want to, of course."

"You're not joking?"

"I'm not. I had a ring I'd give it to you. But you didn't say if you'd marry me. We've talked about it, but we haven't really talked about it. We just keep saying someday. I'm saying we've about come to that day."

Brett slid her chair over close to me and put her arm around me.

"I want to. Bad. But you got to pretend on our wedding night that I'm a renewed virgin."

"That won't be easy," I said.

"Most women play that game."

"It still won't be easy."

"Well, considering I been to bed more than a hospitalful of invalids, I know that," Brett said. "But you got to try, just the same. You don't try, well, to put it in simple terms, you don't get any nookie."

"You drive a hard bargain," I said.

We were sitting there snuggling, when we saw Jim Bob and Leonard come along the pedestrian walk.

"Back from César's already," I said. "Things be happenin'."

I went to the door and opened it. Jim Bob and Leonard appeared in the hallway, and I ushered them in.

"How goes it?" I said.

"Good. You got a beer?" Jim Bob said.

He looked rough. He had taken a worse beating than I had. One eye was swollen and there was a bruise the color of smashed plum on his right cheek. The lip on that side was fat and dark. His hat had crease lines all through it.

"There's a beer in the cash bar. What about you, Leonard?"

"I want John."

"He's not in the cash bar," I said.

I got the bar key and retrieved a beer for Jim Bob. He twisted off the cap, dropped down in the only cushioned chair, and pressed the cold bottle against the bruise on his cheek.

"Man," he said, "I could cook an egg on this motherfucker."

Brett and I sat on the edge of the bed. Leonard pulled

one of the wooden chairs over and sat down, crossed his legs and played with the toe of his shoe.

"How'd it go?" Brett asked.

"Well, we hauled Ileana to a pay phone, twisted her arm, had her talk to Juan Miguel a bit," Jim Bob said. "I talked to him then. I set a meeting up. He's so mad he sounds as if he could eat the ass out of a bull and spit out a wallet."

I said, "When?"

"Tonight."

"That's quick. I thought you'd let him sweat."

"I don't think we ought to fuck around."

"And I don't like waiting," Leonard said. "It makes my feet break out in little hives."

"Juan Miguel is supposed to meet us at the souvenir stands on this side of Tulum," Jim Bob said. "He brings the money, we take the money. He thinks that's it. He thinks he gives us the money, then we set up the next meeting, where we give him the girl and he gives us the rest of the money. I was him, that's where I'd think about nailing us. He gets the girl, double-crosses us, kills us. That would be the plan if I were doing it. Maybe I was him I'd torture us to give back the first batch of money."

"So, like us," I said, "you've actually thought about the money?"

"You can't help but think about the money," Jim Bob said. " 'Course, being smarter than the average criminal, the plan should be take the first batch of money and kill the woman—"

"We're not doing that," Brett said. "That's not the deal."

"Of course not," Jim Bob said. "I'm saying if I were really a kidnapper."

"You really are," I said.

"You know what I mean. I was really out for the money, I'd take the half, let the girl go free, or kill her, and get away with what I got. Best thing to do would be to actually let her go. That way Juan Miguel doesn't have a way to magnify the grudge."

"Since there's supposed to actually be some real money," I said, "what do we do about that?"

"Yeah," Brett said. "What about that?"

"I've been giving that some thought."

"So have we," I said.

"Crossed my mind too," Leonard said.

"My belief is this," Jim Bob said. "We take just enough to pay for our expenses, we give the rest to Ferdinand."

"I thought maybe give it all to Ferdinand," Leonard said, "but I got to admit, that sounds pretty fair."

"We got the hotels, car rentals, and we owe César for the guns," I said.

"Where are the guns?" Brett asked

"In the trunk of the rental," Jim Bob said.

"What time does it happen?"

"We meet at midnight."

"Why midnight?"

"Because where the tourist stand is there's a cross-roads."

"Yeah. So?"

"I like the idea of it," Jim Bob said. "It's an artistic touch to the job. Devil takes a man's soul at the cross-roads, and this bastard's gonna sell his soul there."

"How will it work?" I asked.

Jim Bob looked at his watch. "It's eight o'clock. We go over and pick up Ferdinand at César's so he can have his chance to see it come down—"

"He wants to do the killing," Leonard said. "Not see it."

"He may have to settle for a back seat," Jim Bob said. "Perhaps Juan Miguel doesn't go down for good right off, we let Ferdinand deliver the coup de grâce. A bullet to the head. That kind of thing."

"No torture," I said. "I don't care what Ferdinand wants. Juan Miguel knows why we took Ileana, and that's as close as we're going to get to explaining it. It meant nothing to him anyway."

"At the moment of death, it may," Jim Bob said. "Anyway, we load up Ferdinand. We go out to the drop sight early, before dark. This time of year it gets dark, say, nine-thirty, true dark a little later. There are some good places to hide, and you, Ferdinand, and Leonard can get somewhere you can't be seen."

"Won't they get there early too?" Brett asked.

"They will," Jim Bob said. "You can count on it. But we'll be earlier yet. They see us, they see us. We deal with that when we get there. Thing on our side is Juan Miguel doesn't know our real plan is to kill his sorry ass. If it goes well and he doesn't get there early, doesn't see you guys, I'll appear to be there alone. When Juan Miguel delivers the money, you drop him, Hap."

"Me?" I said.

"Leonard says you can shoot the nuts off a squirrel when all you can see is shape."

"Thanks for volunteering me, Leonard."

"You're welcome, Hap. You're the best shot, and that's all there is to it."

"But if I'm going to shoot him in hiding, what's so wrong with my idea of picking him off from a distance? It's because he wouldn't have the money, isn't it? It's about the money, isn't it?"

"It's about him deserving it," Jim Bob said. "Then there's the money. I told you what I wanted to do with it. I don't think that's selfish. We get our expenses, Ferdinand gets the big cut, and Juan Miguel is dead. That okay with you, Hap?"

"I suppose."

"They'll search me for weapons, so I won't carry.

Leonard will be hidden with the shotgun in the bushes. When I clench my fist, you shoot, Hap, and I'll jump. Leonard can open up then. I'll stash the nine mil close by in the weeds so I can get to it, and play cleanup. We still got Ferdinand and César as insurance. Brett, there's not enough guns, so you're going to stay at César's with Ileana. Someone has to watch her."

"All right," Brett said.

"You can bet Juan Miguel will have his boys with him, so no fuckin' around. Be sure, be double-sure, to take out that Hammerhead motherfucker."

"What if Juan Miguel sends someone?" I said. "Doesn't show himself?"

"When I called, I told him he had to come with the money. Said we didn't trust any of his sidekicks. So he'll show. Like I said, he'll bring them with him, but he'll show. No matter how cool he plays it, he's got it bad for this Ileana. She's got his nose wide open, buddy, you can count on that."

"Now that we got it all talked out, how about we go do it," Leonard said.

34

W<small>E DROVE UP</small> in César's yard at about eight-thirty. When we got out of the car a cold feeling went over me. Something was out of kilter.

I said, "Something sucks."

"Yeah," Leonard said. "But what is it? It doesn't look any different."

Jim Bob stared at the house for a moment. "Yes it does. The blinds are closed. They haven't been closed before."

"Maybe they wanted them closed," Brett said.

"Yeah," Jim Bob said. "Crushed shells up by the porch are pitted. Like maybe there was a struggle there. See, there's shells on the porch. More than would have come off someone's shoes. It's like they were rolled in them, got dragged on the porch and the shells fell off their clothes. Screen door is unlocked and it's slightly open."

Jim Bob strolled to the rear of the car, opened the trunk. He popped one of the suitcases. He took two nine mils from the case and gave one to me, one to Leonard. He got the shotgun parts out of the other case and put it together. He gave us ammo clips, took a fistful of shells and stuffed them in his shirt pocket. He loaded two in the double-barrel.

"I'll just stroll around back," Jim Bob said. "You and Leonard take the front."

Jim Bob trotted off. I said, "Brett, you get behind the wheel. You see anyone come out of the door you don't want to see, you back out and go. Go away fast."

Brett nodded, climbed in behind the wheel, closed the door softly.

Me and Leonard moved toward the front door.

I thought: It could be they wanted the shades closed. Maybe César or Hermonie fell in the drive, brushed themselves off on the porch. Went in and didn't close the door well. In a hurry. It could be that.

I moved the door with my foot. It swung open with a sound that would have made a can of WD40 cry.

Easing inside, crouching, the gun held before me, I saw why things were quiet, and I felt my knees wobble. I kept the gun at ready, but I knew I wouldn't need it.

Leonard came in behind me about the time Jim Bob reached the back patio glass. I strolled over and let him in, using my shirttail to work the latch.

I went around what was on the floor, stepping carefully, eased to the bedroom, pushed the half-open door the rest of the way with my foot.

The room was empty, of course.

I checked out the bathroom, just in case Hammerhead might be using the commode, found nothing, went back to the living room.

I sat down on the brick ridge of the fireplace and looked at what was before me.

Hermonie was dressed in her white pants suit, seated on the couch, looking pretty much the way she always looked, except one side of her head poked out in a funny way. That was because a bullet entering the other side had come out on the side facing me, splintered the bone, lifted her hair. Where her hair was lifted it was slick, as if she had been hit with a tomato. Her right eye had moved a little too far to the right and was almost hidden. The left looked straight ahead. A splotch of blood like another shot from a tomato was splattered on the right shoulder of her outfit. There was red on the wall and the back of the couch.

César lay on the floor. He had been tied to a chair. In his final agonies, most likely, he had turned it over.

His fingers had been chopped off close to the knuckles, and I could see the skin on his hands had been filleted all the way to his elbows. He was shirtless and there were burns on his chest. His eyes were open, as if he had just discovered he had gotten exactly what he wanted for Christmas, but his mouth was wide and gummy and his tongue poked out of it, fat and gray as an old piece of liver. His pants had large globs of blood on the knees where they had dripped off the chair when it was upright. His shoes were gone. So were his toes. The skin on his feet had been peeled all the way to his calves, and his pants were cuffed high to allow it. There were little bits of crushed shells from the drive stuck to his clothes and on the floor around the chair.

Leonard leaned against the wall and let the nine mil hang by his side. Jim Bob bent over César, stood up, looked at Hermonie.

"You have some intuition," I said to Jim Bob. "You were right about there being a struggle in the yard."

"Intuition is really just the unconscious mind learning to talk to the conscious." He gestured toward Hermonie. "One for her and it's over with. César, not so easy. What's that tell you?"

"He didn't talk," I said. "So they gave him hell."

"Shit, he talked. I would have. I tell you what happened. Hermonie here, she called Juan Miguel and told where the girl was."

"But why?" I asked.

"Because she wanted what she thought Juan Miguel could give her," Leonard said.

"Yep," Jim Bob said. "Leonard, you aren't as dumb as you look."

"Thanks."

"I never really trusted her," Jim Bob said, "but I didn't think this. I didn't think she was this stupid. I just thought she was a shit and a bad pick for César. Goddamn, César didn't deserve this."

"Who the hell does?" Leonard said.

"You actually think she called Juan Miguel?" I said.

"They finished her easy," Jim Bob said. "No torture. They just popped her. That tells me she thought maybe she could make the big money. Maybe Ileana talked Hermonie into it. Said I'll see you get paid good. I'll get you in good with Juan Miguel you get me out of this."

"Who did she think she was dealing with?" I said.

"She had no idea," Leonard said.

"No," Jim Bob said, "she didn't. She didn't like us, and according to César, she didn't like him much either. But I don't think this is what she expected. Maybe she thought César would get his, but she figured she was doing Juan Miguel a favor, so she thought she was all right. Would make some big money out of the deal. Get a chance to end up with what she thought she deserved. Juan Miguel had other plans. He decided to thank her by not torturing her. He gave her what he thought she deserved."

"So now Juan Miguel knows we were going to ambush him?" I said.

Jim Bob nodded. "I'm sure César said what he had to say."

"And now," Leonard said, "we don't have our bargaining chip. And we aren't going to get any money, and we aren't going to surprise him . . . Ferdinand . . . where is he?"

"Out back," Jim Bob said. "They took him out there and hacked him to pieces. I wish he'd had a machete. I wish he'd had his chance . . . Probably that goddamn giant did it."

"What now?" I said, and was surprised at how hoarse my voice was.

Jim Bob took off his battered hat and ran a hand through his hair. "Well, three things occur to me. Let's wipe our fingerprints up, and hope there aren't too many old ones. They come up, we get hauled in, we were visiting César. He's a friend of mine, so maybe we can swing it. I doubt anything's missing. I don't thing Juan Miguel would give a shit about anything César owned.

"Second thing is we get the hell out of here quickly. Third thing is César might have told him we were staying at the hotel. Since we got everything we own in the car, I say we check in somewhere else. We don't go back."

We wiped down what we knew we had touched, eased out of there, and with Brett at the wheel, we drove briskly away.

35

WE MOVED to a smaller hotel. Jim Bob carried the suitcase with the shotgun in it to his and Leonard's room.
Leonard kept the nine mil. I kept mine. I kept the suitcase with the rifle.

We were too stunned to eat. Too shocked to think.
That was good. I had been thinking too much. I may not
come up with class plans, but I could at least come up
with something. I had been trying to be too damn smart.
I had let Jim Bob the pro do what the pro knew how to
do, and it hadn't been enough. The pro was good. He
was grand. But sometimes the way you kill a bug is just
step on it. You don't think about it too much. You don't
go get bug spray or call the exterminator, or talk to the
bug and tell it why it must die, or try to bargain money
from it, you just step on it.

Brett watched a Mexican television show for a while,
not understanding a word of it, then fell asleep. I sat and
watched her sleep. I thought about poor Beatrice, how
she looked after that animal Hammerhead had had at her.
It had to be him. Hammerhead was the one. He was the
one that had come for me and killed Charlie instead. That's

what Juan Miguel said. I thought of César. He had done his best to help us. He had tried to be a friend. And Hermonie. How horrible it must have been for César to have been betrayed by her. More horrible than the torture.

And Ferdinand. If they had given him a machete like Jim Bob said, let him fight it out with Hammerhead, he would have died happy. And he might not have died. He had been a terror with a machete.

God. All that blood. The skin peeled back on César's hands and feet. I kept thinking about his eyes. His mouth. The way his pants cuffs were rolled up. Somehow that hit me the hardest. Just that simple little thing, the careful rolling up of the cuffs so they could peel the flesh higher.

I got up quietly, checked on Brett. She was snoring like a lumberjack. I got some of the hotel's stationery out of the desk drawer, a pen. I wrote.

Brett, I love you.

You wake up and read this note, you be cautious. I'm leaving the nine millimeter on the desk. You keep it, go stay with Leonard and Jim Bob. Trust me on this. Tell Leonard I love him. A man couldn't ask for a better brother. Don't tell him that unless I don't come back. No use giving him the big head. Tell him I love him, but that doesn't mean I forgive him for everything. He won't know what he needs forgiving for, but I like the idea of making him nervous.

This isn't a suicide note. This isn't a so-long note. It's a just-in-case note. You read it, you remember that. It's just in case. I'm going to do what always sounds so hokey, but tonight sounds exactly right.

I'm gonna do what a man's got to do, and I'm going to do it without dragging anyone else into it.

If you figure what I'm doing, try and help me, you'll just fuck it up. But if I'm not back by tomorrow, then I didn't do it. It's best you just take a plane home and forget about all this. Leonard and Jim Bob will do whatever. And I have a pretty good idea what that will be. I want them to. But better yet, I want them to end up going home with you. I want Leonard to be with John and Jim Bob to be with his pigs. Leonard and John in a carnal sense, and for all I care, Jim Bob and his pigs in a carnal sense. Actually, I kind of like that idea.

So go home and forget about all this.

Except for me. Remember me awhile. Then forget me.

I keep writing because I don't want to go.

I've got to go. I keep waiting, keep messing around here, I'll be waking you up asking you to proofread this. I go now, I may get back before you know I'm gone, then I can tear up this silly tripe and we can go home.

Love, Hap.

P.S. I don't come back tomorrow disregard what I said before. Have Jim Bob and Leonard kill that sonofabitch. But you go home.

The keys to the car were on the table where Brett had left them. It was easy for me to walk out with the suitcase containing the rifle, scope, and silencer. I drove along the highway, half expecting to see a dark car filled with Juan Miguel's two thugs and the impossibly large Hammerhead.

How would he fit in a car? Did they have to drive a convertible? Did they pull him behind them in a trailer?

I kept thinking about all kinds of stupid things. I felt as if I was coming undone, a piece at a time.

The moon laid greasy patches of light along the road and the road rose up and curved. I could see Juan Miguel's great house standing tall with its palms and its thick high wall, the moon above and behind it like a chunk of suspended lard.

Then the road dipped and I could only see the rise of land on which it was positioned. The road went that way awhile, then rose again. I took a cutoff that was all dirt and steered through tight trees that scraped the car, finally came to a widening in the road that was below Juan Miguel's wall.

I pulled over and got out with the suitcase.

I walked up the road apiece, where the brush and trees cleared, looked up. There was moonlight and man-made light spilling over the vine-covered wall. I could see it was no easy task to go up the side of that big hill, which was maybe two hundred feet high to the wall.

I took off my belt and ran it through the suitcase handle and fastened it, slipped the belt over my head and one shoulder, started to climb.

At first there was vines and brush to hold on to, then some rocks and little plants that sometimes jerked free of the dirt the moment I touched them.

When I was about halfway, I thought I was going to have to give up and start down. I lay tight against the hill, my face touching a cool rock, and gave that a lot of thought. I could get down from here now, give up this silly idea, go back to the hotel, throw away my note, shower, get in bed with Brett and make love to her, and tomorrow, no matter what Jim Bob or Leonard thought, I could take her home and live happily ever after.

I took a deep breath, started up again.

I had gone about twenty more feet when I decided I definitely couldn't make it and had to go back. The suitcase was killing me. Atlas and the world on his shoulders was nothing compared to that goddamn suitcase.

But by then I had gone too far. I was committed.

I continued climbing. It was slow, exhausting work. My fingers ached something horrible. I was losing feeling in them. I wasn't even sure if I was holding on to anything. I decided to look neither up nor down, but to concentrate on the moment, on what was in front of me.

I had no idea how long I had been climbing. Wasn't wearing my watch. Couldn't look at it if I had been. Too dark. Couldn't spare the handhold.

The moonlight shifted. Maybe two hours had passed. I needed to pee. My hands hurt and they were bleeding.

I kept at it. Inch by inch. And then I touched the rough rock wall and the vines that grew over it.

I clutched a fistful of vines and tugged. The wall didn't come loose. Neither did the vines.

I pulled and scuttled and pretty soon I was near the top.

I reached an arm over the wall, hauled up slowly, poked my face over the edge, looked down on Juan Miguel's property.

There was no one there. The pools were blue and shiny and the growth around their edges was thick and green.

I dropped over the wall, managed to get a shaft of a shrub nearly up my ass, fell, clattered against some tall elephant ears and lay still.

I got up slowly, hustled around on my hands and knees until I could see through a split in the shrubs:

Still no one.

I opened the suitcase and took out the rifle parts and, in the glow of the pool lights, I put it together, pushed in the clip, put on the silencer. I didn't bother with the scope. This close I didn't need a scope.

I pulled the suitcase back with me, found a place less obvious. It was a thick swathe of hedge next to a palm tree that afforded me about six feet between it and the wall, and was a good hiding place. It was a good position. I could see all of the side pool. Across the way, I could see the backyard pool.

He said he swam every night.

Would he swim tonight?

Was he off celebrating having Hermonie shot, having César's feet and hands skinned, Ferdinand chopped up like a fish at the market?

Maybe he was celebrating by staying over with his mistress.

The bitch. Jim Bob was right. She knew what Juan Miguel did. What he was like. She didn't care.

I took a pee in the bushes, picked some prickles out of my hands as best I could.

It was hot even for so late at night, so I sat with my back against the cool stone wall, watching through my split in the shrubbery.

There were lights on in the house. They looked orange instead of yellow. I watched the lights until I decided they were causing me to focus too hard. I began watching left and right, waiting, listening.

I must have dozed for a while. I came awake to the sound of the back door opening.

Some ambusher I was.

A woman came out. The wife. She was nude. She walked out to the back pool, leaped in, swam for a while.

This nude business was starting to seem common to me. Maybe I should strip off now. I could be the nude ambusher.

I kept waiting for Juan Miguel, but he didn't show.

She must have swum half an hour. She climbed out, snatched a towel off the back of a chair and slowly dried herself, running the towel the length of her legs, drying between her legs, her breasts, her hair. When she was finished, I felt like I should leave her money.

She went inside. The orange lights soon went out. The moon was starting to drop low in the sky.

I leaned against the wall and dozed.

I dreamed of trying to go back over the wall, of falling. Then I dreamed I was eating a banana.

I hoped to God I was smart enough to never tell Leonard about that dream. He'd give me shit.

I awoke, hungry, in spite of my nocturnal banana. My stomach growled. Loud.

Trying to shift to get comfortable, I heard a car door. I peeked through my leafy peephole. Beyond the pool, about where Jim Bob and I had taken a beating from Juan Miguel's two assholes, was a long black car. Juan Miguel got out. So did Hammerhead and one of the ass-holes.

The other asshole drove the car to the other side of the house, to the garage. The remaining three walked up the drive and the big stone steps before I could say to myself, "Where the hell is my gun?"

They went inside.

Some shooter I was.

I waited awhile. They didn't come out. I stood up, stretched my legs behind some tall plants, took a leak again, went back to my spot, lay on my side with my back against the wall. I knew it was not a good idea, but I couldn't help myself. I was exhausted. I slept.

When I awoke I had a taste in my mouth like a well-used cat box. The greasy moon was gone and the sun was a ball of flaming lead burning away the clouds, heading up toward high noon.

I was sweaty and my face was dirty where I had slept with it pressed to the ground. I brushed myself off, moved my tongue around in my mouth trying to move the rotten taste about.

I peeked through the slit in the shrubs, saw nothing. He was probably sleeping in. Maybe getting a morning quickie with the wife, then brunch.

I wondered how that worked for the wife. She knew he had a mistress. Did she say, "Hey, did you and Ileana have a good hump last night? You did wash your pecker before we did it, didn't you? What shall I get her for her birthday? Edible underwear?"

It was such a weird situation, and yet to them it was as normal as a nose on a face.

A pocked and diseased nose.

Maybe he wasn't sleeping in. Maybe he had already left, and me, the lone assassin, had slept through it.

I wondered if Brett had seen my note.

Surely.

By the sun it was about ten o'clock I figured.

What was Brett thinking since I hadn't come back?

Had she told Jim Bob and Leonard?

Would they do something foolish like rent a taxi and have it drop them off so they could go into the house, guns blazing, looking for me?

Nope. That was more my kind of plan.

More Leonard's kind of plan. Jim Bob wouldn't let that happen. He might come in guns blazing, but he wouldn't arrive in a taxi. He'd be sneaky.

Hell, I had been sneaky, and in the end I had hidden in the bushes and taken a nap.

I was thinking about that, when suddenly I realized I was looking directly at Juan Miguel.

36

HE SEEMED to just appear, standing at the edge of the pool. He was in all his naked glory and quite fond of himself, stretching his arms, rolling his shoulders. He looked left and right, then checked his package, shook it, let it go.

I could see it in his eyes, in the relaxed way he stood and stretched, the slight smile on his face.

He was happy.

He was the king.

The king's package was fine, ready to be used at any time. The envy of all others, that package. Men feared and admired him, women wanted him.

The universe was his.

A strange feeling came over me. Of watching in slow motion, of moving in slow motion. I had had a similar feeling before. In fights. It's always that way. You may be moving fast, but to you it's slow, and everything around you is moving slow. But life is heightened. It's as if in that moment of violence you feel directly connected to the world around you, as if you are in tumultuous union with the universe.

This moment was stronger than ever before. I remember

wiping my eyes, rubbing out the sleep. I had been sitting on my ass, but I rose up on my left knee, raised my right knee, put the rifle against my shoulder and looked down the sight. The sight was very fine, like a little blackhead in the center of Juan Miguel's face.

He was rolling his neck now. I watched him roll it. I wanted him to stop moving just for a moment. The way you're supposed to shoot someone is you aim at the biggest part of them, but I wanted Juan Miguel's head.

I was putting the little blackhead on his face, when I heard a noise and saw, coming around from the rear of the house, Hammerhead. He was naked except for a white beach towel wrapped between his legs and around his waist. It made him look as if he were wearing a huge diaper.

That's all right, I told myself. That's all right, Mama, that's all right with me.

I put the sight back on Juan Miguel as he lifted his arms and touched his hands in dive fashion, and as he lowered them to make his leap into the pool, his head lowered, I shot him right in the top of it.

There was a cough from the silencer, a flash of red juice, a flurry of hair, a whirl of skull like a hubcap fragment, and Juan Miguel dropped his arms and went into the water. There was a burst of dark blood, like ink from a Technicolor squid.

I shifted, floated the barrel, put the sight on Hammerhead.

He had just removed the towel from himself, probably preparing to swim with his boss. He held it in one hand like an oversized hanky he was passing to someone. His jaw hung low, his eyes were fastened on Juan Miguel's body floating under the water, dropping slowly to the bottom.

Hammerhead crouched, dropped the towel, turned his

head, looked in the direction from which he thought the shot must have come. In that moment he saw me in the foliage. Our eyes snapped together like padlocks. I fired again.

It was a good shot, but not as good as it would have been had he not moved. It went through his throat, low and on the right side. He snapped a hand to the wound and let out a bellow. I put three in his chest as fast as I could pull the trigger.

Where he clutched his throat blood was running through his fingers. Three little holes appeared on his chest without much blood.

The pool was in front of him and he hit the water running, went down, not quite over his head, tried to trudge along the bottom. The water bounced him up and down. I took a bead on his eye and let it rip.

His head snapped back. When it righted itself, he continued forward. Much of the pool's surface was slick with his and Juan Miguel's blood and it kept widening as if its job was to paint the remaining blue red.

As Hammerhead climbed out of the pool, a real feeling of terror went over me. This bastard had three in the chest, one in the throat, and one through the eye, and he was still coming.

As he stepped out of the pool on my side, I aimed for his kneecap, popped him twice. The knee went away. He collapsed, tried to raise up on his elbows, but I shot him again, about where the neck meets the shoulder.

This time there was a big burst of blood, like a pipe full of pressured rusty water had broken.

Hammerhead's head snapped forward on the cement at the edge of the pool. He pulled himself forward another inch or so, then lay with only his foot jerking and one hand vibrating. The hand quit, then the foot.

I took a deep breath.

I looked about.

No wife.

No assholes. They were probably watching bowling on TV.

I took the wrench out of the suitcase and took the rifle apart. My hand was shaking so much it took me longer than it should have. I put the pieces in the suitcase.

I looked up.

Still no one. I tossed the suitcase over the fence. I climbed on a slanting palm near the fence, inched up it with the speed of a ground sloth with its leg in a sling.

I made it to the fence and looked down. It didn't look good. I didn't see the suitcase. I'd need that. It had fingerprints all over it.

I walked along the top of the rock wall until I found a place I felt I could descend, went over and started working my way down. Below I heard a car, looked. It went zooming by. I wondered if they had seen me.

It was easier and faster going down in the light than it was going up in the dark. I made the ground fairly easy, looked for the suitcase, didn't see it.

Worse, the car was gone. There was windshield glass on the ground, so I knew during the night, while I slept, someone had smashed the glass and hotwired the rental.

Typical.

I eventually located the suitcase. It was up the hill, hung up in some roots and bushes.

I took a deep breath, started up again. I got the suitcase, and as it still had my belt through the handle, I slung it over my neck and shoulder and climbed down.

I brushed myself off as best I could and started walking.

*   *   *

It took an hour or so for me to reach the main road. I had walked along about fifteen minutes when a large ancient truck with sideboards appeared. It pulled up beside me. In the seat were five men wearing straw hats. One of them stuck his head out the window and said something in Spanish. He was young-looking, with a split between his teeth. He had taken advantage of the split and had inserted a straw between it. It moved around in his mouth when he spoke.

I finally realized they were asking me if I wanted to ride.

"Sí," I said.

I climbed in the back, over the sideboards, found I was company to three large black and white hogs. In one corner of the truck was a large pile of hog shit, and as we bounced along, so did it, creeping its way toward me.

They let me and my suitcase off in town and I walked to our hotel. I wondered if Brett, Leonard, and Jim Bob were still there.

I went straight to Jim Bob's room and knocked. If it was someone else I'd just claim the wrong room and go away.

Jim Bob answered.

"You asshole," he said. "You thoughtless asshole. We been worried fucking sick. Serve you right if you were dead."

"Hi. Good to see you too."

I went inside. Brett was there, she pushed past Leonard, who was trying to shake my hand, grabbed me, kissed me on the face.

"Wow," she said. "What have you been rolling in, Rex?"

"Hog shit," I said. "Really."

"He has," Jim Bob said. "If there's one smell I know, it's hog shit, and that's hog shit."

"You killed him, didn't you?" Leonard said.

"He and that Hammerhead are two of the deadest motherfuckers you'll ever see."

"Good," Jim Bob said. "Goddamn good."

"Who says you have to have good plans to get the job done?" Leonard said.

"You know," I said, "I sort of thought you guys would charge to my assistance. Note or no note. It was just for dramatic effect."

"I slept late," Brett said.

"We didn't see it until a few minutes ago," Jim Bob said.

"I was considering just how bad I wanted to kill you," Leonard said, "then I thought maybe Juan Miguel and Hammerhead would do it for me, so I went back to sleep."

"He did not," Brett said. "He was having a shit fit. We were just about out the door, come to help."

"Yeah," Leonard said, "but I wasn't going to dress up for it."

"You're a dumbass," Jim Bob said.

"Yeah, and don't ever do it again," Leonard said. "It ain't good for my heart. And besides, since when do you have enough brains to do anything without me?"

"It was lonely without you, brother," I said.

Brett suddenly began crying. She said, "You asshole. You thoughtless asshole."

"I'm sorry," I said.

"Yes, you are," she said. "Now, for goodness sake, shower, then let's go home."

While I showered Jim Bob rented us another car, disposed of the suitcases, and brought us food. We ate, checked out, rode to the airport.

We turned in the car there, Jim Bob talked to the other rental agency, explained our car had been stolen from the hotel, filled out the proper forms, and we sat around in hard plastic chairs waiting for our flight.

"Did they buy the theft story?" Leonard asked Jim Bob.

"I believe they did," Jim Bob said. "When I want, I can charm the ass off someone."

"It's your way with the language," Leonard said.

"You betcha."

We kept watching, half expecting Juan Miguel's two goons to show. Except Jim Bob.

He said, "With Big Daddy dead, those two haven't the sense to get in out of the rain. They're probably still trying to wake Juan Miguel and Hammerhead up."

Our flight was late, so we sat a long time, but once on the plane I fell asleep immediately and by the time we were landing at Houston Intercontinental, I felt as if I had been on board for no more than a few minutes.

37

For about three months I still watched for Juan Miguel's goons. But Jim Bob was probably right. They were lost now, maybe working for the old lady. Or perhaps she blamed them and had used her considerable money to have them whacked. Perhaps they had gone to barber college and were now doing honest work in a border town, cutting hair, powdering the back of customers' necks.

I thought about César, Ferdinand, and Hermonie, left there in that house. We hadn't contacted anyone. How long would they go before they were found? A day? A week? A month?

I guess it didn't matter when you were dead.

It was odd, walking away from all that, going back to being a security guard at the chicken plant. But I hadn't fallen back completely into old habits. I had started part-time at the college, taking courses in history. I wasn't exactly sure why, but for the first time in years I felt like I was doing something that counted, even if I wasn't sure what it counted for.

Leonard got another job, security manager of a bakery. All he does now is sit in the office with his feet up, eat sweet cakes and cookies and make sure everyone else does the work. He's even gotten a little fat.

He and John are happy.

Jim Bob's back with his hogs.

Hanson is walking without a cane now. A little slow, but he's walking. He's still wearing Charlie's hat.

Me and Brett?

Well, we haven't gotten married, but we still talk about it. It doesn't seem quite as urgent as it did in that hotel room in Mexico, but the thought is still there.

The other night Brett and I were sitting out in her yard, which I had mowed and freed the lawn chair from, and I was sitting in that lawn chair, and she in another, just sitting there with the moon and the starlight above, a bug-thronged streetlight in view, when a blue Cadillac pulled up at the house, parked next to the streetlight, and killed the motor.

I had a momentary sinking feeling, thinking those dicks from Mexico had caught up with us, but then I saw Mr. Bond come out from behind the wheel and close his door. He went around and opened the other.

A fragile-looking woman with her hair in a ponytail and a bandage across her face got out of the car carefully, pulling crutches after her.

I stood up, but Mr. Bond held up his hand in a *wait there* signal.

I remained standing. Sarah Bond crutched over to me. Her face was a wreck of stitch tracks and little swellings, that white bulgy swathe across one eye. When she spoke she was missing teeth and her voice was a little airy.

"Thank you for saving my life," she said. "I owe you everything."

"You owe me nothing."

"They say they can fix me good as new with ortho work and plastic surgery. Except for the eye."

"That's good," I said. "That's real good."

"Mr. Collins, you will always be my guardian angel."

She positioned her crutches, leaned toward me, puckered her lips. I lowered my cheek and she kissed it.

"She wanted to tell you that," Mr. Bond said. "And I want to thank you again for sparing my daughter. God bless you, Hap Collins."

When they were gone, Brett and I remained in the yard, sitting in our chairs. My cheeks were wet.

"You're such a softie, Hap Collins," Brett said. "And I love you so much for it."

"Sometimes we do something right in spite of ourselves, don't we?" I said.

"Sometimes," Brett said.

Visit THE ORBIT, the official drive-in theater of champion MOJO STORYTELLER Joe R. Lansdale, located on the web at www.joerlansdale.com. Free stories changed weekly, plus Hap and Leonard links.

All Orion/Phoenix titles are available at your local bookshop or from the following address:

Mail Order Department
Littlehampton Book Services
FREEPOST BR535
Worthing, West Sussex, BN13 3BR
telephone 01903 828503, *facsimile* 01903 828802
e-mail MailOrders@lbsltd.co.uk
(Please ensure that you include full postal address details)

Payment can be made either by credit/debit card (Visa, Mastercard, Access and Switch accepted) or by sending a £ Sterling cheque or postal order made payable to *Littlehampton Book Services*.
DO NOT SEND CASH OR CURRENCY.

Please add the following to cover postage and packing

UK and BFPO:
£1.50 for the first book, and 50p for each additional book to a maximum of £3.50

Overseas and Eire:
£2.50 for the first book plus £1.00 for the second book and 50p for each additional book ordered

---

BLOCK CAPITALS PLEASE

name of cardholder ....

address of cardholder ....

delivery address
(if different from cardholder)
....
....
....
....

postcode ....

postcode ....

☐ I enclose my remittance for £........................

☐ please debit my Mastercard/Visa/Access/Switch (delete as appropriate)

card number ☐☐☐☐☐☐☐☐☐☐☐☐☐☐☐☐

expiry date ☐☐☐☐   Switch issue no. ☐☐

signature ....

prices and availability are subject to change without notice